The Blue Hand

Edgar Wallace

About Wallace:

Richard Horatio Edgar Wallace (April 1, 1875–February 10, 1932) was a prolific British crime writer, journalist and playwright, who wrote 175 novels, 24 plays, and countless articles in newspapers and journals. Over 160 films have been made of his novels, more than any other author. In the 1920s, one of Wallace's publishers claimed that a quarter of all books read in England were written by him. (citation needed) He is most famous today as the co-creator of "King Kong", writing the early screenplay and story for the movie, as well as a short story "King Kong" (1933) credited to him and Draycott Dell. He was known for the J. G. Reeder detective stories, The Four Just Men, the Ringer, and for creating the Green Archer character during his lifetime.

Chapter 1

Mr. Septimus Salter pressed the bell on his table for the third time and uttered a soft growl.

He was a stout, elderly man, and with his big red face and white side-whiskers, looked more like a prosperous farmer than a successful lawyer. The cut of his clothes was queerly out of date, the high white collar and the black satin cravat that bulged above a flowered waistcoat were of the fashion of 1850, in which year Mr. Salter was a little ahead of his time so far as fashions were concerned. But the years had caught him up and passed him, and although there was not a more up-to-date solicitor in London, he remained faithful to the style in which he had made a reputation as a "buck."

He pressed the bell again, this time impatiently.

"Confound the fellow!" he muttered, and rising to his feet, he stalked into the little room where his secretary was usually to be found.

He had expected to find the apartment empty, but it was not. A chair had been drawn sideways up to the big ink-stained table, and kneeling on this, his elbows on the table, his face between his hands, was a young man who was absorbed in the perusal of a document, one of the many which littered the table.

"Steele!" said Mr. Salter sharply, and the reader looked up with a start and sprang to his feet.

He was taller than the average and broad of shoulder, though he gave an impression of litheness. His tanned face spoke eloquently of days spent out of doors, the straight nose, the firm mouth, and the strong chin were all part of the characteristic "soldier face" moulded by four years of war into a semblance of hardness.

Now he was a little confused, more like the guilty school-boy than the V.C. who had tackled eight enemy aeroplanes, and had come back to his aerodrome with a dozen bullets in his body.

"Really, Steele," said Mr. Salter reproachfully, "you are too bad. I have rung the bell three times for you."

"I'm awfully sorry, sir," said Jim Steele, and that disarming smile of his went straight to the old man's heart.

"What are you doing here?" growled Mr. Salter, looking at the papers on the desk, and then with a "tut" of impatience, "Aren't you tired of going over the Danton case?"

"No, sir, I'm not," said Steele quietly. "I have a feeling that Lady Mary Danton can be found, and I think if she is found there will be a very satisfactory explanation for her disappearance, and one which will rather disconcert—" He stopped, fearful of committing an indiscretion.

Mr. Salter looked at him keenly and helped himself to a pinch of snuff.

"You don't like Mr. Groat?" he asked, and Jim laughed.

"Well, sir, it's not for me to like him or dislike him," he replied. "Personally, I've no use for that kind of person. The only excuse a man of thirty can produce for not having been in the war, is that he was dead at the time."

"He had a weak heart," suggested Mr. Salter, but without any great conviction.

"I think he had," said Jim with a little twist of his lips. "We used to call it a 'poor heart' in the army. It made men go sick on the eve of a battle, and drove them into dug-outs when they should have been advancing across the open with their comrades."

Mr. Salter looked down at the papers.

"Put them away, Steele," he said quietly. "You're not going to get any satisfaction out of the search for a woman who—why, she must have disappeared when you were a child of five."

"I wish, sir—" began Steele, and hesitated. "Of course, it's really no business of mine," he smiled, "and I've no right to ask you, but I'd like to hear more details of that disappearance if you can spare me the time—and if you feel inclined. I've never had the courage to question you before. What is the real story of her disappearance?"

Mr. Salter frowned, and then the frown was gradually replaced by a smile.

"I think, Steele, you're the worst secretary I ever had," he said in despair. "And if I weren't your godfather and morally bound to help you, I should write you a polite little note saying your services were not required after the end of this week."

Jim Steele laughed.

"I have expected that ever since I've been here," he said.

There was a twinkle in the old lawyer's eyes. He was secretly fond of Jim Steele; fonder than the boy could have imagined. But it was not only friendship and a sense of duty that held Jim down in his job. The young man was useful, and, despite his seeming inability to hear bells when he was wrapped up in his favourite study, most reliable.

"Shut that door," he said gruffly, and when the other had obeyed, "I'm telling this story to you," and he pointed a warning finger at Jim Steele, "not because I want to satisfy your curiosity, but because I hope that I'm going to kill all interest in the Danton mystery as you call it for evermore! Lady Mary Danton was the only daughter of the Earl of Plimstock—a title which is now extinct. She married, when she was quite a young girl, Jonathan Danton, a millionaire shipowner, and the marriage was not a success. Jonathan was a hard, sour man, and a sick man, too. You talk about Digby Groat having a bad heart, well, Jonathan had a real bad one. I think his ill-health was partly responsible for his harsh treatment of his wife. At any rate, the baby that was born to them, a girl, did not seem to bring them together—in fact, they grew farther apart. Danton had to go to America on business. Before he left, he came to this office and, sitting at that very table, he signed a will, one of the most extraordinary wills that I have ever had engrossed. He left the whole of his fortune to his daughter Dorothy, who was then three or four months old. In the event of her death, he provided that the money should go to his sister, Mrs. Groat, but not until twenty years after the date of the child's death. In the meantime Mrs. Groat was entitled to enjoy the income from the estate."

"Why did he do that?" asked Jim, puzzled.

"I think that is easily understood," said Mr. Salter. Space "He was providing against the child's death in its infancy, and he foresaw that the will might be contested by Lady Mary. As it was drawn up—I haven't explained all the details—it could not be so contested for twenty years. However, it was not contested," he said quietly. "Whilst Danton was in America, Lady Mary disappeared, and with her the baby. Nobody knew where she went to, but the baby and a strange nurse, who for some reason or other had care of the child, were traced to Margate. Possibly Lady Mary was there too, though we have no evidence of this. We do know that the nurse, who was the daughter of a fisherman and could handle a boat, took the child out on the sea one summer day and was overtaken by a fog. All the evidence shows that the little boat was run down by a liner, and its battered wreck was picked up at sea, and a week later the body of the nurse was recovered. We never knew what became of Lady Mary. Danton returned a day or two after the tragedy, and the news was broken to him by Mrs. Groat, his sister. It killed him."

"And Lady Mary was never seen again?"

Salter shook his head.

"So you see, my boy," he rose, and dropped his hand on the other's shoulder, "even if by a miracle you could find Lady Mary, you could not in any way affect the position of Mrs. Groat, or her son. There is only one tiny actress in this drama who could ever have benefited by Jonathan Danton's will, and she," he lowered his voice until it was little more than a whisper, "she is beyond recall—beyond recall!"

There was a moment of silence.

"I realize that, sir," said Jim Steele quietly, "only—"

"Only what?"

"I have a queer feeling that there is something wrong about the whole business, and I believe that if I gave my time to the task I could unveil this mystery."

Mr. Salter looked at his secretary sharply, but Jim Steele met his eyes without faltering.

"You ought to be a detective," he said ironically.

"I wish to heaven I was," was the unexpected reply. "I offered my services to Scotland Yard two years ago when the Thirteen Gangs were holding up the banks with impunity."

"Oh, you did, did you?" said the lawyer sarcastically as he opened the door, and then suddenly he turned. "Why did I ring for you?" he asked. "Oh, I remember! I want you to get out all those Danton leases of the Cumberland property."

"Is Mrs. Groat selling?" asked Steele.

"She can't sell yet," said the lawyer, "but on the thirtieth of May, providing a caveat is not entered, she takes control of the Danton millions."

"Or her son does," said Jim significantly. He had followed his employer back to the big private office with its tiers of deed boxes, its worn furniture and threadbare carpet and general air of mustiness.

"A detective, eh?" snorted Mr. Salter as he sat down at his table. "And what is your equipment for your new profession?"

Jim smiled, but there was an unusual look in his face.

"Faith," he said quietly.

"Faith? What is faith to a detective?" asked the startled Salter.

"'Faith is the substance of things hoped for; the evidence of things unseen.'" Jim quoted the passage almost solemnly, and for a long time Mr. Salter did not speak. Then he took up a slip of paper on which he had scribbled some notes, and passed it across to Jim.

"See if you can 'detect' these deeds, they are in the strong-room," he said, but in spite of his jesting words he was impressed.

Jim took up the slip, examined it, and was about to speak when there came a tap at the door and a clerk slipped into the room.

"Will you see Mr. Digby Groat, sir?" he asked.

Chapter 2

MR. SALTER glanced up with a humorous glint in his eye. "Yes," he said with a nod, and then to Jim as he was about to make a hurried exit, "you can wait, Steele. Mr. Groat wrote in his letter that he wanted to see the deeds, and you may have to conduct him to the strong-room."

Jim Steele said nothing.

Presently the clerk opened the door and a young man walked in.

Jim had seen him before and had liked him less every time he had met him. The oblong sallow face, with its short black moustache, the sleepy eyes, and rather large chin and prominent ears, he could have painted, if he were an artist, with his eyes shut. And yet Digby Groat was good-looking. Even Jim could not deny that. He was a credit to his valet. From the top of his pomaded head to his patent shoes he was an exquisite. His morning coat was of the most fashionable cut and fitted him perfectly. One could have used the silk hat he carried in his hand as a mirror, and as he came into the room exuding a delicate aroma of Quelques Fleurs, Jim's nose curled. He hated men who scented themselves, however daintily the process was carried out.

Digby Groat looked from the lawyer to Steele with that languid, almost insolent look in his dark eyes, which the lawyer hated as much as his secretary.

"Good morning, Salter," he said.

He took a silk handkerchief from his pocket and, dusting a chair, sat down uninvited, resting his lemon-gloved hands upon a gold-headed ebony cane.

"You know Mr. Steele, my secretary," said Salter.

The other nodded his glossy head.

"Oh, yes, he's a Victoria Cross person, isn't he?" he asked wearily. "I suppose you find it very dull here, Steele? A place like this would bore me to death."

"I suppose it would," said Jim, "but if you'd had four years' excitement of war, you would welcome this place as a calm haven of rest."

"I suppose so," said the other shortly. He was not too well pleased by Jim's reference to the fact that he had escaped the trials of war.

"Now, Dr. Groat—" but the other stopped him with a gesture.

"Please don't call me 'doctor,'" he said with a pained expression. "The fact that I have been through the medical schools and have gained my degrees in surgery is one which I wish you would forget. I qualified for my own amusement, and if people get into the habit of thinking of me as a doctor, I shall be called up all hours of the night by all sorts of wretched patients."

It was news to Jim that this sallow dandy had graduated in medicines.

"I came to see those Lakeside leases, Salter," Groat went on. "I have had an offer—I should say, my mother has had an offer—from a syndicate which is erecting an hotel upon her property. I understand there is some clause in the lease which prevents building operations of that character. If so, it was beastly thoughtless of old Danton to acquire such a property."

"Mr. Danton did nothing either thoughtless or beastly thoughtless," said Salter quietly, "and if you had mentioned it in your letter, I could have telephoned you the information and saved your calling. As it is, Steele will take you to the strong-room, and you can examine the leases at your leisure."

Groat looked at Jim sceptically.

"Does he know anything about leases?" he asked. "And must I really descend into your infernal cellar and catch my death of cold? Can't the leases be brought up for me?"

"If you will go into Mr. Steele's room I dare say he will bring them to you," said Salter, who did not like his client any more than Jim did. Moreover, he had a shrewd suspicion that the moment the Groats gained possession of the Danton fortune, they would find another lawyer to look after their affairs.

Jim took the keys and returned with an armful of deeds, to discover that Groat was no longer with his chief.

"I sent him into your room," said Salter. "Take the leases in and explain them to him. If there's anything you want to know I'll come in."

Jim found the young man in his room. He was examining a book he had taken from a shelf.

"What does 'dactylology' mean?" he asked, looking round as Jim came in. "I see you have a book on the subject."

"Finger-prints," said Jim Steele briefly. He hated the calm proprietorial attitude of the man, and, moreover, Mr. Groat was examining his own private library.

"Finger-prints, eh?" said Groat, replacing the book. "Are you interested in finger-prints?"

"A little," said Jim. "Here are the Lakeside leases, Mr. Groat. I made a sketchy examination of them in the strong-room and there seems to be no clause preventing the erection of the building you mention."

Groat took the document in his hand and turned it leaf by leaf.

"No," he said at last, and then, putting down the document, "so you're interested in finger-prints, eh? I didn't know old Salter did a criminal business."

"He has very little common law practice," said Jim.

"What are these?" asked Groat.

By the side of Jim's desk was a bookshelf filled with thick black exercise books.

"Those are my private notes," said Jim, and the other looked round with a sneering smile.

"What the devil have you got to make notes about, I wonder?" he asked, and before Jim could stop him, he had taken one of the exercise books down.

"If you don't mind," said Jim firmly, "I would rather you left my private property alone."

"Sorry, but I thought everything in old Salter's office had to do with his clients."

"You're not the only client," said Jim. He was not one to lose his temper, but this insolent man was trying his patience sorely.

"What is it all about?" asked the languid Groat, as he turned one page.

Jim, standing at the other side of the table watching him, saw a touch of colour come into the man's yellow face. The black eyes hardened and his languid interest dropped away like a cloak.

"What is this?" he asked sharply. "What the hell are you—"

He checked himself with a great effort and laughed, but the laugh was harsh and artificial.

"You're a wonderful fellow, Steele," he said with a return to his old air of insouciance. "Fancy bothering your head about things of that sort."

He put the book back where he had found it, picked up another of the leases and appeared to be reading it intently, but Jim, watching him, saw that he was not reading, even though he turned page after page.

"That is all right," he said at last, putting the lease down and taking up his top-hat. "Some day perhaps you will come and dine with us, Steele. I've had rather a stunning laboratory built at the back of our house in Grosvenor Square. Old Salter called me doctor!" He chuckled quietly as though at a big joke. "Well, if you come along, I will show you something that will at least justify the title."

The dark brown eyes were fixed steadily upon Jim as he stood in the doorway, one yellow-gloved hand on the handle.

"And, by the way, Mr. Steele," he drawled, "your studies are leading you into a danger zone for which even a second Victoria Cross could not adequately compensate you."

He closed the door carefully behind him, and Jim Steele frowned after him.

"What the dickens does he mean?" he asked, and then remembered the exercise book through which Groat had glanced, and which had had so strange an effect upon him. He took the book down from the shelf and turning to the first page, read: "Some notes upon the Thirteen Gang."

Chapter 3

THAT afternoon Jim Steele went into Mr. Salter's office. "I'm going to tea now, sir," he said.

Mr. Salter glanced up at the solemn-faced clock that ticked audibly on the opposite wall.

"All right," he grumbled; "but you're a very punctual tea-drinker, Steele. What are you blushing about—is it a girl?"

"No, sir," said Jim rather loudly. "I sometimes meet a lady at tea, but—"

"Off you go," said the old man gruffly. "And give her my love."

Jim was grinning, but he was very red, too, when he went down the stairs into Marlborough Street. He hurried his pace because he was a little late, and breathed a sigh of relief as he turned into the quiet tea-shop to find that his table was as yet unoccupied.

As his tall, athletic figure strode through the room to the little recess overlooking Regent Street, which was reserved for privileged customers, many heads were turned, for Jim Steele was a splendid figure of British manhood, and the grey laughing eyes had played havoc in many a tender heart.

But he was one of those men whose very idealism forbade trifling. He had gone straight from a public school into the tragic theatre of conflict, and at an age when most young men were dancing attendance upon women, his soul was being seared by the red-hot irons of war.

He sat down at the table and the beaming waitress came forward to attend to his needs.

"Your young lady hasn't come yet, sir," she said.

It was the first time she had made such a reference to Eunice Weldon, and Jim stiffened.

"The young lady who has tea with me is not my 'young lady,'" he said a little coldly, and seeing that he had hurt the girl, he added with a gleam of mirth in those irresistible eyes, "she's your young lady, really."

"I'm sorry," said the waitress, scribbling on her order pad to hide her confusion. "I suppose you'll have the usual?"

"I'll have the usual," said Jim gravely, and then with a quick glance at the door he rose to meet the girl who had at that moment entered.

She was slim of build, straight as a plummet line from chin to toe; she carried herself with a dignity which was so natural that the men who haunt the pavement to leer and importune, stood on one side to let her pass, and then, after a glimpse of her face, cursed their own timidity. For it was a face Madonna-like in its purity. But a blue-eyed, cherry-lipped Madonna, vital and challenging. A bud of a girl breaking into the summer bloom of existence. In those sapphire eyes the beacon fires of life signalled her womanhood; they were at once a plea and a warning. Yet she carried the banners of childhood no less triumphantly. The sensitive mouth, the round, girlish chin, the satin white throat and clean, transparent skin, unmarked, unblemished, these were the gifts of youth which were carried forward to the account of her charm.

Her eyes met Jim's and she came forward with outstretched hand.

"I'm late," she said gaily. "We had a tiresome duchess at the studio who wanted to be taken in seventeen different poses—it is always the plain people who give the most trouble."

She sat down and stripped her gloves, with a smile at the waitress.

"The only chance that plain people have of looking beautiful is to be photographed beautifully," said Jim.

Eunice Weldon was working at a fashionable photographer's in Regent Street. Jim's meeting with her had been in the very room in which they were now sitting. The hangings at the window had accidentally caught fire, and Jim, in extinguishing them, had burnt his hand. It was Eunice Weldon who had dressed the injury.

A service rendered by a man to a woman may not lead very much farther to a better acquaintance. When a woman helps a man it is invariably the beginning of a friendship. Women are suspicious of the services which men give, and yet feel responsible for the man they have helped, even to the slightest extent.

Since then they had met almost daily and taken tea together. Once Jim had asked her to go to a theatre, an invitation which she had promptly but kindly declined. Thereafter he had made no further attempt to improve their acquaintance.

"And how have you got on with your search for the missing lady?" she asked, as she spread some jam on the thin bread-and-butter which the waitress had brought.

Jim's nose wrinkled—a characteristic grimace of his.

"Mr. Salter made it clear to me to-day that even if I found the missing lady it wouldn't greatly improve matters," he said.

"It would be wonderful if the child had been saved after all," she said. "Have you ever thought of that possibility?"

He nodded.

"There is no hope of that." he said, shaking his head, "but it would be wonderful, as you say, and more wonderful," he laughed, "if you were the missing heiress!"

"And there's no hope of that either." she said, shaking her head. "I'm the daughter of poor but honest parents, as the story-books say."

"Your father was a South African, wasn't he?"

She nodded.

"Poor daddy was a musician, and mother I can hardly remember, but she must have been a dear."

"Where were you born?" asked Jim.

She did not answer immediately because she was busy with her jam sandwich.

"In Cape Town— Rondebosch, to be exact," she said after a while. "Why are you so keen on finding your long-lost lady?"

"Because I am anxious that the most unmitigated cad in-the world should not succeed to the Danton millions."

She sat bolt upright.

"The Danton millions?" she repeated slowly. "Then who is your unmitigated cad? You have never yet mentioned the names of these people."

This was perfectly true. Jim Steele had not even spoken of his search until a few days before.

"A man named Digby Groat."

She stared at him aghast.

"Why, what's the matter?" he asked in surprise.

"When you said 'Danton' I remembered Mr. Curley—that is our chief photographer—saying that Mrs. Groat was the sister of Jonathan Danton?" she said slowly.

"Do you know the Groats?" he asked quickly.

"I don't know them," she said slowly, "at least, not very well, only—" she hesitated, "I'm going to be Mrs. Groat's secretary."

He stared at her.

"You never told me this," he said, and as she dropped her eyes to her plate, he realized that he had made a faux pas. "Of course," he said hurriedly, "there's no reason why you should tell me, but—"

"It only happened to-day," she said. "Mr. Groat has had some photographs taken—his mother came with him to the studio. She's been several times, and I scarcely noticed them until to-day, when Mr. Curley called me into the office and said that Mrs. Groat was in need of a secretary and that it was a very good position; £5 a week, which is practically all profit, because I should live in the house."

"When did Mrs. Groat decide that she wanted a secretary?" asked Jim, and it was her turn to stare.

"I don't know. Why do you ask that?"

"She was at our office a month ago," said Jim, "and Mr. Salter suggested that she should have a secretary to keep her accounts in order. She said then she hated the idea of having anybody in the house who was neither a servant nor a friend of the family."

"Well, she's changed her views now," smiled the girl.

"This means that we shan't meet at tea any more. When are you going?"

"To-morrow," was the discouraging reply.

He went back to his office more than a little dispirited. Something deep and vital seemed to have gone out of his life.

"You're in love, you fool," he growled to himself.

He opened the big diary which it was his business to keep and slammed down the covers savagely.

Mr. Salter had gone home. He always went home early, and Jim lit his pipe and began to enter up the day's transactions from the scribbled notes which his chief had left on his desk.

He had made the last entry and was making a final search of the desk for some scrap which be might have overlooked.

Mr. Salter's desk was usually tidy, but he had a habit of concealing important memoranda, and Jim turned over the law books on the table in a search for any scribbled memo he might have missed. He found between two volumes a thin gilt-edged notebook, which he did not remember having seen before. He opened it to discover that it was a diary for the year 1901. Mr. Salter was in the habit of making notes for his own private reading, using a queer legal shorthand which no clerk had ever been able to decipher. The entries in the diary were in these characters.

Jim turned the leaves curiously, wondering how so methodical a man as the lawyer had left a private diary visible. He knew that in the big green safe in the lawyer's office were stacks of these books, and possibly the old man had taken one out to refresh his memory. The writing was Greek to Jim, so that he felt no compunction in turning the pages, filled as they were with indecipherable and meaningless scrawls, punctuated now and again with a word in longhand.

He stopped suddenly, for under the heading "June 4th" was quite a long entry. It seemed to have been written in subsequently to the original shorthand entry, for it was in green ink. This almost dated the inscription. Eighteen months before, an oculist had suggested to Mr. Salter, who suffered from an unusual form of astigmatism, that green ink would be easier for him to read, and ever since then he had used no other.

Jim took in the paragraph before he realized that he was committing an unpardonable act in reading his employers' private notes.

"One month imprisonment with hard labour. Holloway Prison. Released July 2nd. Madge Benson (this word was underlined), 14, Palmer's Terrace, Paddington. 74, Highcliffe Gardens, Margate. Long enquiries with boatman who owned Saucy Belle. No further trace—"

"What on earth does that mean?" muttered Jim. "I must make a note of that."

He realized now that he was doing something which might be regarded as dishonourable, but he was so absorbed in the new clues that he overcame his repugnance.

Obviously, this entry referred to the missing Lady Mary. Who the woman Madge Benson was, what the reference to Holloway Gaol meant, he would discover.

He made a copy of the entry in the diary at the back of a card, went back to his room, locked the door of his desk and went home, to think out some plan of campaign.

He occupied a small flat in a building overlooking Regent's Park. It is true that his particular flat overlooked nothing but the backs of other houses, and a deep cutting through which were laid the lines of the London, Midland and Scottish Railway—he could have dropped a penny on the carriages as they passed, so near was the line. But the rent of the flat was only one-half of that charged for those in a more favourable position. And his flat was smaller than any. He had a tiny private income, amounting to two or three pounds a week, and that, with his salary, enabled him to maintain himself in something like comfort. The three rooms he occupied were filled with priceless old furniture that he had saved from the wreckage of his father's home, when that easy-going man had died, leaving just enough to settle his debts, which were many.

Jim had got out of the lift on the fourth floor and had put the key in the lock when he heard the door on the opposite side of the landing open, and turned round.

The elderly woman who came out wore the uniform of a nurse, and she nodded pleasantly.

"How is your patient, nurse?" asked Jim.

"She's very well, sir, or rather as well as you could expect a bedridden lady to be," said the woman with a smile. "She's greatly obliged to you for the books you sent in to her."

"Poor soul," said Jim sympathetically. "It must be terrible not to be able to go out."

The nurse shook her head.

"I suppose it is," she said, "but Mrs. Fane doesn't seem to mind. You get used to it after seven years."

A "rat-tat" above made her lift her eyes.

"There's the post," she said. "I thought it had gone. I'd better wait till he comes down."

The postman at Featherdale Mansions was carried by the lift to the sixth floor and worked his way to the ground floor. Presently they heard his heavy feet coming down and he loomed in sight.

"Nothing for you, sir," he said to Jim, glancing at the bundle of letters in his hand.

"Miss Madge Benson—that's you, nurse, isn't it?"

"That's right," said the woman briskly, and took the letter from his hand, then with a little nod to Jim she went downstairs.

Madge Benson! The name that had appeared in Salter's diary!

Chapter 4

"I'm sick to death of hearing your views on the subject, mother," said Mr. Digby Groat, as he helped himself to a glass of port. "It is sufficient for you that I want the girl to act as your secretary. Whether you give her any work to do or not is a matter of indifference to me. Whatever you do, you must not leave her with the impression that she is brought here for any other purpose than to write your letters and deal with your correspondence."

The woman who sat at the other side of the table looked older than she was. Jane Groat was over sixty, but there were people who thought she was twenty years more than that. Her yellow face was puckered and lined, her blue-veined hands, folded now on her lap, were gnarled and ugly. Only the dark brown eyes held their brightness undimmed. Her figure was bent and there was about her a curious, cringing, frightened look which was almost pitiable. She did not look at her son—she seldom looked at anybody.

"She'll spy, she'll pry," she moaned.

"Shut up about the girl!" he snarled, "and now we've got a minute to ourselves, I'd like to tell you something, mother."

Her uneasy eyes went left and right, but avoided him. There was a menace in his tone with which she was all too familiar.

"Look at this."

He had taken from his pocket something that sparkled and glittered in the light of the table lamp.

"What is it?" she whined without looking.

"It is a diamond bracelet," he said sternly. "And it is the property of Lady Waltham. We were staying with the Walthams for the week-end. Look at it!"

His voice was harsh and grating, and dropping her head she began to weep painfully.

"I found that in your room," he said, and his suave manner was gone. "You old thief!" he hissed across the table, "can't you break yourself of that habit?"

"It looked so pretty," she gulped, her tears trickling down her withered face. "I can't resist the temptation when I see pretty things."

"I suppose yon know that Lady Waltham's maid has been arrested for stealing this, and will probably go to prison for six months?"

"I couldn't resist the temptation," she snivelled, and he threw the bracelet on the table with a growl.

"I'm going to send it back to the woman and tell them it must have been packed away by mistake in your bag. I'm not doing it to get this girl out of trouble, but to save myself from a lot of unpleasantness."

"I know why you're bringing this girl into the house," she sobbed; "it is to spy on me."

His lips curled in a sneer.

"To spy on you!" he said contemptuously, and laughed as he rose. "Now understand," his voice was harsh again, "you've got to break yourself of this habit of picking up things that you like. I'm expecting to go into Parliament at the next election, and I'm not going to have my position jeopardized by an old fool of a kleptomaniac. If there's something wrong with your

13

brain," he added significantly, "I've a neat little laboratory at the back of this house where that might be attended to."

She shrank back in terror, her face grey.

"You—you wouldn't do it—my own son!" she stammered. "I'm all right, Digby; it's only—"

He smiled, but it was not a pleasant smile to see.

"Probably there is a little compression," he said evenly, "some tiny malgrowth of bone that is pressing on a particular cell. We could put that right for you, mother—"

But she had thrown her chair aside and fled from the room before he had finished. He picked up the jewel, looked at it contemptuously and thrust it into his pocket. Her curious thieving propensities he had known for a very long time and had fought to check them, and as he thought, successfully.

He went to his library, a beautiful apartment, with its silver grate, its costly rosewood bookshelves and its rare furnishings, and wrote a letter to Lady Waltham. He wrapped this about the bracelet, and having packed letter and jewel carefully in a small box, rang the bell. A middle-aged man with a dark forbidding face answered the summons.

"Deliver this to Lady Waltham at once, Jackson," said Digby. "The old woman is going out to a concert to-night, by the way, and when she's out I want you to make a very thorough search of her room."

The man shook his head. "I've already looked carefully, Mr. Groat," he said, "and I've found nothing."

He was on the point of going when Digby called him back.

"You've told the housekeeper to see to Miss Weldon's room?"

"Yes, sir," was the reply. "She wanted to put her on the top floor amongst the servants, but I stopped her."

"She must have the best room in the house," said Groat. "See that there are plenty of flowers in the room and put in the bookcase and the Chinese table that are in my room."

The man nodded.

"What about the key, sir?" he asked after some hesitation.

"The key?" Digby looked up. "The key of her room?"

The man nodded.

"Do you want the door to lock?" he asked significantly.

Mr. Groat's lips curled in a sneer.

"You're a fool," he said. "Of course, I want the door to lock. Put bolts on if necessary."

The man looked his surprise. There was evidently between these two something more than the ordinary relationship which existed between employer and servant. "Have you ever run across a man named Steele?" asked Digby, changing the subject.

Jackson shook his head.

"Who is he?" he asked.

"He is a lawyer's clerk. Give him a look up when you've got some time to spare. No, you'd better not go—ask—ask Bronson. He lives at Featherdale Mansions."

The man nodded, and Digby went down the steps to the waiting electric brougham.

Eunice Weldon had packed her small wardrobe and the cab was waiting at the door. She had no regrets at leaving the stuffy untidy lodging which had been her home for two years, and her farewell to her dishevelled landlady, who seemed always to have dressed in a violent hurry, was soon over. She could not share Jim Steele's dislike of her new employers. She was too young to regard a new job as anything but the beginning of an adventure which held all sorts of fascinating possibilities. She sighed as she realized that the little tea-table talks which had been so pleasant a feature of her life were now to come to an end, and yet—surely he would make some effort to see her again?

She would have hours—perhaps half-days to herself, and then she remembered with dismay that she did not know his address! But he would know hers. That thought comforted her, for she wanted to see him again. She wanted to see him more than she had ever dreamt she would. She could close her eyes, and his handsome face, those true smiling eyes of his, would look into hers. The swing of his shoulders as he walked, the sound of his voice as he spoke—every characteristic of his was present in her mind.

And the thought that she might not see him again!

"I will see him—I will!" she murmured, as the cab stopped before the imposing portals of No. 409, Grosvenor Square.

She was a little bewildered by the army of servants who came to her help, and just a little pleased by the deference they showed to her.

"Mrs. Groat will receive you, miss," said a swarthy-looking man, whose name she afterwards learnt was Jackson.

She was ushered into a small back drawing-room which seemed poorly furnished to the girl's eye, but to Mrs. Groat was luxury.

The old woman resented the payment of a penny that was spent on decoration and furniture, and only the fear of her son prevented her from disputing every account which was put before her for settlement. The meeting was a disappointment to Eunice. She had not seen Mrs. Groat except in the studio, where she was beautifully dressed. She saw now a yellow-faced old woman, shabbily attired, who looked at her with dark disapproving eyes.

"Oh, so you're the young woman who is going to be my secretary, are you?" she quavered dismally. "Have they shown you your room?"

"Not yet, Mrs. Groat," said the girl.

"I hope you will be comfortable," said Mrs. Groat in a voice that suggested that she had no very great hopes for anything of the sort.

"When do I begin my duties?" asked Eunice, conscious of a chill.

"Oh, any time," said the old woman off-handedly.

She peered up at the girl.

"You're pretty," she said grudgingly, and Eunice flushed. Somehow that compliment sounded like an insult. "I suppose that's why," said Mrs. Groat absently.

"Why what?" asked the girl gently.

She thought the woman was weak of intellect and had already lost whatever enthusiasm she had for her new position.

"Nothing," said the old woman, and with a nod dismissed her.

The room into which Eunice was shown left her speechless for a while.

"Are you sure this is mine?" she asked incredulously.

"Yes, miss," said the housekeeper with a sidelong glance at the girl.

"But this is beautiful!" said Eunice.

The room would have been remarkable if it had been in a palace. The walls were panelled in brocade silk and the furniture was of the most beautiful quality. A small French bed, carved and gilded elaborately, invited repose. Silk hangings hung at either side of the head, and through the

French windows she saw a balcony gay with laden flower-boxes. Under her feet was a carpet of blue velvet pile that covered the whole of the room. She looked round open-mouthed at the magnificence of her new home; The dressing-table was an old French model in the Louis Quinze style, inlaid with gold, and the matching wardrobe must have been worth a fortune. Near one window was a lovely writing-table, and a well-filled bookcase would almost be within reach of her hand when she lay in bed.

"Are you sure this is my room?" she asked again.

"Yes, miss," said the housekeeper, "and this," she opened a door, "is your bathroom. There is a bath to every room. Mr. Groat had the house reconstructed when he came into it."

The girl opened one of the French windows and stepped on to the balcony which ran along to a square and larger balcony built above the porch of the house. This, she discovered, opened from a landing above the stairs.

She did not see Mrs. Groat again that afternoon, and when she inquired she discovered that the old lady was lying down with a bad headache. Nor was she to meet Digby Groat. Her first meal was eaten in solitude.

"Mr. Groat has not come back from the country," explained Jackson, who waited on her. "Are you comfortable, miss?"

"Quite, thank you," she said.

There was an air about this man which she did not like. It was not that he failed in respect, or that he was in any way familiar, but there was something proprietorial in his attitude. It almost seemed as though he had a financial interest in the place, and she was glad when her meal was finished. She went straight up to her room a little dis-satisfied that she had not met her employer. There were many things which she wanted to ask Mrs. Groat; and particularly did she wish to know what days she would be free.

Presently she switched out the light, and opening the French windows, stepped out into the cool, fragrant night. The after-glow of the sun still lingered in the sky. The square was studded with lights; an almost incessant stream of motor-car traffic passed under her window, for Grosvenor Square is the short cut between Oxford Street and Piccadilly.

The stars spangled the clear sky with a million specks of quivering light. Against the jewelled robe of the northern heavens, the roofs and steeples and stacks of London had a mystery and wonder which only the light of day could dispel. And in the majestic solitude of the night, Eunice's heart seemed to swell until she could scarcely breathe. It was not the magic of stars that brought the blood flaming to her face; nor the music of the trees. It was the flash of understanding that one half of her, one splendid fragment of the pattern on which her life was cut, was somewhere there in the darkness asleep perhaps—thinking of her, she prayed. She saw his face with startling distinctness, saw the tender kindness of his eyes, felt on her moist palm the pressure of those strong brown fingers... .

With a sigh which was half a sob, she closed the window and drew the silken curtains, shutting out the immortal splendours of nature from her view.

Five minutes later she was asleep.

How long she slept she did not know. It must have been hours, she thought. The stream of traffic had ceased and there was no sound from outside, save the distant hoot of a motor-horn. The room was in darkness, and yet she was conscious that somebody was there!

She sat up in bed and a cold shiver ran down her spine. Somebody was in the room! She reached out to turn on the light and could have shrieked, for she touched a hand, a cold, small hand that was resting on the bedside table. For a second she was paralysed and then the hand was suddenly withdrawn. There was a rustle of curtain rings and the momentary glimpse of a figure against the lesser gloom of the night, and, shaking in every limb, she leapt from the bed and switched on the light. The room was empty, but the French window was ajar.

And then she saw on the table by her side, a grey card. Picking it up with shaking hands she read:

"One who loves you, begs you for your life and honour's sake to leave this house."

It bore no other signature than a small blue hand. She dropped the card on the bed and stood staring at it for a while, and then, slipping into her dressing-gown, she unlocked the door of her room and went out into the passage. A dim light was burning at the head of the stairs. She was terror-stricken, hardly knew what she was doing, and she seemed to fly down the stairs.

She must find somebody, some living human creature, some reality to which she could take hold. But the house was silent. The hall lamp was burning, and by its light she saw the old clock and was dimly conscious that she could hear its solemn ticking. It was three o'clock. There must be somebody awake in the house. The servants might still be up, she thought wildly, and ran down a passage to what she thought was the entrance to the servants' hall. She opened a door and found herself in another passage illuminated by one light at the farther end, where further progress was arrested by a white door. She raced along until she came to the door and tried to open it. There was no handle and it was a queer door. It was not made of wood, but of padded canvas.

And then as she stood bewildered, there came from behind the padded door a squeal of agony, so shrill, so full of pain, that her blood seemed to turn to ice.

Again it shrieked, and turning she fled back the way she had come, through the hall to the front door. Her trembling fingers fumbled at the key and presently the lock snapped and the door flew open. She staggered out on to the broad steps of the house and stopped, for a man was sitting on the head of those steps.

He turned his face as the door opened, and in the light from the hall he was revealed. It was Jim Steele!

Chapter 5

JIM came stumbling to his feet, staring in blank amazement at the unexpected apparition, and for a moment thus they stood, facing one another, the girl stricken dumb with fear and surprise.

She thought he was part of a dreadful dream, an image that was conjured by her imagination and would presently vanish.

"Jim—Mr. Steele!" she gasped.

In a stride he was by her bide, his arm about her shoulders.

"What is wrong?" he asked quickly, and in his anxiety his voice was almost harsh.

She shuddered and dropped her face on his breast.

"Oh, it was dreadful, dreadful!" she whispered, and he heard the note of horror in her low voice.

"May I ask what is the meaning of this?" demanded a suave voice, and with a start the girl turned.

A man was standing in the doorway and for a second she did not recognize him. Even Jim, who had seen Digby Groat at close quarters, did not know him in his unusual attire. He was dressed in a long white overall which reached from his throat to his feet; over his head was a white cap which fitted him so that not a particle of his hair could be seen. Bands of white elastic held his cuffs dose to his wrists and both hands were hidden in brown rubber gloves.

"May I again ask you, Miss Weldon, why you are standing on my doorstep in the middle of the night, attired in clothes which I do not think are quite suitable for street wear? Perhaps you will come inside and explain," he said stepping back. "Grosvenor Square is not quite used to this form of midnight entertainment."

Still clutching Jim's arm, the girl went slowly back to the passage and Digby shut the door.

"And Mr. Steele, too," said Digby with ironic surprise, "you're a very early caller."

Jim said nothing. His attention was wholly devoted to the girl. She was trembling from head to foot, and he found a chair for her.

"There are a few explanations due," he said coolly, "but I rather think they are from you, Mr. Groat."

"From me?"' Mr. Groat was genuinely unprepared for that demand.

"So far as my presence is concerned, that can be explained in a minute," said Jim. "I was outside the house a few moments ago when the door swung open and Miss Weldon ran out in a state of abject terror. Perhaps you will tell me, Mr. Groat, why this lady is reduced to such a condition?"

There was a cold menace in his tone which Digby Groat did not like to hear.

"I have not the slightest idea what it is all about," he said. "I have been working in my laboratory for the last half-hour, and the first intimation I had that anything was wrong was when I heard the door open."

The girl had recovered now, and some of the colour had returned to her face, yet her voice shook as she recited the incidents of the night, both men listening attentively.

Jim took particular notice of the man's attitude, and he was satisfied in his mind that Digby Groat was as much in ignorance of the visit to the girl's room as he himself. When she had finished, groat nodded.

"The terrifying cry you heard from my laboratory," he smiled, "is easily explained. Nobody was being hurt; at least, if he was being hurt, it was for his own good. When I came back to my house to-night, I found my little dog had a piece of glass in its paw, and I was extracting it."

She drew a sigh of relief.

"I'm so sorry I made such a fuss," she said penitently, "but I—I was frightened."

"You are sure somebody was in your room?" asked Digby.

"Absolutely certain." She had not told him about the card.

"They came through the French window from the balcony?" She nodded. "May I see your room?"

She hesitated for a moment.

"I will go in first to tidy it," she said. She remembered the card was on the bed, and she was particularly anxious that it should not be read.

Uninvited Jim Steele followed Digby upstairs into the beautiful room. The magnificence of the room, its hangings and costly furniture, did not fail to impress him, but the impression he received was not favourable to Digby Groat.

"Yes, the window is ajar. You are sure you fastened it?"

The girl nodded.

"Yes. I left both fanlights down to get the air," she pointed above, "but I fastened these doors. I distinctly remember that."

"But if this person came in from the balcony," said Digby, "how did he or she get there?"

He opened the French door and stepped out into the night, walking along the balcony until he came to the square space above the porch. There was another window here which gave on to the landing at the head of the stairs. He tried it—it was fastened. Coming back through the girl's room he discovered that not only was the catch in its socket, but the key was turned.

"Strange," he muttered.

His first impression had been that it was his mother who, with her strange whims, had been searching the room for some trumpery trinket which had taken her fancy. But the old woman was not sufficiently agile to climb a balcony, nor had she the courage to make a midnight foray.

"My own impression is that you dreamt it. Miss Weldon," he said, with a smile. "And now I advise you to go to bed and to sleep. I'm sorry that you've had this unfortunate introduction to my house."

He had made no reference to the providential appearance of Jim Steele, nor did he speak of this until they had said good night to the girl and had passed down the stairs into the hall again.

"Rather a coincidence, your being here, Mr. Steele," he said. "What were you doing? Studying dactylology?"

"Something like that," said Jim coolly.

Mr. Digby Groat searched for a cigarette in his pocket and lit it.

"I should have thought that your work was so arduous that you would not have time for early morning strolls in Grosvenor Square."

"Would you really?" said Jim, and then suddenly Digby laughed.

"You're a queer devil," he said. "Come along and see my laboratory."

Jim was anxious to see the laboratory, and the invitation saved him from the necessity of making further reference to the terrifying cry which Eunice had heard.

They turned down a long passage through the padded door and came to a large annexe, the walls of which were of white glazed brick. There was no window, the light in the daytime being admitted through a glass roof. Now, however, these were covered by blue blinds and the room owed its illumination to two powerful lights which hung above a small table. It was not an ordinary table; its legs were of thin iron, terminating in rubber-tyred castors. The top was of white enamelled iron, with curious little screw holds occurring at intervals.

It was not the table so much as the occupant which interested Jim. Fastened down by two iron bands, one of which was about its neck and one about the lower portion of its body, its four paws fastened by thin cords, was a dog, a rough-haired terrier who turned its eyes upon Jim with an expression of pleading so human that Jim could almost feel the message that the poor little thing was sending.

"Your dog, eh?" said Jim.

Digby looked at him.

"Yes," he said. "Why?"

"Haven't you finished taking the glass out of his paw?"

"Not quite," said the other coolly.

"By the way, you don't keep him very clean," Jim said.

Digby turned.

"What the devil are you hinting at?" he asked.

"I am merely suggesting that this is not your dog, but a poor stray terrier which you picked up in the street half an hour ago and enticed into this house."

"Well?"

"I'd save you further trouble by saying that I saw you pick it up."

Digby's eyes narrowed.

"Oh, you did, did you?" he said softly. "So you were spying on me?"

"Not exactly spying on you," said Jim calmly, "but merely satisfying my idle curiosity."

His hand fell on the dog and he stroked its ears gently.

Digby laughed.

"Well, if you know that, I might as well tell you that I am going to evacuate the sensory nerve. I've always been curious to—"

Jim looked round.

"Where is your anaesthetic?" he asked gently, and he was most dangerous when his voice sank to that soft note.

"Anaesthetic? Good Lord," scoffed the other, "you don't suppose I'm going to waste money on chloroform for a dog, do you?"

His fingers rested near the poor brute's head and the dog, straining forward, licked the torturer's hand.

"Filthy little beast!" said Digby, picking up a towel.

He took a thick rubber band, slipped it over the dog's mouth and nose.

"Now lick," he laughed; "I think that will stop his yelping. You're a bit chicken-hearted, aren't you, Mr. Steele? You don't realize that medical science advances by its experiments on animals."

"I realize the value of vivisection under certain conditions," said Jim quietly, "but all decent doctors who experiment on animals relieve them of their pain before they use the knife; and all doctors, whether they are decent or otherwise, receive a certificate of permission from the Board of Trade before they begin their experiments. Where is your certificate?"

Digby's face darkened.

"Look here, don't you come here trying to bully me," he blustered. "I brought you here just to show you my laboratory—"

"And if you hadn't brought me in," interrupted Jim. "I should jolly well have walked in, because I wasn't satisfied with your explanation. Oh, yes, I know, you're going to tell me that the dog was only frightened and the yell she heard was when you put that infernal clamp on his neck. Now, I'll tell you something, Mr. Digby Groat. I'll give you three minutes to get the clamp off that dog."

Digby's yellow face was puckered with rage.

"And if I don't?" he breathed.

"I'll put you where the dog is," said Jim. "And please don't persuade yourself that I couldn't do it?"

There was a moment's silence.

"Take the clamps off that dog." said Jim.

Digby looked at him.

For a moment they gazed at one another and there was a look of malignity in the eyes that dropped before Jim's. Another minute and the dog was free.

Jim lifted the shivering little animal in his arms and rubbed its bony head, and Digby watched him glowering, his teeth showing in his rage.

"I'll remember this," he snarled. "By God, you shall rue the day you ever interfered with me!"

Jim's steady eyes met the man's.

"I have never feared a threat in my life," he said quietly. "I'm not likely to be scared now. I admit that vivisection is necessary under proper conditions, but men like you who torture harmless animals from a sheer lust of cruelty, are bringing discredit upon the noblest of professions. You hurt in order to satisfy your own curiosity. You have not the slightest intention of using the knowledge you gain for the benefit of suffering humanity. When I came into this laboratory," he said—he was standing at the door as he spoke—"there were two brutes here. I am leaving the bigger one behind."

He slammed the padded door and walked out into the passage, leaving a man whose vanity was hurt beyond forgiveness.

Then to his surprise Groat heard Jim's footsteps returning and his visitor came in.

"Did you close your front door when you went upstairs?"

Digby's eyebrows rose. He forgot for the moment the insult that had been offered him.

"Yes—why?"

"It is wide open now," said Jim. "I guess your midnight visitor has gone home."

Chapter 6

IN the cheerful sunlight of the morning all Eunice's fear had vanished and she felt heartily ashamed of herself that she had made such a commotion in the night. And yet there was the card. She took it from under her pillow and read it again, with a puzzled frown. Somebody had been in the room, but it was not a somebody whom she could regard as an enemy. Then a thought struck her that made her heart leap. Could it have been Jim? She shook her head. Somehow she was certain it was not Jim, and she flushed at the thought. It was not his hand she had touched. She knew the shape and contour of that. It was warm and firm, almost electric; that which she had touched had been the hand of somebody who was old, of that she was sure.

She went down to breakfast to find Groat standing before the fire, a debonair, perfectly dressed man, who showed no trace of fatigue, though he had not gone to bed until four o'clock.

He gave her a cheery greeting.

"Good morning, Miss Weldon," he said. "I hope you have recovered from your nightmare."

"I gave you a lot of trouble," she said with a rueful smile. "I am so very sorry."

"Nonsense," he said heartily. "I am only glad that our friend Steele was there to appease you. By the way, Miss Weldon, I owe you an apology. I told you a lie last night."

She looked at him open-eyed.

"Did you, Mr. Groat?" she said, and then with a laugh, "I am sure it wasn't a very serious one."

"It was really. I told you that my little dog had a piece of glass in his paw; the truth was that it wasn't my dog at all, but a dog that I picked up in the street. I intended making an experiment upon him; you know I am a doctor."

She shivered.

"Oh, that was the noise?" she asked with a wry little face.

He shook his head.

"No, he was just scared, he hadn't been hurt at all—and in truth I didn't intend hurting him. Your friend, however, persuaded me to let the little beggar go."

She drew a long sigh of relief.

"I'm so glad," she said. "I should have felt awful."

He laughed softly as he took his place at the table.

"Steele thought I was going to experiment without chloroform, but that, of course, was absurd. It is difficult to get the unprofessional man to realize what an enormous help to medical science these experiments are. Of course," he said airily, "they are conducted without the slightest pain to the animal. I should no more think of hurting a little dog than I should think of hurting you."

"I'm sure you wouldn't," she said warmly.

Digby Groat was a clever man. He knew that Jim would meet the girl again and would give her his version of the scene in the laboratory. It was necessary, therefore, that he should get his story in first, for this girl whom he had brought to the house for his amusement was more lovely than he had dreamt, and he desired to stand well with her.

Digby, who was a connoisseur in female beauty, had rather dreaded the morning meal. The beauty of women seldom survives the cruel searchlight which the grey eastern light throws upon their charms. Love had never touched him, though many women had come and gone in his life.

Eunice Weldon was a more thrilling adventure, something that would surely brighten a dreary week or two; an interest to stimulate him until another stimulation came into sight.

She survived the ordeal magnificently, he thought. The tender texture of the skin, untouched by an artificial agent, was flawless; the eyes, bright and vigorous with life, sparkled with health; the hands that lay upon the table, when she was listening to him, were perfectly and beautifully moulded.

She on her side was neither attracted nor repelled. Digby Groat was just a man. One of the thousands of men who pass and repass in the corridor of life; some seen, some unnoticed, some interesting, some abhorrent. Some stop to speak, some pass hurriedly by and disappear through strange doors never to be seen again. He had "stopped to speak," but had he vanished from sight through one of those doors of mystery she would have been neither sorry nor glad.

"My mother never comes to breakfast," said Digby halfway through the meal. "Do you think you will like your work?"

"I don't know what it is yet," she answered, her eyes twinkling.

"Mother is rather peculiar," he said, "and just a little eccentric, but I think you will be sensible enough to get on with her. And the work will not be very heavy at first. I am hoping later that you will be able to assist me in my anthropological classification."

"That sounds terribly important." she said. "What does it mean?"

"I am making a study of faces and heads," he said easily, "and to that end I have collected thousands of photographs from all parts of the world. I hope to get a million. It is a science which is very much neglected in this country. It appears to be the exclusive monopoly of the Italians. You have probably heard of Mantaganza and Lombroso?"

She nodded.

"They are the great criminal scientists, aren't they?" she said to his surprise.

"Oh, I see, you know something about it. Yes, I suppose you would call them criminal scientists."

"It sounds fascinating," she said, looking at him in wonder, "and I should like to help you if your mother can spare me."

"Oh, she'll spare you," he said.

Her hand lay on the table invitingly near to his, but he did not move. He was a quick, accurate judge of human nature. He knew that to touch her would be the falsest of moves. If it had been another woman—yes, his hand would have closed gently over hers, there would have been a giggle of embarrassment, a dropping of eyes, and the rest would have been so easy. But if he had followed that course with her, he knew that evening would find her gone. He could wait, and she was worth waiting for. She was gloriously lovely, he thought. Half the pleasure of life lies in the chase, and the chase is no more than a violent form of anticipation. Some men find their greatest joy in visions that must sooner or later materialize, and Digby Groat was one of these.

She looked up and saw his burning eyes fixed on her and flushed. With an effort she looked again and he was a normal man.

Was it an illusion of hers, she wondered?

Chapter 7

THE first few days of her engagement were very trying to Eunice Weldon.

Mrs. Groat did not overwork her, indeed Eunice's complaint was that the old woman refused to give her any work at all.

On the third day at breakfast she spoke on the matter to Digby Groat.

"I'm afraid I am not very much use here, Mr. Groat," she said; "it is a sin to take your money."

"Why?" he asked quickly.

"Your mother prefers to write her own letters," she said, "and really those don't seem to be very many!"

"Nonsense," he said sharply, and seeing that be had startled the girl he went on in a much gentler tone: "You see, my mother is not used to service of any kind. She's one of those women who prefer to do things for themselves, and she has simply worn herself to a shadow because of this independence of hers. There are hundreds of jobs that she could give you to do! You must make allowance for old women, Miss Weldon. They take a long time to work up confidence in strangers."

"I realize that," she nodded.

"Poor mother is rather bewildered by her own magnificence," he smiled, "but I am sure when she gets to know you, you will find your days very fully occupied."

He left the morning-room and went straight into his mother's little parlour, and found her in her dressing-room crouching over a tiny fire. He closed the door carefully and walked across to her and she looked up with a little look of fear in her eyes.

"Why aren't you giving this girl work to do?" he asked sharply.

"There's nothing for her to do," she wailed. "My dear, she is such an expense, and I don't like her."

"You'll give her work to do from to-day," he said, "and don't let me tell you again!"

"She'll only spy on me," said Mrs. Groat fretfully, "and I never write letters, you know that. I haven't written a letter for years until you made me write that note to the lawyer."

"You'll find work for her to do," repeated Digby Groat. "Do you understand? Get all the accounts that we've had for the past two years, and let her sort them out and make a list of them. Give her your bank account. Let her compare the cheques with the counterfoils. Give her anything. Damn you! You don't want me to tell you every day, do you?"

"I'll do it, I'll do it, Digby," she said hurriedly. "You're very hard on me, my boy. I hate this house," she said with sudden vehemence. "I hate the people in it. I looked into her room this morning and it is like a palace. It must have cost us thousands of pounds to furnish that room, and all for a work-girl—it is sinful!"

"Never mind about that," he said. "Find something to occupy her time for the next fortnight."

The girl was surprised that morning when Mrs. Groat sent for her.

"I've one or two little tasks for you, miss—I never remember your name."

"Eunice," said the girl, smiling.

"I don't like the name of Eunice," grumbled the old woman. "The last one was Lola! A foreign girl. I was glad when she left. Haven't you got another name?"

"Weldon is my other name," said the girl good-humouredly, "and you can call me 'Weldon' or 'Eunice' or anything you like, Mrs. Groat."

The old woman sniffed.

She had in front of her a big drawer packed with cheques which had come back from the bank.

"Go through these," she said, "and do something with them. I don't know what."

"Perhaps you want me to fasten them to the counterfoils," said the girl.

"Yes, yes, that's it," said Mrs. Groat. "You don't want to do it here, do you? Yes, you'd better do it here," she went on hastily. "I don't want the servants prying into my accounts."

Eunice put the drawer on the table, gathered together the stubs of the cheque books, and with a little bottle of gum began her work, the old woman watching her.

When, for greater comfort, the girl took off the gold wrist-watch which she wore, a present from her dead father, Mrs. Groat's greedy eyes focussed upon it and a look of animation came into the dull face.

It looked like being a long job, but Eunice was a methodical worker, and when the gong in the hall sounded for lunch, she had finished her labours.

"There, Mrs. Groat," she said with a smile, "I think that is the lot. All your cheques are here."

She put away the drawer and looked round for her watch, but it had disappeared. It was at that moment that Digby Groat opened the door and walked in.

"Hullo, Miss Weldon," he said with his engaging smile. "I've come back for lunch. Did you hear the gong, mother? You ought to have let Miss Weldon go."

But the girl was looking round.

"Have you lost anything?" asked Digby quickly.

"My little watch. I put it down a few minutes ago, and it seems to have vanished," she said.

"Perhaps it is in the drawer," stammered the old woman, avoiding her son's eye.

Digby looked at her for a moment, then turned to Eunice.

"Will you please ask Jackson to order my car for three o'clock?" he asked gently.

He waited until the door closed behind the girl and then: "Where is that watch?" he asked.

"The watch, Digby?" quavered the old woman.

"The watch, curse you!" he said, his face black with rage.

She put her hand into her pocket reluctantly and produced it.

"It was so pretty," she snivelled, and he snatched it from her hand.

A minute later Eunice returned.

"We have found your watch," he said with a smile. "You had dropped it under the table."

"I thought I'd looked there," she said. "It is not a valuable watch, but it serves a double purpose."

She was preparing to put it on.

"What other purpose than to tell you the time?" asked Digby.

"It hides a very ugly scar," she said, and extended her wrist. "Look." She pointed to a round red mark, the size of a sixpence. It looked like a recent burn.

"That's queer," said Digby, looking, and then he heard a strangled sound from his mother. Her face was twisted and distorted, her eyes were glaring at the gilt's wrist.

"Digby, Digby!" Her voice was a thin shriek of sound. "Oh, my God!"

And she fell across the table and before he could reach her, had dropped to the floor in an inert heap.

Digby stooped over his mother and then turned his head slowly to the frightened girl.

"It was the scar on your hand that did it," he said slowly. "What does it mean?"

Chapter 8

THE story of the scar and the queer effect it had produced on Mrs. Groat puzzled Jim almost as much as it had worried the girl. He offered his wild theory again and she laughed.

"Of course I shall leave," she said, "but I must stay until all Mrs. Groat's affairs are cleared up. There are heaps of letters and documents of all kinds which I have to index," she said, "at least Mr. Groat told me there were. And it seems so unfair to run away whilst the poor old lady is so ill. As to my being the young lady of fortune, that is absurd. My parents were South Africans. Jim, you are too romantic to be a good detective."

He indulged in the luxury of a taxi to carry her back to Grosvenor Square, and this time went with her to the house, taking his leave at the door.

Whilst they were talking on the step, the door opened and a man was shown out by Jackson. He was a short, thick-set man with an enormous brown beard.

Apparently Jackson did not see the two people on the step, at any rate he did not look toward them, but said in a loud voice:

"Mr. Groat will not be home until seven o'clock, Mr. Villa."

"Tell him I called," said the bearded man with a booming voice, and stepped past Jim, apparently oblivious to his existence.

"Who is the gentleman with the whiskers?" asked Jim, but the girl could give him no information.

Jim was not satisfied with the girl's explanation of her parentage. There was an old school-friend of his in business in Cape Town, as an architect, and on his return to his office, Jim sent him a long reply-paid cablegram. He felt that he was chasing shadows, but at present there was little else to chase, and he went home to his flat a little oppressed by the hopelessness of his task.

The next day he had a message from the girl saying that she could not come out that afternoon, and the day was a blank, the more so because that afternoon he received a reply to his cable. The reply destroyed any romantic dreams he might have had as to Eunice Weldon's association with the Danton millions. The message was explicit. Eunice May Weldon had been born at Rondebosch; on the 12th June, 1899; her parents were Henry William Weldon, musician, and Margaret May Weldon. She had been christened at the Wesleyan Chapel at Rondebosch, and both her parents were dead.

The final two lines of the cable puzzled him:

"Similar inquiries made about parentage Eunice Weldon six months ago by Selenger & Co., Brade Street Buildings."

"Selenger & Co.," said Jim thoughtfully. Here was a new mystery. Who else was making inquiries about the girl? He opened a Telephone Directory and looked up the name. There were several Selengers, but none of Brade Street Buildings. He put on his hat, and hailing a taxi, drove to Brade Street, which was near the Bank, and with some difficulty found Brade Street Buildings. It was a moderately large block of offices, and on the indicator at the door he discovered Selenger & Co. occupied No. 6 room on the ground floor.

The office was locked and apparently unoccupied. He sought the hall-keeper.

"No, sir," said that man, shaking his head. "Selengers' aren't open. As a matter of fact, nobody's ever there except at night."

"At night," said Jim, "that's an extraordinary time to do business."

The hall-keeper looked at him unfavourably.

"I suppose it is the way they do their business, sir," he said pointedly.

It was some time before Jim could appease the ruffled guardian, and then he learnt that Selengers were evidently privileged tenants. A complaint from Selengers had brought the dismissal of his predecessor, and the curiosity of a house-keeper as to what Selengers did so late at night had resulted in that lady being summarily discharged.

"I think they deal with foreign stock," said the porter. "A lot of cables come here, but I've never seen the gentleman who runs the office. He comes in by the side door."

Apparently there was another entrance to Selengers' office, an entrance reached by a small courtyard opening from a side passage. Selengers were the only tenants who had this double means of egress and exit, and also, it seemed, they were the only tenants of the building who were allowed to work all night.

"Even the stockbrokers on the second floor have to shut down at eight o'clock," explained the porter, "and that's pretty hard on them, because when the market is booming, there's work that would keep them going until twelve o'clock. But at eight o'clock, it is 'out you go' with the company that owns this building. The rents aren't high and there are very few offices to be had in the city nowadays. They have always been very strict, even in Mr. Danton's time."

"Mr. Danton's time," said Jim quickly. "Did he own this building? Do you mean Danton the shipowner millionaire?"

The man nodded.

"Yes, sir," he said, rather pleased with himself that he had created a sensation. "He sold it, or got rid of it in some way years ago. I happen to know, because I used to be an office-boy in these very buildings, and I remember Mr. Danton—he had an office on the first floor, and a wonderful office it was, too."

"Who occupies it now?"

"A foreign gentleman named Levenski. He's a fellow who's never here, either."

Jim thought the information so valuable that he went to the length of calling up Mr. Salter at his home. But Mr. Salter knew nothing whatever about the Brade Street Buildings, except that it had been a private speculation of Danton's. It had come into his hands as the result of the liquidation of the original company, and he had disposed of the property without consultation with Salter & Salter.

It was another blank wall.

Chapter 9

"I SHALL not be in the office to-day, sir. I have several appointments which may keep me occupied," said Jim Steele, and Mr. Salter sniffed.

"Business, Steele?" he asked politely.

"Not all of them, sir," said Jim. He had a shrewd idea that Mr. Salter guessed what that business was.

"Very good," said Salter, putting on his glasses and addressing himself to the work on his desk.

"There is one thing I wanted to ask, and that is partly why I came, because I could have explained my absence by telephone."

Mr. Salter put down his pen patiently.

"I cannot understand why this fellow Groat has so many Spanish friends," said Jim. "For example, there is a girl he sees a great deal, the Comtessa Manzana; you have heard of her, sir?"

"I see her name in the papers occasionally," said Mr. Salter.

"And there are several Spaniards he knows. One in particular named Villa. Groat speaks Spanish fluently, too."

"That is curious," said Mr. Salter, leaning back in his chair. "His grandfather had a very large number of Spanish friends. I think that somewhere in the background there may have been some Spanish family connection. Old man Danton, that is, Jonathan Danton's father, made most of his money in Spain and in Central America, and was always entertaining a houseful of grandees. They were a strange family, the Dantons. They lived in little water-tight compartments, and I believe on the day of his death Jonathan Danton hadn't spoken more than a dozen words to his sister for twenty years. They weren't bad friends, if you understand. It was just the way of the Dantons. There are other families whom I know who do exactly the same thing. A reticent family, with a keen sense of honour."

"Didn't Grandfather Danton leave Mrs. Groat any money? She was one of his two children, wasn't she?"

Septimus Salter nodded.

"He never left her a penny," he said. "She practically lived on the charity of her brother. I never understood why, but the old man took a sudden dislike to her. Jonathan was as much in the dark as I am. He used to discuss it with me and wondered what his sister had done to incur the old man's enmity. His father never told him—would never even discuss the sister with him. It was partly due to the old man's niggardly treatment of Mrs. Groat that Jonathan Danton made his will as he did.

"Probably her marriage with Groat was one of the causes of the old man's anger. Groat was nothing, a shipping clerk in Danton's Liverpool office. A man ill at ease in good society, without an 'h' to his name, and desperately scared of his wife. The only person who was ever nice to him was poor Lady Mary. His wife hated him for some reason or other. Curiously enough when he died, too, he left all his money to a distant cousin—and he left about £5,000. Where he got it from heaven knows. And now be off, Steele. The moment you come into this office," said Mr. Salter in despair, "you start me on a string of reminiscences that are deplorably out of keeping with a lawyer's office."

Jim's first call that morning was at the Home Office. He was anxious to clear up the mystery of Madge Benson. Neither Scotland Yard nor the Prisons Commissioners were willing to supply an unofficial investigator with the information he had sought, and in desperation he had applied to the Secretary of State's Department. Fortunately he had a "friend at court" in that building, a middle-aged barrister he had met in France, and his inquiry, backed by proof that he was not merely satisfying his personal curiosity, had brought him a note asking him to call.

Mr. Fenningleigh received him in his room with a warmth which showed that he had not forgotten the fact that on one occasion Jim had saved him from what might have been a serious injury, if not death, for Jim had dragged him to cover one night when the British headquarters were receiving the unwelcome attentions of ten German bombers.

"Sit down, Steele. I can't tell you much," said the official, picking up a slip of paper from his blotting-pad, "and I'm not sure that I ought to tell you anything! But this is the information which 'prisons' have supplied."

Jim took the slip from the barrister's hand and read the three lines.

"'Madge Benson, age 26. Domestic Servant. One month with H.L. for theft. Sentenced at Marylebone Police Court. June 5th, 1898. Committed to Holloway. Released July 2nd. 1898.'"

"Theft?" said Jim thoughtfully. "I suppose there is no way of learning the nature of the theft?"

Mr. Fenningleigh shook his head.

"I should advise you to interview the gaoler at Marylebone. These fellows have extraordinary memories for faces, and besides, there is certain to be a record of the conviction at the court. You had better ask Salter to apply; they will give permission to a lawyer."

But this was the very thing Jim did not want to do.

Chapter 10

EUNICE WELDON was rapidly settling down in her new surroundings. The illness of her employer, so far from depriving her of occupation, gave her more work than she had ever expected. It was true, as Digby Groat had said, that there were plenty of small jobs to fill up her time. At his suggestion she went over the little account books in which Mrs. Groat kept the record of her household expenses, and was astounded to find how parsimonious the old lady had been.

One afternoon when she was tidying the old bureau, she stopped in her work to admire the solid workmanship which the old furniture builders put into their handicraft.

The bureau was one of those old-fashioned affairs, which are half desk and half bookcase, the writing-case being enclosed by glass doors covered on the inside with green silk curtains.

It was the thickness of the two side-pieces enclosing the actual desk, which, unlike the writing-flap of the ordinary secretaire, was immovable, that arrested her attention. She was rubbing her hand admiringly along the polished mahogany surface when she felt a strip of wood give way under the pressure of her finger-tips. To her surprise a little flap about an inch wide and about six inches long had fallen down and hung on its in visible hinges, leaving a black cavity. A secret drawer in a secretaire is not an extraordinary discovery, but she wondered whether she ought to explore the recess which her accidental touch had revealed. She put in her fingers and drew out a folded paper. There was nothing else in the drawer, if drawer it could be called.

Ought she to read it, she wondered? If it had been so carefully put away, Mrs. Groat would not wish it to be seen by a third person. Nevertheless, it was her duty to discover what the document was, and she opened it.

To the top a piece of paper was attached on which a few words wire written in Mrs. Groat's hand:

"This is the will referred to in the instructions contained in the sealed envelope which Mr. Salter has in his possession."

The word "Salter" had been struck out and the name of the firm of solicitors, which had supplanted the old man had been substituted.

The will was executed on one of those forms, which can be purchased at any law stationer's. But apart from the preamble it was short:

"I give to my son, Digby Francis Groat, the sum of 20,000 pounds and my house and furniture at 409, Grosvenor Square. The remainder of my estate I give to Ramonez—Marquis of Estremeda, of Calle Receletos, Madrid."

It was witnessed by two names, unknown to the girl, and as they had described themselves as domestic servants it was probable that they had long since left her employment, for Mrs. Groat did not keep a servant very long.

What should she do with it? She determined to ask Digby.

Later, when going through the drawers on her desk she discovered a small miniature and was startled by the dark beauty of the subject. It was a head and shoulders of a girl wearing her hair in a way, which was fashionable in the late seventies. The face was bold, but beautiful, the dark eyes seemed to glow with life. The face of a girl who had her way, thought Eunice, as she noted the firm round chin. She wondered who it was and showed it to Digby Groat at lunch.

"Oh, that is a picture of my mother," he said carelessly.

"Your mother," said Eunice in astonishment, and he chuckled.

"You'd never think she was never like that; but she was, I believe, a very beautiful girl."—his face darkened—"just a little too beautiful," he said, without explaining what he meant.

Suddenly, he snatched the miniature from and looked on the back.

"I'm sorry," he apologized, and a sudden pallor had come to his face. "Mother sometimes writes things on the back of pictures, and I was rather—" he was going to say "scared "—"and I was rather embarrassed."

He was almost incoherent, an unusual circumstance, for Digby Groat was the most self-possessed of men.

He changed the subject by introducing an inquiry which he had meant to make some time before.

"Miss Weldon, can you explain that scar on your wrist?" he asked.

She shook her head laughingly.

"I'm almost sorry I showed it to you," she said. "It is ugly, isn't it?"

"Do you know how it happened?"

"I don't know," she said, "mother never told me. It looks rather like a burn."

He examined the little red place attentively.

"Of course," she went on, "it is absurd to think that the sight of my birthmark was the cause of your mother's stroke."

"I suppose it is," he nodded, "but it was a remarkable coincidence."

He had endeavoured to find from the old woman the reason of her sudden collapse, but without success. For three days she had laid in her bed speechless and motionless and apparently had neither heard nor seen him when he had made his brief visits to the sick room.

She was recovering now, however, and he intended, at the first opportunity, demanding a full explanation.

"Did you find anything else?" he asked suspiciously. He was never quite sure what new folly his mother might commit. Her passion for other people's property might have come to light.

Should she tell him? He saw the doubt and trouble in her face and repeated his question.

"I found your mother's will," she said.

He had finished his lunch, had pushed back his chair and was smoking peacefully. The cigar dropped from his hand and she saw his face go black.

"Her will?" he said. "Are you sure? Her will is at the lawyer's. It was made two years ago."

"This will was made a few months ago," said Eunice, troubled. "I do hope I haven't betrayed any secret of hers."

"Let me see this precious document," said Digby, starting up.

His voice was brusque, almost to rudeness. She wondered what had brought about this sudden change. They walked back to the old woman's shabby room and the girl produced a document from the drawer.

He read it through carefully.

"The old fool," he muttered. "The cussed drivelling old fool! Have you read this?" he asked sharply.

"I read a little of it," admitted the girl, shocked by the man's brutal reference to his mother.

He examined the paper again and all the time he was muttering something under his breath.

"Where did you find this?" he asked harshly.

"I found it by accident," explained Eunice. "There is a little drawer here "—she pointed to the seemingly solid side of the bureau in which gaped an oblong cavity.

"I see," said Digby Groat slowly as he folded the paper. "Now, Miss Weldon, perhaps you will tell me how much of this document you have read? "—he tapped the will on his palm.

She did not know exactly what to say. She was Mrs. Groat's servant and she felt it was disloyal even to discuss her private affairs with Digby.

"I read beyond your legacy," she admitted, "I did not read it carefully."

"And you saw that my mother had left me £20,000?" said Digby Groat, "and the remainder to—somebody else."

She nodded.

"Do you know who that somebody else was?"

"Yes," she said. "To the Marquis of Estremeda."

His face had changed from sallow to red, from red to a dirty grey, and his voice as he spoke shook with the rage he could not altogether suppress.

"Do you know how much money my mother will be worth?" he asked.

"No, Mr. Groat," said the girl quietly, "and I don't think you ought to tell me. It is none of my business."

"She will be worth a million and a quarter," he said between his teeth, "and she's left me £20,000 and this damned house!"

He swung round and was making for the door, and the girl, who guessed his intentions, went after him and caught his arm.

"Mr. Groat," she said seriously, "you must not go to your mother. You really must not!"

Her intervention sobered him and he walked slowly back to the fireplace, took a match from his pocket, lit it, and before the astonished eyes of the girl applied it to one corner of the document. He watched it until it was black ash and then put his foot upon the debris.

"So much for that!" he said, and turning caught the amazed look in the face of Eunice. "You think I've behaved disgracefully, I suppose," he smiled, his old debonair self. "The truth is, I am saving my mother's memory from the imputation of madness. There is no Marquis of Estremeda, as far as I know. It is one of the illusions which my mother has, that a Spanish nobleman once befriended her. That is the dark secret of our family, Miss Weldon," he laughed, but she knew that he was lying.

Chapter 11

The door of Digby Groat's study was ajar, and he caught a glimpse of Eunice as she came in and made her way up to her room. She had occupied a considerable amount of his thoughts that afternoon, and he had cursed himself that he had been betrayed into revealing the ugly side of his nature before one whom he wished to impress. But there was another matter troubling him. In his folly he had destroyed a legal document in the presence of a witness and had put himself into her power. Suppose his mother died, he thought, and the question of a will arose? Suppose Estremeda got hold of her, her testimony in the courts of law might destroy the value of his mother's earlier will and bring him into the dock at the Old Bailey.

It was an axiom of his that great criminals are destroyed by small causes. The spendthrift who dissipates hundreds of thousands of pounds, finds himself made bankrupt by a paltry hundred pounds, and the clever organizer of the Thirteen who had covered his traces so perfectly that the shrewdest police in the world had not been able to associate him with their many crimes, might easily be brought to book through a piece of stupidity which was dictated by rage and offended vanity. He was now more than ever determined that Eunice Weldon should come within his influence, so that her power for mischief should be broken before she knew how crushingly it might be employed.

It was not an unpleasant task he set himself, for Eunice exercised a growing fascination over him. Her beauty and her singular intelligence were sufficient lures, but to a man of his temperament the knowledge that she added to these gifts a purity of mind and soul gave her an added value. That she was in the habit of meeting the man he hated, he knew. His faithful Jackson had trailed the girl twice, and on each occasion had returned with the same report. Eunice Weldon was meeting Steele in the park. And the possibility that Jim loved her was the greatest incentive of all to his vile plan.

He could strike at Jim through the girl, could befoul the soul that Jim Steele loved best in the world. That would be a noble revenge, he thought, as he sat, pen in hand, and heard her light footsteps pass up the stairs. But he must be patient and the game must be played cautiously. He must gain her confidence. That was essential, and the best way of securing this end, was to make no reference to these meetings, to give her the fullest opportunity for seeing Jim Steele and to avoid studiously any suggestion that he himself had an interest in her.

He had not sought an interview with his mother. She had been sleeping all the afternoon, the nurse had told him, and he felt that he could be patient here also. At night, when he saw the girl at dinner, he made a reference to the scene she had witnessed in the old woman's sitting-room.

"You'll think I'm an awful cad, Miss Weldon," he said frankly, "but mother has a trick of making me more angry than any other person I have met. You look upon me as a very unfilial son?" he smiled.

"We do things we're ashamed of sometimes when we are angry," said Eunice, willing to find an excuse for the outburst. She would have gladly avoided the topic altogether, for her conscience was pricking her and she felt guilty when she remembered that she had spoken to Jim on the subject. Digby Groat was to make her a little more uncomfortable by his next remark.

"It is unnecessary for me to tell you, Miss Weldon," he said, with his smile, "that all which happens within these four walls is confidential. I need not express any fear that you will ever speak to an outsider about our affairs."

He had only to look at the crimson face, at the downcast eyes and the girl's fingers playing nervously with the silver, to realize that she had already spoken of the will, and again he cursed himself for his untimely exhibition of temper.

He passed on, to the girl's great relief, to another subject. He was having certain alterations made in his laboratory and was enthusiastic about a new electrical appliance which he had installed.

"Would you like to see my little den, Miss Weldon?" he asked.

"I should very much," said the girl.

She was, she knew, being despicably insincere. She did not want to see the laboratory. To her, since Jim had described the poor little dog who had been stretched upon the table, it was a place of horror. But she was willing to agree to anything that would take Digby Groat from the topic of the will, and the thought of her own breach of faith.

There was nothing very dreadful in the laboratory, she discovered. It was so white and clean and neat that her womanly instinct for orderliness could admire the well-arranged little room, with its shelves packed with bottles, its delicate glass retorts and its strange and mysterious instruments.

He did not open the locked doors that hid one cupboard which stood at one end of the laboratory, so she knew nothing of the grisly relics of his investigations. She was now glad she had seen the place, but was nevertheless as pleased to return to the drawing-room.

Digby went out at nine o'clock and she was left alone to read and to amuse herself as best she could. She called at Mrs. Groat's room on her way up and learnt from the nurse that the old lady was rapidly recovering.

"She will be quite normal to-morrow or the next day," said the nurse.

Here was another relief. Mrs. Groat's illness had depressed the girl. It was so terrible to see one who had been as beautiful as the miniature proved her to have been, struck down and rendered a helpless mass, incapable of thought or movement.

Her room, which had impressed her by its beauty the day she had arrived, had now been enhanced by the deft touches which only a woman's fingers can give. She had read some of the books which Digby Groat had selected for her entertainment, and some she had dipped into only to reject.

She spent the evening with The Virginian, and here Digby had introduced her to one of the most delightful creations of fiction. The Virginian was rather like Jim, she thought—but then all the heroes of all the books she read were rather like Jim.

Searching in her bag for her handkerchief her fingers closed on the little card which had been left on her table the night of her introduction to the Grosvenor Square household. She took it out and read it for the twentieth time, puzzling over the identity of the sender and the object he had in view.

What was the meaning of that little card, she wondered? And what was the story which lay behind it?

She put down her book and, rising, switched on the lamp over her writing-table, examining the card curiously. She had not altered her first impression that the hand had been made by a rubber stamp. It was really a beautiful little reproduction of an open palm and every line was distinct.

Who was her mysterious friend—or was he a friend? She shook her head. It could not be Jim, and yet—it worried her even to think of Jim in this connection. Whoever it was, she thought with a little smile, they had been wrong. She had not left the house and nothing had happened to her, and she felt a sense of pride and comfort in the thought that the mysterious messenger could know nothing of Jim, her guardian angel.

She heard a step in the passage and somebody knocked at her door. It was Digby Groat. He had evidently just come in.

"I saw your light," he said, "so I thought I would give you something I have brought back from the Ambassadors' Club."

The "something" was a big square box tied with lavender ribbon.

"For me?" she said in surprise.

"They were distributing them to the guests," he said, "and I thought you might have a taste for sweeties. They are the best chocolates in England."

She laughed and thanked nun. He made no further attempt to continue the conversation, but, with a nod, went to his room. She heard the door open and close, and five minutes later it opened again and his soft footsteps faded away.

He was going to his laboratory, she thought, and wondered, with a shiver, what was the experiment he was attempting that night.

She had placed the box on the table and had forgotten about it until she was preparing for bed, then she untied the pretty ribbons and displayed the contents.

"They're delicious," she murmured, and took one up in her fingers.

Thump!

She turned quickly and dropped the chocolate from her fingers.

Something had hit against her window, it sounded like a fist. She ran to the silken curtains which covered the glass doors from view and hesitated nervously for a moment; then with a little catch of breath she thought that possibly some boys had thrown a ball.

She pulled back the curtains violently and for a moment saw nothing. The balcony was clear and she unfastened the latch and stepped out. There was nobody in sight. She looked on the floor of the balcony for the object which had been thrown but could find nothing.

She went slowly back to her room and was closing the door when she saw and gasped. For on one of the panes was the life-size print of the Blue Hand!

Again that mysterious warning!

Chapter 12

EUNICE gazed at the hand spell-bound, but she was now more curious than alarmed. Opening the window again she felt gingerly at the impression. It was wet, and her finger-tip was stained a deep greasy blue, which wiped off readily on her handkerchief. Again she stepped out on to the balcony, and following it along, came to the door leading to the head of the stairs. She tried it. It was locked. Leaning over the parapet she surveyed the square. She saw a man and a woman walking along and talking together and the sound of their laughter came up to her. At the corner of the square she saw passing under a street-lamp a helmeted policeman who must, she calculated, have been actually in front of the house when the imprint was made.

She was about to withdraw to her room when, looking down over the portico, she saw the figure of a woman descending the steps of the house. Who was she? Eunice knew all the servants by now and was certain this woman was a stranger. She might, of course, be one of Digby Groat's friends or a friend of the nurse, but her subsequent movements were so unusual that Eunice was sure that this was the mysterious stranger who had left her mark on the window. So it was a woman, after all, thought Eunice in amazement, as she watched her cross the square to where a big limousine was waiting.

Without giving any instructions to the chauffeur the woman in black stepped into the car, which immediately moved off.

Eunice came back to the room and sat down in a chair to try to straighten her tangled mind. That hand was intended as a warning, she was sure of that. And now it was clear which way the visitor had come. She must have entered the house by the front door and have got on to the balcony through the door on the landing, locking it after her when she made her escape.

Looking in the glass, Eunice saw that her face was pale, but inwardly she felt more thrilled than frightened, and she had also a sense of protection, for instinctively she knew that the woman of the was a friend. Should she go downstairs and tell Digby Groat? She shook her head at the thought. No, she would reserve this little mystery for Jim to unravel. With a duster, which she kept in one of the cupboards, she wiped the blue impression from the window and then sat down on the edge of her bed to puzzle out the intricate and baffling problem.

Why had the woman chosen this method of warning her? Why not employ the mundane method of sending her a letter? Twice she had taken a risk to impress Eunice with the sense of danger, when the same warning might have been conveyed to her through the agency of the postman.

Eunice frowned at this thought, but then she began to realize that, had an anonymous letter arrived, she would have torn it up and thrown it into her waste-paper basket. These midnight visitations were intended to impress upon the girl the urgency of the visitor's fear for her.

It was not by any means certain that the woman who had left the house was the mysterious visitor. Eunice had never troubled to inquire into Digby Groat's character, nor did she know any of his friends. The lady in black might well have been an acquaintance of his, and to tell Digby of the warning and all that she had seen could easily create a very embarrassing situation for all concerned.

She went to bed, but it was a long time before sleep came to her. She dozed and woke and dozed again and at last decided to get up. She pulled aside the curtains to let in the morning light.

The early traffic was rumbling through the street, and the clear fragrance of the unsullied air came coldly as she stood and shivered by the open window. She was hungry, as hungry as a healthy girl can be in that keen atmosphere, and she bethought herself of the box of chocolates which Digby had brought to her. She had taken one from its paper wrapping and it was between her teeth when she remembered with a start that the warning had come at the very moment she was about to eat a chocolate! She put it down again thoughtfully, and went back to bed to pass the time which must elapse before the servants were about and any kind of food procurable.

Jim Steele was about to leave his little flat in Featherdale Mansions that morning when he was met at the door by a district messenger carrying a large parcel and a bulky letter. He at once recognized the handwriting of Eunice and carried the parcel into his study. The letter was written hurriedly and was full of apologies. As briefly as possible Eunice had related the events of the night.

"I cannot imagine that the chocolates had anything to do with it, but somehow you are communicating your prejudice against Digby Groat to me. I have no reason whatever to suspect him of any bad design toward me, and in sending these I am merely doing as you told me, to communicate everything unusual. Aren't I an obedient girl! And, please, Jim, will you take me out to dinner to-night. It is 'my night out,' and I'd love to have a leisurely meal with you, and I'm simply dying to talk about the Blue Hand! Isn't it gorgeously mysterious! What I shall try to catch up some of my arrears of sleep this afternoon so that I shall be fresh and brilliant." (She had written "and beautiful" in mockery but had scratched it out.)

Jim Steele whistled. Hitherto he had regarded the Blue Hand as a convenient and accidental method which the unknown had chosen for his or her signature. Now, however, it obtained a new significance. The Blue Hand had been chosen deliberately and for some reason which must be known to one of the parties concerned. To Digby Groat? Jim shook his head. Somehow he knew for certain that the Blue Hand would be as much of a mystery to Digby Groat as it was to the girl and himself. He had no particular reason for thinking this. It was one of those immediate instincts which carry their own conviction. But who else was concerned? He determined to ask his partner that morning if the Blue Hand suggested anything to him.

In the meantime there were the chocolates. He examined the box carefully. The sweetmeats were beautifully arranged and the box bore the label of a well-known West End confectioner. He took out three or four of the chocolates, placed them carefully in an envelope, and put the envelope in his pocket. Then he set forth for the city. As he closed his own door his eye went to the door on the opposite side of the landing, where dwelt Mrs. Fane and the mysterious Madge Benson. The door was ajar and he thought he heard the woman's voice on the ground floor below talking to the porter of the flats.

His foot was extended to descend the first of the stairs when from the flat came a sharp scream and a voice: "Madge, Madge, help!"

Without a second's hesitation he pushed open the door and ran down the passage. There were closed doors on either side, but the last on the right was open and a thin cloud of smoke was pouring forth. He rushed in, just as the woman, who was lying on the bed, was rising on her elbow as though she were about to get up, and tearing down the blazing curtains at one of the windows, stamped out the fire. It was all over in a few seconds and he had extinguished the last spark of fire from the blackened lace before he looked round at the occupant of the bed, who was staring at him wide-eyed.

She was a woman of between forty and forty-five, he judged, with a face whose delicate moulding instantly impressed him. He thought he had seen her before, but knew that he must have been mistaken. The big eyes, grey and luminous, the dark brown hair in which a streak of grey had appeared, the beautiful hands that lay on the coverlet, all of these he took in at one glance.

"I'm very greatly obliged to you, Mr. Steele," said the lady in a voice that was little above a whisper. "That is the second accident we have had. A spark from one of the engines must have blown in through the open window."

Just beneath her was the cutting of the London, Midland and Scottish Railway, and Jim, who had watched the heavily laden trains toiling slowly and painfully up the steep incline, had often wondered if there was any danger from the showers of sparks which the engines so frequently threw up.

"I must apologize for my rather rough intrusion," he said with his sweet smile. "I heard your screams. You are Mrs. Fane, aren't you?"

She nodded, and there was admiration in the eyes that surveyed his well-knit figure.

"I won't start a conversation with you under these embarrassing circumstances," said Jim with a laugh, "but I'd like to say how sorry I am that you are so ill, Mrs. Fane. Could I send you some more books?"

"Thank you," she whispered. "You have done almost enough."

He heard the door close as the servant, unconscious that anything was wrong, came in, and heard her startled exclamation as she smelt the smoke. Coming out into the passage he met Madge Benson's astonished face.

A few words explained his presence and the woman hustled him to the door a little unceremoniously.

"Mrs. Fane is not allowed to see visitors, sir," she said. "She gets so excited."

"What is the matter with her?" asked Jim, rather amused at the unmistakable ejection.

"Paralysis in both legs," said Madge Benson, and Jim uttered an exclamation of pity.

"Don't think I'm not grateful to you, Mr. Steele," said the woman earnestly; "when I saw that smoke coming out into the passage my heart nearly stopped beating. That is the second accident we have had."

She was so anxious for him to be off that he made no attempt to continue talking.

So that was Mrs. Fane, thought Jim, as he strode along to his office. A singularly beautiful woman. The pity of it! She was still young and in the bloom of health save for this terrible affliction.

Jim had a big heart for suffering humanity, and especially for women and children on whom the burden of sickness fell. He was half-way to the office when he remembered that Mrs. Fane had recognized him and called him by name! How could she have known him—she who had never left her sick-room?

Chapter 13

"Mr Groat will not be down to breakfast. He was working very late, miss."

Eunice nodded. She preferred the conversation of Digby Groat to the veiled familiarity of his shrewd-faced servant. It would be difficult for her to define in what way Jackson offended her. Outwardly he was respect itself, and she could not recall any term or word he had employed to which she could reasonably take offence. It was the assurance of the man, his proprietorial attitude, which irritated her. He reminded her of a boarding-house at which she had once stayed, where the proprietor acted as butler and endeavoured, without success, to combine the deference of the servant with the authority of the master.

"You were out very early this morning, miss," said Jackson with his sly smile as he changed her plates.

"Is there any objection to my going out before breakfast?" asked Eunice, her anger rising.

"None at all, miss," said the man blandly. "I hope I haven't offended you, only I happened to see you coming back."

She had been out to send the parcel and the letter to Jim, the nearest district messenger office being less than a quarter of a mile from Grosvenor Square. She opened her lips to speak and closed them again tightly. There was no reason in the world why she should excuse herself to the servant.

Jackson was not ready to take a rebuff, and besides, he had something important to communicate.

"You weren't disturbed last night, were you, miss?" he asked.

"What do you mean?" demanded Eunice, looking with a start.

His keen eye was on her and without any reason she felt guilty.

"Somebody was having a joke here last night, miss," he said, "and the governor is as wild as… well, he's mad!"

She put down her knife and fork and sat back in her chair.

"I don't quite understand you, Jackson," she said coldly. "What is the joke that somebody was having, and why do you ask me if I was disturbed? Did anything happen in the night?"

The man nodded.

"Somebody was in the house," he said, "and it is a wonder that Mr. Groat didn't hear it, because he was working in his laboratory. I thought perhaps you might have heard him searching the house afterwards."

She shook her head. Had the Blue Hand been detected, she wondered?

"How do you know that a stranger was in the house?" she asked.

"Because he left his mark," said the man grimly. "You know that white door leading to the laboratory, miss?"

She nodded.

"Well, when Mr. Groat came out about half-past two this morning he was going to turn out the hall lights when he saw a smudge of paint on the door. He went back and found that it was the mark of a Blue Hand. I've been trying to get it off all the morning, but it is greasy and can't be cleaned."

"The mark of a Blue Hand?" she repeated slowly and felt herself change colour. "What does that mean?"

"I'm blessed if I know," said Jackson, shaking his head. "The governor doesn't know either But there it was as plain as a pike-staff. I thought it was a servant who did it. There is one under notice and she might have been up to her tricks, but it couldn't have been her. Besides, the servants' sleeping-rooms are at the back of the house, and the door between the front and the back is kept locked."

So the mysterious visitor had not been satisfied with warning her. She had warned Digby Groat as well!

Eunice had nearly finished breakfast when Digby made his appearance. He was looking tired and haggard, she thought. He never looked his best in the early hours, but this morning he was more unprepossessing than usual. He shot a swift suspicious glance at the girl as he took his place at the table.

"You have finished, I'm afraid, miss Weldon," he said briefly. "Has Jackson told you what happened in the night?"

"Yes," said Eunice quietly. "Have you any idea what it means?"

He shook his head.

"It means trouble to the person who did it, if I catch him." he said; then, changing the conversation, he asked how his mother was that morning.

Eunice invariably called at Mrs. Groat's room on her way down, and she was able to tell him that his mother was mending rapidly and had passed a very good night.

"She can't get well too soon," he said. "How did you sleep, Miss Weldon?"

"Very well," she prevaricated.

"Have you tried my chocolates?" he smiled.

She nodded.

"They are beautiful."

"Don't eat too many at once, they are rather rich," he said, and made no further reference either to that matter or to the midnight visitor.

Later in the morning, when she was going about her work, Eunice saw workmen engaged on cleaning the canvas door. Apparently the blue stain could not be eradicated, and after a consultation with Digby the canvas was being painted a dull blue colour.

She knew that Digby was perturbed more than ordinarily. When she had met him, as she had occasionally that morning, he had worn a furtive, hunted look, and once, when she had gone into his study to bring to his notice an account which she had unearthed, he was muttering to himself.

That afternoon there was a reception at Lord Waltham's house in Park Lane, in honour of a colonial premier who was visiting England. Digby Groat found it convenient to cultivate the acquaintance of the aesthetic Lord Waltham, who was one of the great financial five of the City of London. Digby had gone cleverly to work to form a small syndicate for the immediate purchase of the Danton estate. The time had not yet come when he could dispose of this property, but it was fast approaching.

There were many women in that brilliant assembly who would have been glad to know a man reputedly clever, and certainly the heir to great wealth; but in an inverted sense Digby was a fastidious man. Society which met him and discussed him over their dinner-tables were puzzled by his avoidance of woman's society. He could have made a brilliant marriage, had he so desired, but apparently the girls of his own set had no attraction for him. There were intimates, men about

41

town, who were less guarded in their language when they spoke across the table after the women had gone, and these told stories of him which did not redound to his credit. Digby in his youth had had many affairs—vulgar, sordid affairs which had left each victim with an aching heart and no redress.

He had only come to "look in," he explained. There was heavy work awaiting him at home, and he hinted at the new experiment he was making which would take up the greater part of the evening.

"How is your mother, Groat?" asked Lord Waltham.

"Thank you, sir, I think she is better," replied Digby. He wanted to keep off the subject of his mother.

"I can't understand the extraordinary change that has come over her in late years," said Lord Waltham with a little frown. "She used to be so bright and cheerful, one of the wittiest women I have ever met. And then, of a sudden, all her spirits seemed to go and if you don't mind my saying so, she seemed to get old."

"I noticed that," said Digby with an air of profound concern, "but women of her age frequently go all to pieces in a week."

"I suppose there's something in that. I always forget you're a doctor," smiled Lord Waltham.

Digby took his leave and he, too, was chuckling softly to himself as he went down the steps to his waiting car. He wondered what Lord Waltham would say if he had explained the secret of his mother's banished brightness. It was only by accident that he himself had made the discovery. She was a drug-taker, as assiduous a "dope" as he had ever met in his professional career.

When he discovered this he had set himself to break down the habit. Not because he loved her, but because he was a scientist addicted to experiments. He had found the source of her supply and gradually had extracted a portion of the narcotic from every pellet until the drug had ceased to have its effect.

The result from the old woman's point of view was deplorable. She suddenly seemed to wither, and Digby, whom she had ruled until then with a rod of iron, had to his surprise found himself the master. It was a lesson of which he was not slow to take advantage, every day and night she was watched and the drug was kept from her. With it she was a slave to her habit; without it she was a slave to Digby. He preferred the latter form of bondage.

Mr. Septimus Salter had not arrived when Jim had reached the office that morning, and he waited, for he had a great deal to say to the old man, whom he had not seen for the better part of the week.

When he did come, a little gouty and therefore more than a little petulant, he was inclined to pooh-pooh the suggestion that there was anything in the sign of the Blue Hand.

"Whoever the poison is, he or she must have had the stamp by them—you say it looks like a rubber stamp—and used it fortuitously. No, I can't remember any Blue Hand in the business. If I were you I should not attach too much importance to this."

Although Jim did not share his employer's opinion he very wisely did not disagree.

"Now, what is this you wore telling me about a will? You say Mrs. Groat has made a new will, subsequent to the one she executed in this office?"

Jim assented.

"And left all her money away from the boy, eh?" said old Mr. Salter thoughtfully. "Curiously enough, I always had an idea that there was no love lost between that pair. To whom do you say the money was left?"

"To the Marquis of Estremeda."

"I know the name," nodded Mr. Salter. "He is a very rich grandee of Spain and was for some time an attache at the Spanish Embassy. He may or may not have been a friend of the Dantons, I cannot recall. There is certainly no reason why she should leave her money to one who, unless my memory is at fault, owns half a province and has three or four great houses in Spain. Now, here you are up against a real mystery. Now, what is your news?" he asked.

Jim had a little more to tell him.

"I am taking the chocolates to an analyst—a friend of mine," he said, and Mr. Salter smiled.

"You don't expect to discover that they are poisoned, do you?" he asked dryly. "You are not living in the days of Caesar Borgia, and with all his poisonous qualities I have never suspected Digby Groat of being a murderer."

"Nevertheless," said Jim, "I am leaving nothing to chance. My own theory is that there is something wrong with those innocent-looking sweetmeats, and the mysterious Blue Hand knew what it was and came to warn the girl."

"Rubbish," growled the old lawyer. "Get along with you. I have wasted too much time on this infernal case."

Jim's first call was at a laboratory in Wigmore Street, and he explained to his friend just enough to excite his curiosity for further details, which, however, Jim was not prepared to give.

"What do you expect to find?" said the chemist, weighing two chocolates in his palm.

"I don't know exactly what I expect," said Jim. "But I shall be very much surprised if you do not discover something that should not be there."

The scientist dropped the chocolates in a big test-tube, poured in a liquid from two bottles and began heating the tube over a Bunsen burner.

"Call this afternoon at three o'clock and I will give you all the grisly details," he said.

It was three o'clock when Jim returned, not expecting, it must be confessed, any startling results from the analysis. He was shown into the chemist's office, and there on the desk were three test-tubes, standing in a little wooden holder.

"Sit down, Steele," said Mendhlesohn. He was, as his name implied, a member of a great Jewish fraternity which has furnished so many brilliant geniuses to the world. "I can't quite make out this analysis," he said. "But, as you thought, there are certainly things in the chocolates which should not be there."

"Poison?" said Jim, aghast.

Mendhlesohn shook his head.

"Technically, yes," he admitted. "There is poison in almost everything, but I doubt whether the eating of a thousand of these would produce death. I found traces of bromide of potassium and traces of hyacin, and another drug which is distilled from cannabis indica."

"That is hashish, isn't it?"

Mendhlesohn nodded.

"When it is smoked it is called hashish; when it is distilled we have another name for it. These three drugs come, of course, into the category of poisons, and in combination, taken in large doses, they would produce unconsciousness and ultimately death, but there is not enough of the drug present in these sweets to bring about that alarming result."

"What result would it produce?" asked Jim.

"That is just what is puzzling me and my friend, Dr. Jakes," said Mendhlesohn, rubbing his unshaven chin. "Jakes thinks that, administered in small continuous doses, the effect of this drug would be to destroy the will-power, and, what for a better term I would describe in the German fashion, as the resistance-to-evil-power of the human mind. In England, as you probably know, when a nervous and highly excitable man is sentenced to death, it is the practice to place minute doses of bromide in everything he eats and drinks, in order to reduce him to such a low condition of mental resistance that even the thought of an impending doom has no effect upon him."

Jim's face had gone suddenly pale, as the horror of the villainous plot dawned upon him.

"What effect would this have upon a high-spirited girl, who was, let us say, being made love to by a man she disliked?"

The chemist shrugged his shoulders.

"I suppose that eventually her dislike would develop into apathy and indifference. She would not completely forgo her resistance to his attentions, but at the same time that resistance would be more readily overcome. There are only two types of mind," he went on, "the 'dominant' and the 'recessive.' We call the 'dominant' that which is the more powerful, and the 'recessive' that which is the less powerful. In this world it is possible for a little weak man to dominate a big and vigorous man, by what you would call the sheer force of his personality. The effect of this drug would ultimately be to turn a powerful mind into a weak mind. I hope I am not being too scientific," he smiled.

"I can follow you very well." said Jim quietly. "Now tell me this, Mendhlesohn, would it be possible to get a conviction against the person who supplied these sweets?"

Mendhlesohn shook his head.

"As I told you, the doses are in such minute quantities that it is quite possible they may have got in by accident. I have only been able to find what we chemists call a 'trace' so far, but probably the doses would be increased from week to week. If in three weeks' time you bring me chocolates or other food that has been tampered with, I shall be able to give you a very exact analysis."

"Were all the chocolates I brought similarly treated?"

Mendhlesohn nodded.

"If they have been doped," he went on, "the doping has been very cleverly done. There is no discoloration of the interior, and the drug must have been introduced by what we call saturation, which only a very skilful chemist or a doctor trained in chemistry would attempt."

Jim said nothing. Digby Groat was both a skilled chemist and a doctor trained in chemistry.

On leaving the laboratory he went for his favourite walk in Hyde Park. He wanted to be alone and think this matter out. He must act with the greatest caution, he thought. To warn the girl on such slender foundation was not expedient. He must wait until, the dose had been increased, though that meant that she was to act as a bait for Digby Groat's destruction, and he writhed at the thought. But she must not know; he was determined as to this.

That night he had arranged a pleasant little dinner, and he was looking forward eagerly to a meeting with one whose future absorbed his whole attention and thoughts. Even the search for Lady Mary Danton had receded into the background, and might have vanished altogether as a matter of interest were it not for the fact that Digby Groat and his affairs were so inextricably mixed up with the mystery. Whilst Eunice Weldon was an inmate of the Groats' house, the Danton mystery would never be completely out of his thoughts.

Chapter 14

JIM had never seen the girl in evening clothes, and he was smitten dumb by her ethereal beauty. She wore a simple dress of cream charmeuse, innocent of colour, except for the touch of gold at her waist. She looked taller to Jim's eyes, and the sweet dignity of her face was a benison which warmed and comforted his heart.

"Well," she asked as the cab was proceeding towards Piccadilly. "Am I presentable?"

"You're wonderful!" breathed Jim.

He sat stiffly in the cab, scarcely daring to move lest the substance of this beautiful dream be touched by his irreverent hands. Her loveliness was unearthly and he, too, could adore, though from a different standpoint, the glorious promise of her womanhood, the delicious contours of her Madonna-like face. She was to him the spirit and embodiment of all that womanhood means. She was the truth of the dreams that men dream, the divine substance of shadowy figures that haunt their thoughts and dreams.

"Phew!" he said, "you almost frighten me, Eunice."

He heard her silvery laugh in the darkness.

"You're very silly, Jim," she said, slipping her arm into his.

Nevertheless, she experienced a thrill of triumph and happiness that she had impressed him so.

"I have millions of questions to ask you," she said after they had been ushered to a corner of the big dining-room of the Ritz-Carlton. "Did you get my letter? And did you think I was mad to send you those chocolates? Of course, it was terribly unfair to Mr. Groat, but really, Jim, you're turning me into a suspicious old lady!"

He laughed gently.

"I loved your letter," he said simply. "And as for the chocolates——" he hesitated.

"Well?"

"I should tell him that you enjoyed them thoroughly," he smiled.

"I have," said the girl ruefully. "I hate telling lies, even that kind of lie."

"And the next box you receive," Jim went on, "you must send me three or four of its contents."

She was alarmed now, looking at him, her red lips parted, her eyebrows crescents of inquiry.

"Was there anything wrong with them?" she asked.

He was in a dilemma. He could not tell her the result of the analysis, and at the same time he could not allow her to run any farther into needless danger. He had to invent something on the spur of the moment and his excuse was lame and unconvincing.

Listening, she recognized their halting nature, but was sensible enough not to insist upon rigid explanations, and, moreover, she wanted to discuss the hand and its startling appearance in the middle of the night.

"It sounds almost melodramatic," said Jim, but his voice was grave, "and I find a great difficulty in reconciling the happening to the realities of life. Of one thing I'm sure," he went on, "and it is that this strange woman, if woman it be, has a reason for her acts. The mark of the hand is deliberately designed. That it is blue has a meaning, too, a meaning which apparently is not clear to Digby Groat. And now let us talk about ourselves," he smiled, and his hand rested for a moment over hers.

She did not attempt to withdraw her own until the waiter came in sight, and then she drew it away so gently as to suggest reluctance.

"I'm going to stay another month with the Groats," she informed him, "and then if Mrs. Groat doesn't find some real work for me to do I'm going back to the photographers'—if they'll have me."

"I know somebody who wants you more than the photographer," he said quietly, "somebody whose heart just aches whenever you pass out of his sight."

She felt her own heart beating thunderously, and the hand that he held under the cover of the table trembled.

"Who is that—somebody?" she asked faintly.

"Somebody who will not ask you to marry him until he can offer you an assured position," said Jim. "Somebody who loves the very ground you walk upon so much that he must have carpets for your dear feet and a mansion to house you more comfortably than the tiny attic overlooking the London, Midland and Scottish Railway."

She did not speak for a long time, and he thought he had offended her. The colour came and went in her face, the soft rounded bosom rose and fell more quickly than was usual, and the hand that he held closed so tightly upon his fingers that they were almost numb when she suddenly released her hold.

"Jim," she said, still averting her eyes, "I could work very well on bare boards, and I should love to watch the London, Midland and Scottish trains—go past your attic."

She turned her head to his and he saw that her eyes were bright with tears.

"If you're not very careful, Jim Steele," she said, with an attempt at raillery, "I shall propose to you!"

"May I smoke?" said Jim huskily, and when she nodded, and he lit his match, she saw the flame was quivering in his shaking hand.

She wondered what made him so quiet for the rest of the evening. She could not know that he was stunned and shaken by the great fortune that had come to him, that his heart was as numb with happiness as his fingers had been in the pressure of her hand.

When they drove back to the house that night she wanted him to take her in his arms in the darkness of the cab and crush her against his breast: she wanted to feel his kisses on her lips, her eyes. If he had asked her at that moment to run away with him, to commit the maddest folly, she would have consented joyously, for her love for the man was surging up like a bubbling stream of subterranean fire that had found its vent, overwhelming and burning all reason, all tradition.

Instead, he sat by her side, holding her hand and dreaming of the golden future which awaited him.

"Good night, Jim." Her voice sounded cold and a little dispirited as she put her gloved hand in his at the door of 409.

"Good night," he said in a low voice, and kissed her hand. She was nearly in tears when she went into her room and shut the door behind her. She walked to her dressing-table and looked in the glass, long and inquiringly, and then she shook her head. "I wish he wasn't so good," she said, "or else more of a hero!"

Chapter 15

JIM continued his journey to the flat, so enveloped in the rosy clouds which had descended upon him that he was unconscious of time or space, and it seemed that he had only stepped into the cab when it jerked to a halt before the portals of Featherdale Mansions. He might have continued in his dream without interruption had not the cabman, with some asperity, called him back to remind him that he had not paid his fare.

That brought him back to the earth.

As he was about to open the outer door of the flats (it was closed at eleven every night) the door opened of its own accord and he stepped back to allow a lady to pass. She was dressed from head to foot in black and she passed him without a word, he staring after her as she walked with quick steps to a motor-car that he had noticed drawn up a few yards from where his cab had stopped. Who was she? he wondered as the car passed out of sight.

He dismissed her from his thoughts, for the glamour of the evening was not yet passed, and for an hour he sat in his big chair, staring into vacancy and recalling every incident of that previous evening. He could not believe it was true that this half-divine being was to be his; and then, with a deep sigh, he aroused himself to a sense of reality.

There was work to be done, he thought, as he rose to his feet, and it was work for her. His income was a small one, and must be considerably augmented before he dare ask this beautiful lady to share his lot.

He glanced idly at the table. That afternoon he had been writing up his notes of the case and the book was still where he had left it, only—

He could have sworn he had left it open. He had a remarkable memory for little things, tiny details of placements and position, and he was sure the book had not only been closed, but that its position had been changed.

A woman came in the mornings to clean the flat and make his bed and invariably he let her in himself. She usually arrived when he was making his own breakfast—another fad of his. She had no key, and under any circumstances never came at night.

He opened the book and almost jumped.

Between the pages, marking the place where he had been writing, was a key of a peculiar design. Attached to the handle was a tiny label on which was written: "D.G.'s master key."

This time there was no sign of the Blue Hand, but he recognized the writing. It was the same which had appeared on the warning card which the girl had received.

The woman in black had been to his flat—and had left him the means to enter Digby Groat's premises!

"Phew!" whistled Jim in amazement.

Chapter 16

EUNICE woke in the morning with a queer little sense of disappointment. It was not until she was thoroughly awake, sitting up in bed and sipping the fragrant tea which the maid had brought her, that she analysed the cause. Then she laughed at herself.

"Eunice Weldon," she said, shaking her head sadly, "you're a bold woman! Because the best man in the world was too good, too silly, or too frightened, to kiss you, you are working up a grievance. In the first place, Eunice Weldon, you shouldn't have proposed to a man. It was unladylike and certain to lead to your feeling cheap. You should have been content to wait for the beautiful carpet under your feet and the mansion over your head, and should have despised the bare boards of an attic overlooking the railway. I don't suppose they are bare boards, Eunice," she mused. "They are certain to be very nicely covered and there will be all sorts of mementos of Jim's campaigns hanging on the walls or tucked away in odd little cupboards. And I'm sure, when the trains are not rattling past, that the view from the window is beautiful, and, anyway, I shouldn't have time to look out of the window. There would be Jim's shirts to mend, Jim's socks to dam, and—Eunice Weldon, get up!" she said hurriedly as she slipped out of bed.

Going along the corridor Digby Groat heard the sound of her fresh young voice singing in the bathroom, and he smiled.

The ripe beauty of the girl had come on him with a rush. She was no longer desirable, she was necessary. He had intended to make her his plaything, he was as determined now that she should be his decoration. He laughed aloud at the little conceit! A decoration! Something that would enhance him in the eyes of his fellows. Even marriage would be a small price to pay for the possession of that jewel.

Jackson saw him smiling as he came down the stairs.

"Another box of chocolates has arrived, sir," he said in a low voice, as though he were imparting a shameful secret.

"Throw them in the ashpit, or give them to my mother," said Digby carelessly, and Jackson stared at him.

"Aren't you—" he began.

"Don't ask so many questions, Jackson." Digby turned his glittering eyes upon his servant and there was an ugly look in his face. "You are getting just a little too interested in things, my friend. And whilst we are on this matter, let me say, Jackson, that when you speak to Miss Weldon I want you to take that damned grin off your face and talk as a servant to a lady; do you understand that?"

"I'm no servant," said the man sullenly.

"That is the part you are playing now, so play it," said Digby, "and don't sulk with me, or—"

His hand went up to a rack hanging on the wall, where reposed a collection of hunting-crops, and his fingers closed over the nearest.

The man started back.

"I didn't mean anything," he whined, his face livid. "I've tried to be respectful—"

"Get my letters," said Digby curtly, "and bring them into the dining-room."

Eunice came into the room at that moment.

"Good morning. Miss Weldon," said Digby, pulling out her chair from the table. "Did you have a nice dinner?"

"Oh, splendid," she said, and then changed the conversation.

She was dreading the possibility of his turning the conversation to the previous night, and was glad when the meal was finished.

Digby's attitude, however, was most correct. He spoke of general topics, and did not touch upon her outing, and when she went to Mrs. Groat's room to play at work, for it was only playing, the real work had been done, he did not, as she feared he might, follow her.

Digby waited until the doctor called, and waylaying him in the passage learnt that his mother had completely recovered, and though a recurrence of the stroke was possible, it was not immediately likely. He had a few words to say to her that morning.

Old Mrs. Groat sat by the window in a wheeled chair, a huddled, unlovely figure, her dark gloomy eyes surveyed without interest the stately square with its green leafy centrepiece. The change of seasons had for her no other significance than a change of clothing. The wild heart which once leapt to the call of spring, beat feebly in a body in which passion had burnt itself to bitter ashes. And yet the gnarled hands, crossing and re-crossing each other on her lap, had once touched and blessed as they had touched and blasted.

Once or twice her mind went to this new girl, Eunice Weldon. There was no ray of pity in her thought. If Digby wanted the girl, he would take her, and her fate interested old Jane Groat no more than the fate of the fly that buzzed upon the window, and whom a flick of her handkerchief presently swept from existence. There was more reason why the girl should go if... she frowned. The scar on the wrist was much bigger than a sixpence. It was probably a coincidence.

She hoped that Digby would concentrate on his new quest and leave her alone. She was mortally afraid of him, fearing in her own heart the length to which he would go to have his will. She knew that her life would be snuffed out, like the flame of a candle, if it were expedient for Digby to remove her. When she had recovered consciousness and found herself in charge of a nurse, her first thought had been of wonder that Digby had allowed her to revive. He knew nothing of the will, she thought, and a twisted smile broke upon the lined face. There was a surprise in store for him. She would not be there to see it, that was the pity. But she could gloat in anticipation over his chagrin and his impotent rage.

The handle of the door turned and there followed a whispered conversation. Presently the door closed again.

"How are you this morning, mother?" said the pleasant voice of Digby, and she blinked round at him in a flutter of agitation.

"Very well, my boy, very well," she said tremulously. "Won't you sit down?" She glanced nervously about for the nurse, but the woman had gone. "Will you tell the nurse I want her, my boy?" she began.

"The nurse can wait," said her dutiful son coolly. "There are one or two things I want to talk to you about before she returns. But principally I want to know why you executed a will in favour of Estremeda and left me with a beggarly twenty thousand pounds to face the world?"

She nearly collapsed with the shock.

"A will, my boy?" She whined the words. "What on earth are you talking about?"

"The will which you made and put into that secret drawer of your cabinet," he said patiently, "and don't tell me that I'm dreaming, or that you did it for a joke, or that it was an act of mental aberration on your part. Tell me the truth!"

49

"It was a will I made years ago, my dear," she quavered. "When I thought twenty thousand pounds was all the money I possessed."

"You're a liar," said Digby without heat. "And a stupid old liar. You made that will to spite me, you old devil!"

She was staring at him in horror.

Digby was most dangerous when he talked in that cool, even tone of his.

"I have destroyed the precious document," said Digby Groat in the same conversational voice, "and when you see Miss Weldon, who witnessed its destruction, I would be glad if you would tell her that the will she saw consumed was one which you made when you were not quite right in your head."

Mrs. Groat was incapable of speech. Her chin trembled convulsively and her only thought was how she could attract the attention of the nurse.

"Put my chair back against the bed, Digby," she said faintly. "The light is too strong."

He hesitated, but did as she asked, then seeing her hand close upon the bell-push which hung by the side of the bed, he laughed.

"You need not be afraid, mother," he said contemptuously, "I did not intend taking any other action than I have already taken. Remember that your infernal nurse will not be here all the time, and do as I ask you. I will send Miss Weldon up to you in a few minutes on the excuse of taking instructions from you and answering some letters which came for you this morning. Do you understand?"

She nodded, and at that moment the nurse came in.

Summoned to the sick-room, Eunice found her employer looking more feeble than she had appeared before she was stricken down. The old woman's eyes smouldered their hate, as the girl came into the room. She guessed it was Eunice who had discovered the will and loathed her, but fear was the greater in her, and after the few letters had been formally answered, Mrs. Groat stopped the girl, who was in the act of rising.

"Sit down again, miss Weldon," she said. "I wanted to tell you about a will of mine that you found. I'm very glad you discovered it. I had forgotten that I had made it."

Every word was strained and hateful to utter.

"You see, my dear young woman, I sometimes suffer from a curious lapse of memory, and—and—that will was made when I was suffering from an attack—"

Eunice listened to the halting words and was under the impression that the hesitation was due to the old woman's weakness.

"I quite understand, Mrs. Groat," she said sympathetically. "Your son told me."

"He told you, did he?" said Jane Groat, returning to her contemplation of the window; then, when Eunice was waiting for her dismissal, "Are you a great friend of my son's?"

Eunice smiled.

"No, not a great friend, Mrs. Groat," she said.

"You will be," said the woman, "greater than you imagine," and there was such malignity in the tone that the girl shuddered.

Chapter 17

JIM loved London, the noise and the smell of it. He loved its gentle thunders, its ineradicable good-humour, its sublime muddle. Paris depressed him, with its air of gaiety and the underlying fierceness of life's struggle. There was no rest in the soul of Paris. It was a city of strenuous bargaining, of ruthless exploitation. Brussels was a dumpy undergrown Paris, Berlin a stucco Gomorrah, Madrid an extinct crater beneath which a new volcanic stream was seeking a vent.

New York he loved, a city of steel and concrete teeming with sentimentalists posing as tyrants. There was nothing quite like New York in the world. Dante in his most prodigal mood might have dreamt New York and da Vinci might have planned it, but only the high gods could have materialized the dream or built to the master's plan. But London was London—incomparable, beautiful. It was the history of the world and the mark of civilization. He made a detour and passed through Covent Garden.

The blazing colour and fragrance of it! Jim could have lingered all the morning in the draughty halls, but he was due at the office to meet Mr. Salter.

Almost the first question that the lawyer asked him was:

"Have you investigated Selengers?"

The identity of the mysterious Selengers had been forgotten for the moment, Jim admitted.

"You ought to know who they are," said the lawyer. "You will probably discover that Groat or his mother are behind them. The fact that the offices were once the property of Danton rather supports this idea—though theories are an abomination to me!"

Jim agreed. There were so many issues to the case that he had almost lost sight of his main object.

"The more I think of it," he confessed "the more useless my search seems to me, Mr. Salter. If I find Lady Mary, you say that I shall be no nearer to frustrating the Groats?"

Mr. Septimus Salter did not immediately reply. He had said as much, but subsequently had amended his point of view. Theories, as he had so emphatically stated, were abominable alternatives to facts, and yet he could not get out of his head that if the theory he had formed to account for Lady Mary Danton's obliteration were substantiated, a big step would have been taken toward clearing up a host of minor mysteries.

"Go ahead with Selengers," he said at last; "possibly you may find that their inquiries are made as much to find Lady Mary as to establish the identity of your young friend. At any rate, you can't be doing much harm."

Chapter 18

AT twelve o'clock that night Eunice heard a car draw up in front of the house. She had not yet retired, and she stepped out on to the balcony as Digby Groat ascended the steps.

Eunice closed the door and pulled the curtains across. She was not tired enough to go to bed. She had very foolishly succumbed to the temptation to take a doze that afternoon, and to occupy her time she had brought up the last bundle of accounts, unearthed from a box in the wine-cellar, and had spent the evening tabulating them.

She finished the last account, and fixing a rubber band round them, rose and stretched herself, and then she heard a sound; a stealthy foot upon the stone of the balcony floor. There was no mistaking it. She had never heard it before on the occasion of the earlier visits. She switched out the light, drew back the curtains noiselessly and softly unlocked the French window. She listened. There it was again. She felt no fear, only the thrill of impending discovery. Suddenly she jerked open the window and stepped out, and for a time saw nothing, then as her eyes grew accustomed to the darkness, she saw something crouching against the wall.

"Who is that?" she cried.

There was no reply for a little time; then the voice said:

"I am awfully sorry to have frightened you, Eunice."

It was Jim Steele.

"Jim!" she gasped incredulously, and then a wave of anger swept over her. So it had been Jim all the time and not a woman! Jim, who had been supporting his prejudices by these contemptible tricks. Her anger was unreasonable, but it was very real and born of the shock of disillusionment. She remembered in a flash how sympathetic Jim had been when she told him of the midnight visitor and how he had pretended to be puzzled. So he was fooling her all the time. It was hateful of him!

"I think you had better go." she said coldly.

"Let me explain, Eunice."

"I don't think any explanation is necessary," she said. "Really, Jim, it is despicable of you."

She went back to her room with a wildly beating heart. She could have wept for vexation. Jim! He was the mysterious Blue Hand, she thought indignantly, and he had made a laughing-stock of her! Probably he was the writer of the letters, too, and had been in her room that night. She stamped her foot in her anger. She hated him for deceiving her. She hated him for shattering the idol she had set up in her heart. She had never felt so unutterably miserable as she was when she flung herself on her bed and wept until she fell asleep from sheer exhaustion.

"Damn!" muttered Jim as he slipped out of the house and strode in search of his muddy little car. An unprofitable evening had ended tragically.

"Bungling, heavy-footed jackass," he growled savagely, as he spun perilously round a comer and nearly into a taxi-cab which had ventured to the wrong side of the road. But he was not cursing the cab-driver. It was his own stupidity which had led him to test the key which had made a remarkable appearance on his table the night before. He had gone on to the balcony, merely to examine the fastenings of the girl's window, with the idea of judging her security.

He felt miserable and would have been glad to talk his trouble over with somebody. But there was nobody he could think of, nobody whom he liked well enough, unless it was—Mrs. Fane.

He half smiled at the thought and wondered what that invalid lady would think of him if he knocked her up at this hour to pour his woes into her sympathetic ears! The sweet, sad-faced woman had made a very deep impression upon him; he was surprised to find how often she came into his thoughts.

Half-way up Baker Street he brought his car to a walking pace and turned. He had remembered Selengers, and it had just occurred to him that at this hour he was more likely to profit by a visit than by a daytime call. It was nearly two o'clock when he stopped in Brade Street and descended.

He remembered the janitor had told him that there was a side entrance, which was used alone by Selengers. He found the narrow court which led to the back of the building, and after a little search discovered what was evidently the door which would bring him through the courtyard to the back of Brade Street Buildings. He tried the door, and to his surprise it was unlocked. Hearing the soft pad of the policeman's feet in the street, and not wishing to be discovered trying strange doors at that hour, he passed through and dosed it behind him, waiting till the officer had passed before he continued his investigations.

In preparation for such a contingency, he had brought with him a small electric lamp, and with the aid of this he found his way across the paved yard to a door which opened into the building. This was locked, he discovered to his dismay. There must be another, he thought, and began looking for it. There were windows overlooking the courtyard, but these were so carefully shuttered that it was impossible to tell whether lights shone behind them or not.

He found the other entrance at an angle of two walls, tried it, and to his delight it opened. He was in a short stone corridor and at the farther end was a barred gate. Short of this and to the right was a green door. He turned the handle softly, and as it opened he saw that a brilliant light was burning within. He pushed it farther and stepped into the room.

He was in an office which was unfurnished except for a table and a chair, but it was not the desolate appearance of the apartment which held his eye.

As he had entered a woman, dressed from head to foot in black, was passing to a second room, and at the sound of the door she turned quickly and drew her veil over her face. But she had delayed that action a little too long, and Jim, with a gasp of amazement, had looked upon the face of that "incurable invalid" Mrs. Fane!

Chapter 19

"Who are you, and what do you want?" she asked. He saw her hand drop to the fold of her dress, then: "Mr. Steele," she said as she recognized him.

"I'm sorry to disturb you," said Jim as he closed the door behind him, "but I wanted to see you pretty badly."

"Sit down, Mr. Steele. Did you see my—" she hesitated, "see my face?"

He nodded gravely.

"And did you recognize me?"

He nodded again.

"Yes, you are Mrs. Fane," he said quietly.

Slowly her hands rose and she unpinned the veil.

"You may lock the door," she said; "yes, I am Mrs. Fane."

He was so bewildered, despite his seeming self-possession, that he had nothing to say.

"You probably think that I have been practising a wicked and mean deception," she said, "but there are reasons—excellent reasons—why I should not be abroad in the daytime, and why, if I were traced to Featherdale Mansions, I should not be identified with the woman who walks at night."

"Then it was you who left the key?" he said.

She nodded, and all the time her eyes never left his face.

"I am afraid I cannot enlighten you any farther," she said, "partly because I am not prepared at this moment to reveal my hand and partly because there is so little that I could reveal if I did."

And only a few minutes before he had been thinking how jolly it would be if he could lay all his troubles and perplexities before her. It was incredible that he should be talking with her at this midnight hour in a prosaic city office. He looked at the delicate white hand which rested against her breast and smiled, and she, with her quick perceptions, guessed the cause of his amusement.

"You are thinking of the Blue Hand?" she said quickly.

"Yes, I am thinking of the Blue Hand," said Jim.

"You have an idea that that is just a piece of chicanery and that the hand has no significance?" she asked quietly.

"Curiously enough, I don't think that," said Jim. "I believe behind that symbol is a very interesting story, but you must tell it in your own time, Mrs. Fane."

She paced the room deep in thought, her hands clasped before her, her chin on her breast, and he waited, wondering how this strange discovery would develop.

"You came because you heard from South Africa that I had been making inquiries about the girl—she is not in danger?"

"No," said Jim with a wry face. "At present I am in danger of having offended her beyond pardon."

She looked at him sharply, but did not ask for an explanation.

"If you had thought my warnings were theatrical and meaningless, I should not have blamed you," she said after a while, "but I had to reach her in some way that would impress her."

"There is something I cannot understand, Mrs. Fane," said Jim. "Suppose Eunice had told Digby Groat of this warning?"

She smiled.

"He knows," she said quietly, and Jim remembered the hand on the laboratory door. "No, he is not the person who will understand what it all means," she said. "As to your Eunice," her lips parted in a dazzling little smile, "I would not like any harm to come to the child."

"Have you any special reason for wishing to protect her?" asked Jim.

She shook her head.

"I thought I had a month ago," she said. "I thought she was somebody whom I was seeking. A chance resemblance, fleeting and elusive, brought me to her; she was one of the shadows I pursued," she said with a bitter little smile, "one of the ghosts that led nowhere. She interested me. Her beauty, her fresh innocence and her character have fascinated me, even though she has ceased to be the real object of my search. And you, Mr. Steele. She interests you too?" She eyed him keenly.

"Yes," said Jim, "she interests me too."

"Do you love her?"

The question was so unexpected that Jim for once was not prepared with an answer. He was a reticent man ordinarily, and now that the opportunity presented he could not discuss the state of his feelings towards Eunice.

"If you do not really love her," said the woman, "do not hurt her, Mr. Steele. She is a very young girl, too good to be the passing amusement that Digby Groat intends she shall be."

"Does he?" said Jim between his teeth.

She nodded.

"There is a great future for you, and I hope that you will not ruin that career by an infatuation which has the appearance at the moment of being love."

He looked at the flushed and animated face and thought that next to Eunice she was the most beautiful woman he had ever seen.

"I am almost at the end of my pursuit," she went on, "and once we can bring Digby Groat and his mother to book, my work will be done." She shook her head sadly. "I have no further hope, no further hope," she said.

"Hope of what?" asked Jim.

"Finding what I sought," said Mrs. Fane, and her luminous eyes were fixed on his. "But I was mad, I sought that which is beyond recall, and I must use the remaining years of my life for such happiness as God will send to me. Forty-three years of waste!" she threw out her arms with a passionate gesture. "Forty-three years of suffering. A loveless childhood, a loveless marriage, a bitter betrayal. I have lost everything, Mr. Steele, everything. Husband and child and hope."

Jim started back.

"Good God!" he said, "then you are——"

"I am Lady Mary Danton." She looked at him strangely. "I thought you had guessed that."

Lady Mary Danton!

Then his search was ended, thought Jim with dismay. A queer unsatisfactory ending, which brought him no nearer to reward or advancement, both of which were so vitally necessary now.

"You look disappointed," she said, "and yet you had set yourself out to find Lady Mary." He nodded.

"And you have found her. Is she less attractive than you had imagined?"

He did not reply. He could not tell her that his real search had not been for her, but for her dead child.

"Do you know I have been seeing you every day for months, Mr. Steele?" she asked. "I have sat by your side in railway trains, in tube trains, and even stood by your side in tube lifts," she said with the ghost of a smile. "I have watched you and studied you and I have liked you."

She said the last words deliberately and her beautiful hand rested for a second on his shoulder.

"Search your heart about Eunice," she said, "and if you find that you are mistaken in your sentiments, remember that there is a great deal of happiness to be found in this or world." I There was no mistaking her meaning.

"I love Eunice," said Jim quietly, and the hand that rested on his shoulder was withdrawn, "I love her as I shall never love any other woman in life. She is the beginning and end of my dreams." He did not look up at the woman, but he could hear her quick breathing. Presently she said in a low voice:

"I was afraid so—I was afraid so." And then Jim, whose moral courage was beyond question, rose and faced her.

"Lady Mary," he said quietly, "you have abandoned hope that you will ever find your daughter?" She nodded.

"Suppose Eunice were your daughter? Would you give her to me?" She raised her eyes to his.

"I would give her to you with thankfulness," she said, "for you are the one man in the world whom I would desire any girl I loved to marry "— she shook her head. "But you, too, are pursuing shadows," she said. "Eunice is not my daughter—I have traced her parentage and there is no doubt at all upon the matter. She is the daughter of a South African musician."

"Have you seen the scar on her wrist?" he asked slowly. It was his last hope of identification, and when she shook her head, his heart' sank.

"I did not know that she had a scar on her wrist. What kind of a scar is it?" she asked.

"A small round burn the size of a sixpence," said Jim.

"My baby had no such mark—she had no blemish whatever."

"Nothing that would have induced some evilly disposed person to remove?"

Lady Mary shook her head.

"Oh, no," she said faintly. "You are chasing shadows, Mr. Steele, almost as persistently as I have done. Now let me tell you something about myself," she said, "and I warn you that I am not going to elucidate the mystery of my disappearance—that can wait. This building is mine," she said. "I am the proprietor of the whole block. My husband bought it and in a moment of unexampled generosity presented it to me the day after its purchase. In fact, it was mine when it was supposed to be his. He was not a generous man," she said sadly, "but I will not speak of his treatment of me. This property has provided me with an income ample for my needs, and I have, too, a fortune which I inherited from my father. We were desperately poor when I married Mr. Danton," she explained, "and only a week or two later my father's cousin, Lord Pethingham, died, and father inherited a very large sum of money, the greater portion of which came to me."

"Who is Madge Benson?" he demanded.

"Need you ask that?" she said. "She is my servant."

"Why did she go to prison?"

He saw the woman's ups close tight.

"You must promise not to ask questions about the past until I am ready to tell you, Mr. Steele," she said, "and now I think you can see me home." She looked round the office. "There are usually a dozen cablegrams to be seen and answered. A confidential clerk of mine comes in the morning to attend to the dispatch of wires which I leave for him. I have made myself a nuisance to every town clerk in the world, from Buenos Ayres to Shanghai," she said with a whimsical laugh in which there was a note of pain. "'The shadow he pursueth—' You know the old Biblical lines, Mr. Steele, and I am so tired of my pursuit, so very tired!"

"And is it ended now?" asked Jim.

"Not yet," said Lady Mary, and suddenly her voice grew hard and determined. "No, we've still got a lot of work before us, Jim——" She used the word shyly and laughed like a child when she saw him colour. "Even Eunice will not mind my calling you Jim," she said, "and it is such a nice name, easily remembered, and it has the advantage of not being a popular nickname for dogs and cats."

He was dying to ask her why, if she was so well off, she had taken up her residence in a little fiat overlooking a railway line, and it was probable that had he asked her, he would have received an unsatisfactory reply.

He took leave of her at her door.

"Good night, neighbour," he smiled.

"Good night, Jim," she said softly.

And Jim was still sitting in his big arm-chair pondering the events of the night when the first rays of the rising sun made a golden pattern upon the blind.

Chapter 20

EARLY the next morning a district messenger arrived at the flat with a letter from Eunice, and he groaned before he opened it.

She had written it in the hurt of her discovery and there were phrases which made him wince.

"I never dreamt it was you, and after all the pretence you made that this was a woman! It wasn't fair of you, Jim. To secure a sensation you nearly frightened me to death on my first night here, and made me look ridiculous in order that I might fall into your waiting arms! I see it all now. You do not like Mr. Groat, and were determined that I should leave his house, and this is the method which you have followed. I shall find it very hard to forgive you and perhaps you had better not see me again until you hear from me."

"Oh, damn," said Jim for the fortieth time since he had left her.

What could he do? He wrote half a dozen letters and tore them all up, every one of them into shreds. He could not explain to her how the key came into his possession without betraying Lady Mary Danton's secret. And now he would find it more difficult than ever to convince her that Digby Groat was an unscrupulous villain. The position was hopeless and he groaned again. Then a thought struck him and he crossed the landing to the next flat.

Madge Benson opened the door and this time regarded him a little more favourably.

"My lady is asleep," she said. She knew that Jim was aware of Mrs. Fane's identity.

"Do you think you could wake her? It is rather important."

"I will see," said Madge Benson, and disappeared into the bedroom. She returned in a few moments. "Madame is awake. She heard your knock," she said. "Will you go in?"

Lady Mary was lying on the bed fully dressed, wrapped in a dressing-gown, and she took the letter from Jim's hand which he handed her without a word, and read.

"Have patience," she said as she handed it back. "She will understand in time."

"And in the meanwhile," said Jim, his heart heavy, "anything can happen to her! This is the very thing I didn't want to occur."

"You went to the house. Did you discover anything?"

He shook his head.

"Take no notice and do not worry," said Lady Mary, settling down in the bed and closing her eyes, "and now please let me sleep, Mr. Steele; I have not been to bed for twenty-four hours."

Eunice had not dispatched the messenger with the letter to Jim five minutes before she regretted the impulse which had made her write it. She had said bitter things which she did not really feel. It was an escapade of his which ought to be forgiven, because at the back of it, she thought, was his love for her. She had further reason to doubt her wisdom, when, going into Digby Groat's library she found him studying a large photograph.

"That is very good, considering it was taken in artificial light," he said. It was an enlarged photograph of his laboratory door bearing the blue imprint, and so carefully had the photographer done his work, that every line and whorl of the finger-tips showed.

"It is a woman's hand, of course," he said.

"A woman!" she gasped. "Are you sure?"

He looked up in surprise.

"Of course I'm sure," said Digby; "look at the size of it! It is much too small for a man."

So she had wronged Jim cruelly! And yet what was he doing there in the house? How had he got in? The whole thing was so inexplicable that she gave it up, only—she must tell Jim and ask him to forgive her.

As soon as she was free she went to the telephone. Jim was not in the office.

"Who is it speaking?" asked the voice of the clerk.

"Never mind," said the girl hurriedly, and hung up the receiver.

All day long she was haunted by the thought of the injustice she had done the man she loved. He would send her a note, she thought, or would call her up, and at every ring of the telephone the blood came into her face, only to recede when she heard the answer, and discovered the caller was some person in whom she had no interest.

That day was one of the longest she had ever spent in her life. There was practically no work to do, and even the dubious entertainment of Digby was denied her. He went out in the morning and did not come back until late in the afternoon, going out again as soon as he had changed his clothes.

She ate her dinner in solitude and was comforted by the thought that she would soon be free from this employment. She had written to her old employer and he had answered by return of post, saying how glad he would be if he could get her back. Then they could have their little tea-parties all over again, she thought, and Jim, free of this obsession about Digby Groat, would be his old cheerful self,

The nurse was going out that evening and Mrs. Groat sent for her. She hated the girl, but she hated the thought of being alone much more.

"I want you to sit here with me until the nurse comes home," she said. "You can take a book and read, but don't fidget."

Eunice smiled to herself and went in search of a book.

She came back in time to find Mrs. Groat hiding something beneath her pillow. They sat in silence for an hour, the old woman playing with her hands on her lap, her head sunk forward, deep in thought, the girl trying to read, and finding it very difficult. Jim's face so constantly came between her and the printed page, that she would have been glad for an excuse to put down the book, glad for any diversion.

It was Mrs. Groat who provided her with an escape from her ennui.

"Where did you get that scar on your wrist?" she asked, looking up.

"I don't know," said Eunice. "I have had it ever since I was a baby. I think I must have been burnt."

There was another long silence.

"Where were you born?"

"In South Africa," said the girl.

Again there was an interval, broken only by the creak of Mrs. Groat's chair.

In sheer desperation, for the situation was getting on her nerves, Eunice said: "I found an old miniature of yours the other day, Mrs. Groat."

The woman fixed her with her dark eyes.

"Of me?" she said, and then, "Oh, yes, I remember. Well? Did you think it looks like me?" she asked sourly.

"I think it was probably like you years ago. I could trace a resemblance," said Eunice diplomatically.

The answer seemed to amuse Jane Groat. She had a mordant sense of humour, the girl was to discover.

"Like me when I was like that, eh?" she said. "Do you think I was pretty?"

Here Eunice could speak whole-heartedly and without evasion.

"I think you were very beautiful," she said warmly.

"I was, too," said the woman, speaking half to herself. "My father tried to bury me in a dead-and-alive village. He thought I was too attractive for town. A wicked, heartless brute of a man," she said, and the girl was somewhat shocked.

Apparently the old doctrine of filial piety did not run in Jane Groat's family.

"When I was a girl," the old woman went on, "the head of the family was the family tyrant, and lived for the exercise of his power. My father hated me from the moment I was born and I hated him from the moment I began to think."

Eunice said nothing. She had not invited the confidence, nevertheless it fascinated her to hear this woman draw aside the veil which hid the past. What great tragedy had happened, she speculated, that had turned the beautiful original of the miniature into this hard and evil-looking woman?

"Men would run after me. Miss Weldon," she said with a curious complacence. "Men whose names are famous throughout the world."

The girl remembered the Marquis of Estremeda and wondered whether her generosity to him was due to the part he had played as pursuing lover.

"There was one man who loved me," said the old woman reflectively, "but he didn't love me well enough. He must have heard something, I suppose, because he was going to many me and then he broke it off and married a simpering fool of a girl from Malaga."

She chuckled to herself. She had had no intention of discussing her private affairs with Eunice Weldon, but something had started her on a train of reminiscence. Besides, she regarded Eunice already as an unofficial member of the family. Digby would tell her sooner or later. She might as well know from her, she thought.

"He was a Marquis," she went on, "a hard man, too, and he treated me badly. My father never forgave me after I came back, and never spoke another word in his life, although he lived for nearly twenty years."

After she had come back, thought Eunice. Then she had gone away with this Marquis? The Marquis of Estremeda. And then he had deserted her, and had married this "simpering fool" from Malaga. Gradually the story was revealing itself before her eyes.

"What happened to the girl?" she asked gently. She was almost afraid to speak unless she stopped the loquacious woman.

"She died," said Mrs. Groat with a thin smile. "He said I killed her. I only told her the truth. Besides, I owed him something," she frowned. "I wish I hadn't," she muttered, "I wish I hadn't. Sometimes the ghost of her comes into this room and looks down at me with her deep black eyes and tells me that I killed her!" She mumbled something, and again with that note of complacency in her voice:

"When she heard that my child was the son—" she stopped quickly and looked round. "What am I talking about?" she said gruffly.

Eunice held her breath. Now she knew the secret of this strange household! Jim had told her something about it; told her of the little shipping clerk who had married Mrs. Groat, and for whom she had so profound a contempt. A shipping clerk from the old man's office, whom he had paid to marry the girl that her shame should be hidden.

Digby Groat was actually the son of—the Marquis of Estremeda! In law he was not even the heir to the Danton millions!

Chapter 21

EUNICE could only stare at the old woman. "Get on with your book," grumbled Mrs. Groat pettishly, and the girl, looking up through her lashes, saw the suspicious eyes fixed on her and the tremulous mouth moving as though she were speaking.

She must tell Jim. Despite her sense of loyalty, she realized that this was imperative. Jim was vitally interested in the disposal of the Danton estate, and he must know.

Suddenly the old woman began speaking again.

"What did I tell you just now?" she asked.

"You were talking about your youth," said the girl.

"Did I say anything about—a man?" asked the old woman suspiciously. She had forgotten! Eunice forced the lie to her lips.

"No," she replied, so loudly that anybody but this muddled woman would have known she was not speaking the truth.

"Be careful of my son," said Mrs. Groat after a while. "Don't cross him. He's not a bad lad, not a bad lad "—she shook her head and glanced slyly at the girl. "He is like his father in many ways."

"Mr. Groat?" said Eunice, and felt inexpressively mean at taking advantage of the woman's infirmity, but she steeled her heart with the thought that Jim must benefit by her knowledge.

"Groat," sneered, the old woman contemptuously, "that worm. No—yes, of course he was Groat. Who else could he be; who else?" she asked, her voice rising wrathfully.

There was a sound outside and she turned her head and listened.

"You won't leave me alone. Miss Weldon, until the nurse comes back, will you?" she whispered with pathetic eagerness. "You promise me that?"

"Why, of course I promise you," said Eunice, smiling; "that is why I am here, to keep you company."

The door handle turned and the old woman watched it, fascinated. Eunice heard her audible gasp as Digby came in. He was in evening dress and smoking a cigarette through a long holder.

He seemed for the moment taken aback by the sight of Eunice and then smiled.

"Of course, it is the nurse's night out, isn't it? How are you feeling to-night, mother?"

"Very well, my boy," she quavered, "very well indeed. Miss Weldon is keeping me company."

"Splendid," said Digby. "I hope Miss Weldon hasn't been making your flesh creep."

"Oh, no," said the girl, shocked, "of course I haven't. How could I?"

"I was wondering whether you had been telling mother of our mysterious visitor," he laughed as he pulled up an easy chair and sat down. "You don't mind my smoke, mother, do you?"

Eunice thought that even if old Jane Groat had objected it would not have made the slightest difference to her son, but the old woman shook her head and again turned her pleading eyes on Eunice.

"I should like to catch that lady," said Digby, watching a curl of smoke rise to the ceiling.

"What lady, my boy?" asked Mrs. Groat.

"The lady who has been wandering loose round this house at night, leaving her mark upon the panels of my door."

"A burglar," said the old woman, and did not seem greatly alarmed.

Digby shook his head.

"A woman and a criminal, I understand. She left a clear finger-print, and Scotland Yard have had the photograph and have identified it with that of a woman who served a sentence in Holloway Gaol."

A slight noise attracted Eunice and she turned to look at Jane Groat.

She was sitting bolt upright, her black eyes staring, her face working convulsively.

"What woman?" she asked harshly. "What are you talking about?'"

Digby seemed as much surprised as the girl to discover the effect the statement had made upon his mother.

"The woman who has been getting into this house and making herself a confounded nuisance with her melodramatic signature."

"What do you mean?" asked Mrs. Groat with painful slowness.

"She has left the mark of a Blue Hand on my door—"

Before he could finish the sentence his mother was on her feet, staring down at him with terror in her eyes.

"A Blue Hand!" she cried wildly. "What was that woman's name?"

"According to the police report, Madge Benson," said Digby.

For a second she glared at him wildly.

"Blue Hand," she mumbled, and would have collapsed but for the fact that Eunice had recognized the symptoms and was by her side and took her in her strong young arms.

Chapter 22

OUTSIDE the door in the darkened passage a man was listening intently. He had trailed Digby Groat all that evening, and had followed him into the house. Hearing a movement of footsteps within, he slipped into a side passage and waited. Eunice flew past the entrance to the passage and Jim Steele thought it was time that he made a move. In a few minutes the house would be aroused, for he guessed that the old woman had collapsed. It was a desperate, mad enterprise of his, to enter the great household at so early an hour, but he had a particular reason for wishing to discover the contents of a letter which he had seen slipped into Digby's hand that night.

Jim had been following him without success until Digby Groat had alighted at Piccadilly Circus apparently to buy a newspaper. Then a stranger had edged close to him and Jim had seen the quick passage of the white envelope. He meant to see that letter.

He reached the ground floor in safety and hesitated. Should he go into the laboratory whither Digby was certain to come, or should he—? A hurried footstep on the stairs above decided him: he slipped through the door leading to Digby's study. Hiding-place there was none: he had observed the room when he had been in there a few days previously. He was safe so long as nobody came in and turned on the lights. Jim heard the footsteps pass the door, and pulled his soft felt hat further over his eyes. The lower part of his face he had already concealed with a black silk handkerchief, and if the worst came to the worst, he could battle his way out and seek safety in flight. Nobody would recognize him in the old grey suit he wore, and the soft collarless shirt. It would not be a very noble end to the adventure, but it would be less ignominious than being exposed again to the scorn of Eunice.

Suddenly his heart beat faster. Somebody was coming into the library. He saw the unknown open the door and he crouched down so that the big library table covered him from observation. Instantly the room was flooded with light; Jim could only see the legs of the intruder, and they were the legs of Digby Groat. Digby moved to the table, and Jim heard the tear of paper as an envelope was slit, and then an exclamation of anger from the man.

"Mr. Groat, please come quickly!"

It was the voice of Eunice calling from the floor above, and Digby hurried out, leaving the door open. He was scarcely out of sight before Jim had risen; his first glance was at the table. The letter lay as Digby had thrown it down, and he thrust it into his pocket. In a second he was through the doorway and in the passage. Jackson was standing by the foot of the stairs looking up, and for the moment he did not see Jim; then, at the sight of the masked face, he opened his mouth to shout a warning, and at that instant Jim struck at him twice, and the man went down with a crash.

"What is that?" said Digby's voice, but Jim was out of the house, the door slammed behind him, and was racing along the sidewalk toward Berkeley Square, before Digby Groat knew what had happened. He slackened his pace, turned sharp to the right, so that he came back on his track, and stopped under a street light to read the letter.

Parts of its contents contained no information for him. But there was one line which interested him:

"Steele is trailing you: we will fix him to-night."

He read the line again and smiled as he walked on at a more leisurely pace.

Once or twice he thought he was being followed, and turned round, but saw nobody. As he strolled up Portland Place, deserted at this hour of the night save for an occasional car, his suspicion that he was being followed was strengthened. Two men, walking one behind the other, and keeping close to the railings, were about twenty yards behind him.

"I'll give yon a run for your money, my lads," muttered Jim, and crossing Marylebone Road, he reached the loneliest part of London, the outer circle of Regent's Park. And then he began to run: and Jim had taken both the sprint and the two-mile at the 'Varsity sports. He heard swift feet following and grinned to himself. Then came the noise of a taxi door shutting. They had picked up the "crawler" he had passed.

"That is very unsporting," said Jim, and turning, ran in the opposite direction. He went past the cab like a flash, and heard it stop and a loud voice order the taxi to turn, and he slackened his pace. He had already decided upon his plan of action—one so beautifully simple and so embarrassing to Digby Groat and his servitors, if his suspicions were confirmed, that it was worth the bluff. He had dropped to a walk at the sight of a policeman coming toward him. As the taxi came abreast he stepped into the roadway, gripped the handle of the door and jerked it open.

"Come out," he said sternly.

In the reflected light from the taximeter lantern he saw the damaged face of an old friend.

"Come out, Jackson, and explain just why you're following me through the peaceful streets of this great city."

The man was loath to obey, but Jim gripped him by the waistcoat and dragged him out, to the taxi-driver's astonishment.

The second man was obviously a foreigner, a little dark, thin-faced man with a mahogany face, and they stood sheepishly regarding their quarry.

"To-morrow you can go back to Mr. Digby Groat and tell him that the next time he sets the members of the Thirteen Gang to trail me, I'll come after him with enough evidence in each hand to leave him swinging in the brick-lined pit at Wandsworth. Do you understand that?"

"I don't know what you mean about to-morrow," said the innocent Jackson in an aggrieved tone. "We could have the law on you for dragging us out of the cab."

"Try it, here comes a policeman," said Jim. He gripped him by the collar and dragged him toward the interested constable. "I think this man wants to make a charge against me."

"No, I don't," growled Jackson, terrified as to what his master would sav when he heard of this undramatic end to the trailing of Jim.

Chapter 23

THERE is little that is romantic about a Police Station, and Digby Groat, who came in a towering rage to release his servants, was so furious that he could not even see the humorous side of the situation.

Once outside the building he dismissed one, Antonio Fuentes, with a curse, and poured the vials of wrath upon the unhappy Jackson.

"You fool, you blundering dolt," he stormed. "I told you to keep the man in sight; Bronson would have carried out my orders without Steele knowing. Why the hell did you carry a revolver?"

"How did I know he would play a dirty trick on me like that?" growled Jackson; "besides, I've never heard of the Firearms Act."

It was a stupid but a dangerous situation, thought Digby Groat, as he sat gnawing his nails in the library. It was an old theory of his that great schemes come to nought and great crimes are detected through some contemptible little slip on the part of the conspirators. What Jim had done in the simplest, easiest manner, was to set the police moving against the Thirteen, and to bring two of its members into the searching light of a magisterial inquiry. What was worse, he had associated Digby Groat with the proceedings, though Digby had an excuse that Jackson was his valet, and, as such, entitled to his interest. He had disclaimed all knowledge of Fuentes, but, as an act of generosity, as the Spaniard was a friend of his servant, had gone bail for him also.

Had the Thirteen brought off a big coup, their tracks would have been so hidden, their preparations so elaborated, that they would have defied detection. And here through a simple offence, which carried no more than a penalty of a five-pound fine, two of the members of the gang had come under police observation. Madmen!

It was a sleepless night for him—even his three hours was denied him. The doctor attending his mother did not leave until past three o'clock.

"It is not exactly a stroke, but I think a collapse due to some sudden shock."

"Probably you're right," said Digby. "But I thought it best to call you in. Do you think she will recover?"

"Oh. yes. I should imagine she'll be all right in the morning."

Digby nodded. He agreed with that conclusion, without being particularly pleased to hear it.

Difficulties were increasing daily, it seemed; new obstacles were besetting the smooth path of his life, and he traced them one by one and reduced them to a single cause—Jim Steele.

The next morning, after he had telephoned to a shady solicitor whom he knew, ordering him to defend the two men who were to be charged at Marylebone with offences under the Firearms Act, he sent for Eunice Weldon.

"Miss Weldon," he said, "I am making changes in this house, and I thought of taking my mother to the country next week. The air here doesn't seem to agree with her, and I despair of her getting better unless she has a radical change of environment."

She nodded gravely.

"I am afraid I shall not be able to accompany you, Mr. Groat."

He looked up at her sharply.

"What do you mean, Miss Weldon?" he asked.

66

"There is not sufficient work for me to do here, and I have decided to return to my old employment," she said.

"I am sorry to hear that, Miss Weldon," he said quietly, "but, of course, I will put no obstacle in your way. This has been a calamitous house recently, and your experience has not been an exceedingly happy one, and therefore I quite understand why you are anxious to leave us. I could have wished that you would have stayed with my mother until she was settled in my place in the country, but even on this point I will not press you."

She expected that he would have been annoyed, and his courtesy impressed her.

"I shall not, of course, think of leaving until I have done all that I possibly can," she hastened to add, as he expected her to do, "and really I have not been at all unhappy here, Mr. Groat."

"Mr. Steele doesn't like me, does he?" he smiled, and he saw her stiffen.

"Mr. Steele has no voice in my plans," she said, "and I have not seen him for several days."

So there had been a quarrel, thought Digby, and decided that he must know a little more of this. He was too wily to ask her point-blank, but the fact that they had not met on the previous day was known to him.

Eunice was glad to get the interview over and to go up to Mrs. Groat, who had sent for her a little earlier.

The old woman was in bed propped up with pillows, and apparently was her normal self again.

"You've been a long time," she grumbled.

"I had to see your son, Mrs. Groat," said Eunice.

The old woman muttered something under her breath.

"Shut the door and lock it," she said. "Have you got your note-book?"

Eunice pulled up a chair to the bedside, and wondered what was the important epistle that Mrs. Groat had decided to dictate. Usually she hated writing letters except with her own hand, and the reason for her summons had taken the girl by surprise.

"I want you to write in my name to Mary Weatherwale. Write that down." Old Mrs. Groat spelt the name. "The address is in Somerset—Hill Farm, Retherley, Somerset. Now say to her that I am very ill, and that I hope she will forgive our old quarrel and will come up and stay with me—underline that I am very ill," said Jane Groat emphatically. "Tell her that I will pay her expenses and give her £5 a week. Is that too much?" she asked. "No, don't put the salary at all. I'll be bound she'll come; they're poorly on, the Weatherwales. Tell her she must come at once. Underline that, too."

The girl scribbled down her instructions.

"Now listen. Miss Weldon." Jane Groat lowered her voice. "You are to write this letter, and not to let my son know that yon have done it: do you understand? Post it yourself; don't give it to that horrible Jackson. And again I tell you not to let my son know."

Eunice wondered what was the reason for the mystery, but she carried out the old woman's instructions, and posted the letter without Digby's knowledge.

There was no word from Jim, though she guessed he was the masked stranger who had knocked down Jackson in the hall. The strain of waiting was beginning to tell upon Eunice; she had grown oddly nervous, started at every sound, and it was this unusual exhibition of nerves which had finally decided her to leave Grosvenor Square and return to the less exciting life at the photographic studio.

Why didn't Jim write, she asked herself fretfully, and immediately after relentless logic demanded of her why she did not write to Jim.

She went for a walk in the park that afternoon hoping that she would see him, but although she sat for an hour under his favourite tree, he did not put in an appearance and she went home depressed and angry with herself.

A stamp upon a postcard would have brought him, but that postcard she would not write.

The next day brought Mrs. Mary Weatherwale, a stout, cheery woman of sixty, with a rosy apple face. She came in a four-wheeled cab, depositing her luggage in the hall, and greeted Eunice like an old friend.

"How is she, my darling?" ("Darling" was a favourite word of hers, Eunice discovered with amusement.) "Poor old Jane, I haven't seen her for years and years. We used to be good friends once, you know, very good friends, but she—but there, let bygones be bygones, darling; show me to her room, will you?"

It required all the cheerfulness of Mrs. Weatherwale to disguise her shock at the appearance of her one-time friend.

"Why, Jane," she said, "what's the matter with you?"

"Sit down, Mary," said the other pettishly. "All right, young lady, you needn't wait."

This ungrateful dismissal was addressed to Eunice, who was very glad to make her escape. She was passing through the hall later in the afternoon, when Digby Groat came in. He looked at the luggage, which had not been removed from the hall, and turned with a frown to Eunice.

"What is the meaning of this?" he asked. "To whom does this belong?"

"A friend of Mrs. Groat is coining to stay," said Eunice.

"A friend of mother's?" he answered quickly. "Do you know her name?"

"Mrs. Weatherwale."

She saw an instant change come over his face.

"Mrs. Weatherwale, eh," he said slowly. "Coming to stay here? At my mother's invitation, I suppose." He stripped his gloves and flung them on to the hall table and went up the stairs two at a time.

What happened in the sick-room Eunice could only guess. The first intimation she had that all was not well, was the appearance of Mrs. Weatherwale strutting down the stairs, her face as red as a turkey-cock, her bead bonnet trembling with anger. She caught sight of Eunice and beckoned her.

"Get somebody to find a cab for me, my darling," she said. "I'm going back to Somerset. I've been thrown out, my darling! What do you think of that? A woman of my age and my respectability; thrown out by a dirty little devil of a boy that I wouldn't harbour in my cow-yard." She was choleric and her voice was trembling with her righteous rage. "I'm talking about you," she said, raising her voice, and addressing somebody, apparently Digby, who was out of sight of Eunice. "You always were a cruel little beast, and if anything happens to your mother, I'm going to the police."

"You had better get out before I send for a policeman," said Digby's growling voice.

"I know you," she shook her fist at her invisible enemy. "I've known you for twenty-three years, my boy, and a more cruel and nastier man never lived!"

Digby came slowly down the stairs, a smile on his face.

"Really, Mrs. Weatherwale," he said, "you are unreasonable. I simply do not want my mother to be associated with the kind of people she chose as her friends when she was a girl. I can't be responsible for her vulgar tastes then; I certainly am responsible now."

The rosy face of the woman flushed an even deeper red.

"Common! Vulgar!" she spluttered. "You say that? You dirty little foreigner. Ah! That got home. I know your secret, Mr. Digby Groat!"

If eyes could kill, she would have died at that moment. He turned at the foot of the stairs and walked into his study, and slammed the door behind him.

"Whenever yon want to know anything about that!"—Mrs. Weatherwale pointed at the close door—"send for me. I've got letters from his mother about him when he was a child of so high that would make your hair stand on ends, darling."

When at last a cab bore the indignant lady from Grosvenor Square, Eunice breathed a sigh of relief. One more family skeleton, she thought, but she had already inspected the grisly bones. She would not be sorry to follow in Mrs. Weatherwale's footsteps, though, unknown to her, Digby Groat had other plans.

Those plans were maturing, when he heard a sharp rat-tat at the door and came out into the hall. "Was that a telegram for me?" he asked.

"No, for me," said Eunice, and there was no need to ask whom that message was from; her shining eyes, her flushed face, told their own story.

Chapter 24

"JIM!"

Eunice came running across the grass with out-stretched hands, oblivious to the fact that it was broad daylight and that she was being watched by at least a hundred idle loungers in the park.

Jim took both her hands in his and she experienced a moment of serene comfort. Then they both talked at once; they were both apologetic, interrupting one another's explanations with the expression of their own contrition.

"Jim, I'm going to leave Mrs. Groat's house," she said when they had reached sanity.

"Thank God for that," said Jim.

"You are so solemn about it," she laughed. "Did you really think I was in any danger there?"

"I know you were," he said.

She had so much to tell him that she did not know where to begin.

"Were you sorry not to see me?"

"The days I have not seen you are dead, and wiped off the calendar," said Jim.

"Oh, before I forget," said Eunice, "Mrs. Weatherwale has gone."

"Mrs. Weatherwale!" he repeated, puzzled.

"I haven't told you? No, of course not. I did not see you yesterday. But Mrs. Groat asked me to write to Mrs. Weatherwale, who is an old friend of hers, asking her to come and stay. I think Mrs. Groat is rather afraid of Digby."

"And she came?" asked Jim.

The girl nodded.

"She came and stayed about one hour, then arrived my lord Digby, who bundled her unceremoniously into the street. There is no love lost there, either, Jim. The dear old lady hated him. She was a charming old soul and called me 'darling.'"

"Who wouldn't?" said Jim. "I can call you darling even though I am not a charming old soul. Go on. So she went away? I wonder what she knows about Digby?"

"She knows everything. She knows about Estremeda, of that I am sure. Jim, doesn't that make a difference?"

He shook his head.

"If you mean does it make any difference about Digby inheriting his mother's money when she gets it, I can tell you that it makes none. The will does not specify that he is the son of John Groat, and the fact that he was born before she married this unfortunate shipping clerk does not affect the issue."

"When is the money to be made over to the Groats?"

"Next Thursday," said Jim, with a groan, "and I am just as far from stopping the transfer of the property as I have ever been."

He had not told her of his meeting with Lady Mary Danton. That was not his secret alone. Nor could he tell her that Lady Mary was the woman who had warned her.

They strolled across the Park towards the Serpentine and Jim was unusually preoccupied.

"Do you know, Eunice, that I have an uncanny feeling that you really are in some way associated with the Danton fortune?"

She laughed and clung tighter to his arm.

"Jim, you would make me Queen of England if you could," she said, "and you have just as much chance of raising me to the throne as you have of proving that I am somebody else's child. I don't want to be anybody else's, really," she said. "I was very, very fond of my mother, and it nearly broke my heart when she died. And daddy was a darling."

He nodded.

"Of course, it is a fantastic idea," he said, "and I am flying in face of all the facts. I have taken the trouble to discover where you were born. I have a friend in Cape Town who made the inquiries for me."

"Eunice May Weldon," she laughed. "So you can abandon that idea, can't you?" she said.

Strolling along by the side of the Serpentine, they had reached the bridge near the magazine and were standing waiting until a car had passed before they crossed the road. Somebody in the car raised his hat.

"Who was that?" said Jim.

"Digby Groat," she smiled, "my nearly late employer! Don't let us go to the tea-shop, Jim," she said; "let us go to your flat—I'd love to."

He looked at her dubiously.

"It is not customary for bachelors to give tea-parties to young females," he said.

"I'm sure it is"—she waved aside his objection. "I'm perfectly certain it happens every day, only they don't speak about it."

The flat delighted her and she took off her coat and busied herself in the little kitchenette.

"You told me it was an attic with bare boards," she said reproachfully as she was laying the cloth.

To Jim, stretched in his big chair, she was a thing of sheer delight. He wanted no more than to sit for ever and watch her flitting from room to room. The sound of her fresh voice was a delicious narcotic, and even when she called him, as she did, again and again, to explain some curio of his which hung in the hall, the spell was not broken.

"Everything is speckless," she said as she brought in the tea, "and I'm sure you haven't polished up those brasses and cleaned that china."

"You're right first time," said Jim lazily. "An unprepossessing lady comes in every morning at half-past seven and works her fingers to the bone, as she has told me more times than once, though she manages to keep more flesh on those bones than seems comfortable for her."

"And there is your famous train," she said, jumping up and going to the window as an express whizzed down the declivity. "Oh, Jim, look at those boys," she gasped in horror.

Across the line and supported by two stout poles, one of which stood in the courtyard of the flat, was a stretch of thin telegraph wires, and on these a small and adventurous urchin was pulling himself across hand-over-hand, to the joy of his companions seated on the opposite wall of the cutting.

"The young devil," said Jim admiringly.

Another train shrieked past, and running down into Euston trains moved at a good speed. The telegraph wire had sagged under the weight of the boy to such an extent that he had to lift up his legs to avoid touching the tops of the carriages.

"If the police catch him," mused Jim, "they will fine him a sovereign and give him a birching. In reality he ought to be given a medal. These little beggars are the soldiers of the future, Eunice, and some day he will reproduce that fearlessness of danger, and he will earn the Victoria Cross a jolly sight more than I earned it."

She laughed and dropped her head against his shoulder.

"You queer man," she said, and then returned to the contemplation of the young climber, who had now reached the opposite wall amidst the approving yells and shouts of his diminutive comrades.

"Now let us drink our tea, because I must get back," said the girl.

The cup was to her lips when the door opened and a woman came in. Eunice did not hear the turning of the handle, and her first intimation of the stranger's presence was the word "Jim." She looked up. The woman in the doorway was, by all standards, beautiful, she noticed with a pang. Age had not lined or marred the beauty of her face and the strands of grey in her hair added to her attraction. For a moment they looked at one another, the woman and the girl, and then the intruder, with a nod and a smile, said:

"I will see you again. I am sorry," and went out closing the door behind her.

The silence that followed was painful. Jim started three times to speak, but stopped as he realized the futility of explaining to the girl the reason of the woman's presence. He could not tell her she was Lady Mary Danton.

"She called you 'Jim,'" said the girl slowly. "Is she a friend of yours?"

"Er—yes," he replied awkwardly. "She is Mrs. Fane, a neighbour."

"Mrs. Fane," repeated the girl, "but you told me she was paralysed and could not get up. You said she had never been out of doors for years."

Jim swallowed something.

"She called you 'Jim,'" said the girl again. "Are you very great friends?"

"Well, we are rather," said Jim huskily. "The fact is, Eunice—"

"How did she come in?" asked the girl with a frown. "She must have let herself in with a key. Has she a key of your flat?"

Jim gulped.

"Well, as a matter of fact—" he began.

"Has she, Jim?"

"Yes, she has. I can't explain, Eunice, but you've got—"

"I see," she said quietly. "She is very pretty, isn't she?"

"Yes, she is rather pretty," admitted Jim miserably. "You see, we have business transactions together, and frequently I am out and she wants to get to my telephone. She has no telephone in her own flat, you see, Eunice," he went on lamely.

"I see," said the girl, "and she calls you 'Jim'?"

"Because we are good friends," he floundered. "Really, Eunice, I hope you are not putting any misconstruction upon that incident."

She heaved a little sigh.

"I suppose it is all right, Jim," she said, and pushed away her plate. "I don't think I will wait any longer. Please don't come back with me, I'd rather you didn't. I can get a cab; there's a rank opposite the flat, I remember."

Jim cursed the accident which had brought the lady into his room at that moment and cursed himself that he had not made a clean breast of the whole thing, even at the risk of betraying Lady Mary.

He had done sufficient harm by his incoherent explanation and he offered no other as he helped the girl into her coat.

"You are sure you'd rather go alone?" he said miserably.

She nodded.

They were standing on the landing. Lady Mary's front door was ajar and from within came the shrill ring of a telephone bell. She raised her grave eyes to Jim.

"Your friend has the key of your flat because she has no telephone of her own, didn't you say, Jim?"

He made no reply.

"I never thought you would lie to me," she said, and he watched her disappear down the staircase with an aching heart.

He had hardly reached his room and flung himself in his chair by the side of the tea-table, when Lady Mary followed him into the room.

"I'm sorry," she said, "I hadn't the slightest idea she would be here."

"It doesn't matter," said Jim with a wan smile, "only it makes things rather awkward for me. I told her a lie and she found me out, or rather, your infernal telephone did, Lady Mary."

"Then you were stupid," was all the comfort she gave him.

"Why didn't you stay?" he asked. "That made it look so queer."

"There were many reasons why I couldn't stay," said Lady Mary. "Jim, do you remember the inquiries I made about this very girl, Eunice Weldon, and which you made too?"

He nodded.

He wasn't interested in Eunice Weldon's obvious parentage at that moment.

"You remember she was born at Rondebosch?"

"Yes," he said listlessly. "Even she admits it," he added with a feeble attempt at a jest.

"Does she admit this?" asked Lady Mary. She pushed a telegram across the table to Jim, and he picked it up and read:

"Eunice May Weldon died in Cape Town at the age of twelve months and three days, and is buried at Rosebank Cemetery. Plot No. 7963."

Chapter 25

JIM read the cablegram again, scarcely believing his eyes or his understanding,

"Buried at the age of twelve months," he said incredulously, "but how absurd. She is here, alive, besides which, I recently met a man who knew the Weldons and remembered Eunice as a child. There is no question of substitution."

"It is puzzling, isn't it?" said Lady Mary softly, as she put the telegram in her bag. "But here is a very important fact. The man who sent me this cablegram is one of the most reliable private detectives in South Africa."

Eunice Weldon was born, Eunice Weldon had died, and yet Eunice Weldon was very much alive at that moment, though she was wishing she were dead.

Jim leant his elbow on the table and rested his chin on his palm.

"I must confess that I am now completely rattled," he said. "Then if the girl died, it is obvious the parents adopted another girl and that girl was Eunice. The question is, where did she come from, because there was never any question of her adoption, so far as she knew."

She nodded.

"I have already cabled to my agent to ask him to inquire on this question of adoption," she said, "and in the meantime the old idea is gaining ground, Jim."

His eyes met hers.

"You mean that Eunice is your daughter?"

She nodded slowly.

"That circular scar on her wrist? You know nothing about it?"

She shook her head.

"It may have been done after "—she faltered—"after—I lost sight of her."

"Lady Mary, will you explain how you came to lose sight of her?" asked Jim.

She shook her head.

"Not yet." she said.

"Then perhaps you will answer another question. You know Mrs. Groat?"

She nodded.

"Do you know a woman named Weatherwale?"

Lady Mary's eyes opened.

"Mary Weatherwale, yes. She was a farmer's daughter who was very fond of Jane, a nice, decent woman. I often wondered how Jane came to make such a friend. Why do you ask?"

Jim told her what had happened when Mrs. Weatherwale had arrived at Grosvenor Square.

"Let us put as many of our cards on the table as are not too stale to exhibit," she said. "Do you believe that Jane Groat had some part in the disappearance of my daughter?"

"Honestly I do," said Jim. "Don't you?"

She shook her head.

"I used to think so," she said quietly, "but when I made inquiries, she was exonerated beyond question. She is a wicked woman, as wicked as any that has ever been born," she said with a sudden fire that sent the colour flying to her face, "but she was not so wicked that she was responsible for little Dorothy's fate."

"You will not tell me any more about her?"

She shook her head.

"There is something you could say which might make my investigations a little easier," said Jim.

"There is nothing I can say—yet," she said in a low voice, as she rose and, without a word of farewell, glided from the room.

Jim's mind was made up. In the light of that extraordinary cablegram from South Africa, his misunderstanding with Eunice faded into insignificance. If she were Lady Mary's daughter! He gasped at the thought which, with all its consequences, came as a new possibility, even though he had pondered it in his mind.

He fixed upon Jane Groat as one who could supply the key of the mystery, but every attempt he had made to get the particulars of her past had been frustrated by ignorance, or the unwillingness of all who had known her in her early days.

There was little chance of seeing Septimus Salter in his office, so he went round to the garage where he housed his little car, and set forth on a voyage of discovery to Chislehurst, where Mr. Salter lived.

The old gentleman was alone; his wife and his eldest son, an officer, who was staying with him, had gone to Harrogate, and he was more genial in his reception than Jim had a right to expect.

"You'll stay to dinner, of course," he said.

Jim shook his head.

"No thank you, sir, I'm feeling rather anxious just now. I came to ask you if you knew Mrs. Weatherwale."

The lawyer frowned.

"Weatherwale, Weatherwale," he mused, "yes, I remember the name. I seldom forget a name. She appears in Mrs. Groat's will, I think, as a legatee for a few hundred pounds. Her father was one of old Danton's tenants."

"That is the woman," said Jim, and told his employer all that he had learnt about Mrs. Weatherwale's ill-fated visit to London.

"It only shows," said the lawyer when he had finished, "how the terrific secrets which we lawyers think are locked away in steel boxes and stowed below the ground in musty cellars, are the property of Tom, Dick and Harry! We might as well save ourselves all the trouble. Estremeda is, of course, the Spanish Marquis who practically lived with the Dantons when Jane was a young woman. He is, as obviously, the father of Digby Groat, and the result of this woman's mad passion for the Spaniard. I knew there was some sort of scandal attached to her name, but this explains why her father would never speak to her, and why he cut her out of his will. I'm quite sure that Jonathan Danton knew nothing whatever about his sister's escapade, or he would not have left her his money. He was as straitlaced as any of the Dantons, but, thanks to his father's reticence, it would seem that Mrs. Groat is going to benefit."

"And the son?" said Jim, and the lawyer nodded.

"She may leave her money where she wishes—to anybody's son, for the matter of that," said the lawyer. "A carious case, a very curious case"—he shook his grey head. "What do you intend doing?"

"I am going down to Somerset to see Mrs. Weatherwale," said Jim. "She may give us a string which will lead somewhere."

"If she'll give you a string that will lead Mr. Digby Groat to prison," growled the old lawyer, "get hold of it, Steele. and pull like the devil!"

Chapter 26

WHEN his alarm dock turned him out at six in the morning, Jim was both sleepy and inclined to be pessimistic. But as his mind cleared and he realized what results the day's investigations might bring, he faced his journey with a lighter heart.

Catching the seven o'clock from Paddington, he reached the nearest station to Mrs. Weatherwale's residence soon after nine. He had not taken any breakfast, and he delayed his journey for half an hour, whilst the hostess of a small inn facing the station prepared him the meal without which no Englishman could live, as she humorously described it, & dish of eggs and bacon.

It seemed as though he were in another world to that which he had left behind at Paddington. The trees were a little greener, the lush grasses of the meadows were a more vivid emerald, and overhead in the blue sky, defying sight, a skylark trilled passionately and was answered somewhere from the ground. Tiny furry shapes in their bright spring coats darted across the white roadway almost under his feet. He crossed a crumbling stone bridge and paused to look down into the shallow racing stream that foamed and bubbled and swirled on its way to the distant sea.

The old masons who had dressed these powdery ashlars and laid the moss-green stones of the buttresses, were dead when burly Henry lorded it at Westminster. These stones had seen the epochs pass, and the maidens who had leant against the parapet listening with downcast eyes to their young swains had become old women and dust and forgotten.

Jim heaved a sigh as he resumed his trudge. Life would not be long enough for him, if Eunice... if I—

He shook the thought from him and climbed steadily to his destination.

Hill Farm was a small house standing in about three acres of land, devoted mainly to market garden. There was no Mr. Weatherwale. He had been dead for twelve years, Jim learnt at the inn, but the old lady had a son who assisted in the management of the farm.

Jim strode out to what was to prove a pleasant walk through the glories of a Somerset countryside, and he found Mrs. Weatherwale in the act of butter-making. She had a pasture and a dozen cows, as she informed him later.

"I don't want to talk about Jane Groat," she said decisively, when he broached the object of his visit. "I'll never forgive that boy of hers for the trouble he gave me, apart from the insult. I gave up my work and had to hire a woman to take charge here and look after the boy—there's my fare to London—"

"I dare say all that could be arranged, Mrs. Weatherwale," said Jim with a laugh. "Mr. Digby Groat will certainly repay you."

"Are you a friend of his?" she asked suspiciously, "because if you are—"

"I am not a friend of his," said Jim. "On the contrary, I dislike him probably as much as you do."

"That is not possible," she said, "for I would as soon see the devil as that yellow-faced monkey."

She wiped her hands on her apron and led the way to the sunny little parlour.

"Sit ye down, Mr. What-you-may-call-it," she said briskly.

"Steele," murmured Jim.

"Mr. Steele, is it? Just sit down there, will you?" She indicated a window-seat covered with bright chintz. "Now tell me just what you want to know."

"I want to know something about Jane Groat's youth, who were her friends, and what you know about Digby Groat?"

Mrs. Weatherwale shook her head.

"I can't tell you much about that, sir," she said. "Her father was old Danton who owned Kennett Hall. You can see it from here "—she pointed across the country to a grey mass of buildings that showed above the hill-crest.

"Jane frequently came over to the farm. My father ard a bigger one in those days. All Hollyhock Hill belonged to him, but he lost his money through horses, drat them!" she said good-humouredly, and apparently had no particular grievance against the thoroughbred race-horse.

"And we got quite friendly. It was unusual, I admit, she being a lady of quality and me being a farmer's daughter; but lord! I've got stacks of letters from her, or rather, I had. I burnt them this morning."

"You've burnt them?" said Jim in dismay. "I was hoping that I should find something I wanted to know from those."

She shook her head.

"There's nothing there you would find, except a lot of silly nonsense about a man she fell in love with, a Spanish man."

"The Marquis of Estremeda?" suggested Jim.

She closed her lips.

"Maybe it was and maybe it wasn't," she said. "I'm not going to scandalize at my time of life, and at her time of life too. We've all made mistakes in our time, and I dare say you'll make yours, if you haven't made them already. Which reminds me, Mr.—I don't remember your name?"

"Steele," said Jim patiently.

"Well, that reminds me there's a duck of a girl in that house. How Jane can allow a beautiful creature like that to come into contact with a beast like Digby, I don't know. But that is all by the way. No, I burnt the letters, except a few. I kept one or two to prove that a boy doesn't change his character when he grows up. Why, it may be," she said that good-humouredly, "when Digby is hanged the newspaper reporters would like to see these, and they will be worth money to me!"

Jim laughed. Her good-humour was infectious, and when after an absence of five minutes she returned to the room with a small box covered with faded green plush, he asked; "You know nothing of Digby Groat's recent life?"

She shook her head.

"I only knew him as a boy, and a wicked little devil he was, the sort of boy who would pull a fly's wings off for the sport of it. I used to think those stories about boys were lies, but it was true about him. Do you know what his chief delight was as a boy?"

"No, I don't," smiled Jim. "It was something unpleasant, I am sure."

"To come on a Friday afternoon to Fanner Johnson's and see the pigs killed for market," she said grimly. "That's the sort of boy he was."

She took out a bundle of faded letters and fixing her large steel-rimmed spectacles, read them over.

"Here's one," she said; "that will show you the kind of kid he was."

"I flogged Digby to-day. He tied a bunch of crackers round the kitten's neck and let them off. The poor little creature had to be killed."

"That's Digby," said Mrs. Weatherwale, looking over her glasses. "There isn't a letter here which doesn't say that she had to beat him for something or other," she read on, reading half to herself, and Jim heard the word "baby."

"What baby was that?"

She looked at him.

"It wasn't her baby," she said.

"But whose was it?" insisted Jim.

"It was a baby she was looking after."

"Her sister-in-law's?" demanded Jim.

The woman nodded.

"Yes, Lady Mary Danton's, poor little soul—he did a cruel thing to her too."

Jim dare not speak, and without encouragement Mrs. Weatherwale said: "Listen to this, if you want to understand the kind of little devil Digby was."

"I had to give Digby a severe flogging to-day. Really, the child is naturally cruel. What do you imagine he did? He took a sixpence, heated it in the fire and put it on the poor baby's wrist. It left a circular bum."

"Great God!"-said Jim, springing to his feet, his face white. "A circular burn on the rest?"

She looked at him in astonishment.

"Yes, why?"

So that was the explanation, and the heiress to the Danton millions was not Digby Groat or his mother, but the girl who was called Eunice Weldon, or, as the world would know her, Dorothy Danton!

Chapter 27

EUNICE was Lady Mary's daughter! There was no doubt of it, no possible doubt. His instinct had proved to be right. How had she got to South Africa? He had yet to find a solution to the mystery.

Mrs. Weatherwale's rosy face was a picture of astonishment. For a moment she thought her visitor had gone mad.

"Will you read that piece again about Digby Groat burning the baby's wrist," said Jim slowly, and after a troubled glance at him, she complied.

"The little baby was lost soon after," she explained. "It went out with a nurse; one of Jane's girls took it out in a boat, and the boat must have been run down by some ship."

And then a light dawned upon Jim.

What ships passed to the east of the Goodwins (for it was near there that the disaster must have occurred) on the day of the tragedy? He must find it out immediately and he must take the letter from Jane to her friend in order to place it before Septimus Salter. Here, however, the woman demurred, and Jim, sitting down again, told her plainly and frankly all his fears and suspicions.

"What, that beautiful girl I saw in Jane's house?" said Mrs. Weatherwale in amazement. "You don't tell me!"

"I do," said Jim. "She has the mark on her wrist, a burn, and now I remember! Mrs. Groat knows she is the daughter of Lady Mary, too! It was the sight of that scar which brought about her stroke."

"I don't want any harm to happen to Jane, she hasn't been a bad friend of mine, but it seems to me only justice to the young lady that she should have the letter. As a matter of fact, I nearly burnt it."

"Thank God you didn't," said Jim fervently.

He carried his prize back by the first train that left for London and dashed into Salter's office with his news.

"If your theory is correct." said the old man when he had finished. "there ought not to be any difficulty in discovering the link between the child's disappearance and her remarkable appearance in Cape Town as Eunice Weldon. We have had confirmation from South Africa that Eunice Weldon did die at this tender age, so, therefore, your Eunice cannot be the same girl. I should advise you to get busy because the day after to-morrow I hand over the Danton estate to Mrs. Groat's new lawyers, and from what I can see of things," said Mr. Salter grimly, "it is Digby Groat's intention to sell immediately the whole of the Danton property."

"Does that amount to much?"

"It represents more than three-quarters of the estate," said the lawyer to Jim's surprise. "The Lakeside properties are worth four hundred thousand pounds, they include about twenty-four homesteads and six fairly big farms. You remember he came here some time ago to question us as to whether he had the right of sale. I had a talk with Bennetts—they are his new solicitors— only this morning," Mr. Salter went on stroking his big chin thoughtfully, "and it is pretty clear that Digby intends selling out. He showed Bennett the Power of Attorney which his mother gave him this morning."

The lawyer was faithfully interpreting Digby Groat's intentions. The will which Eunice had found had shocked him. He was determined that he should not be at the mercy of a capricious old woman who he knew disliked him as intensely as he hated her, and he had induced his mother to change her lawyers, not so much because he had any prejudice against Salter, but because he needed a new solicitor who would carry through the instructions which Salter would question.

Digby was determined to turn the lands and revenues of the Danton Estate into solid cash—cash which he could handle, and once it was in his bank he would breathe more freely.

That was the secret of his business in the city, the formation of a syndicate to take over the Danton properties on a cash basis, and he had so well succeeded in interesting several wealthy financiers in the scheme, that it wanted but the stroke of a pen to complete the deal.

"Aren't there sufficient facts now," asked Jim, "to prove that Eunice is Lady Mary's daughter?"

Salter shook his head.

"No," he said, "you must get a closer connection of evidence. But as I say, it should not be very difficult for you to do that. You know the date the child disappeared. It was on the 2ist June, 1901. To refresh your memory I would remark that it was in that year the Boar War was being fought out."

Jim's first call was at the Union African Steamship Company, and he made that just when the office was closing.

Fortunately the assistant manager was there, took him into the office and made a search of his records.

"None of our ships left London River on the 20th or 21st June," he said, "and, anyway, only our intermediate boats sail from there. The mail steamers sail from Southampton. The last ship to pass Southampton was the Central Castle. She was carrying troops to South Africa and she called at Plymouth on the 20th, so she must have passed Margate three days before."

"What other lines of steamers run to South Africa?"

The manager gave him a list, and it was a longer one than Jim had expected.

He hurried home to break the news to Lady Mary, but she was out. Her maid, the mysterious Madge Benson, said she had left and did not expect to be back for two or three days, and Jim remembered that Lady Mary had talked of going to Paris.

"Do you know where she would stay in Paris?"

"I don't even know she's gone to Paris, sir," said the woman with a smile. "Lady Mary never tells me her plans."

Jim groaned.

There was nothing to do but wait until to-morrow and pursue his inquiries. In the meantime it was growing upon him that Eunice and he were bad friends. He smiled to himself. What would she say when she discovered that the woman who called him "Jim" was her mother! He must possess his soul in patience for another twenty-four hours.

Suddenly a thought came to him, a thought which struck the smile from his lips. Eunice Weldon might forgive him and might marry him and change the drab roadway of life to a path of flowers, but Dorothy Danton was a rich woman, wealthy beyond her dreams, and Jim Steele was a poor man. He sat back in his chair to consider that disquieting revelation. He could never marry the girl Eunice now, he thought; it would not be fair to her, or to him. Suppose she never knew! He smiled contemptuously at the thought.

"Get thee behind me, Satan." he said to the little dog that crouched at his feet, watching him with eyes that never left his face. He bent down and patted the mongrel, who turned on his back with uplifted paws. "You and I have no particular reason to love Digby Groat, old fellow," he said, for this was the dog he had rescued from Digby's dissecting table, "and if he harms a hair of her head, he will be sorry he was ever born."

He began his search in the morning, almost as soon as the shipping offices opened. One by one they blasted his hopes, and he scarcely dared make his last call which was at the office of the African Coastwise Line.

"And I don't think it is much use going to them," said the clerk at the last but one of his calls. "They don't sail from London, they are a Liverpool firm, and all their packets sail direct from the Mersey. I don't think we have ever had a Coastwise boat in the London docks. I happen to know," he explained, "because I was in the Customs before I came to this firm."

The Coastwise Line was an old-fashioned firm and occupied an old-fashioned office in a part of London which seemed to be untouched by the passing improvements of the age. It was one of those firms which have never succumbed to the blandishments of the Company Promoter, and the two senior partners of the firm, old gentlemen who had the appearance of being dignitaries of the Church, were seated on either side of a big partner's table.

Jim was received with old-world courtesy and a chair was placed for him by a porter almost as ancient as the proprietors of the African Coastwise Line.

Both the gentlemen listened to his requirements in silence.

"I don't think we have ever had a ship pass through the Straits of Dover," said one, shaking his head. "We were originally a Liverpool firm, and though the offices have always been in London, Liverpool is our headquarters."

"And Avonmouth," murmured his partner.

"And Avonmouth, of course," the elder of the two acknowledged the correction with a slight inclination of his head.

"Then there is no reason why I should trouble you, gentlemen," said Jim with a heavy heart.

"It is no trouble, I assure you," said the partner, "but to make absolutely sure we will get our sailings for—June, 1901, I think you said?"

He rang a bell, and to the middle-aged clerk, who looked so young, thought Jim, that he must be the office-boy, he made his request known. Presently the clerk came back with a big ledger which he laid on the partners' desk. He watched the gentleman as his well-manicured finger ran carefully down the pages and suddenly stopped.

"Why, of course," he said, looking up, "do you remember we took over a Union African trip when they were hard pressed with transport work?"

"To be sure," said his partner. "It was the Battledore we sent out, she went from Tilbury. The only ship of ours that has ever sailed from Thames River."

"What date did it sail?" asked Jim eagerly.

"It sailed with the tide, which was apparently about eight o'clock in the morning of the 21st June. Let me see," said the partner, rising and going to a big chart that hung on the wall, "that would bring her up to the North Foreland Light at about twelve o'clock. What time did the accident occur?"

"At noon," said Jim huskily, and the partners looked at one another.

"I don't remember anything peculiar being reported on that voyage," said the senior slowly.

"You were in Switzerland at the time," said the other, "and so was I. Mr. Mansar was in charge."

"Is Mr. Mansar here?" asked Jim eagerly.

"He is dead," said the partner gently. "Yes, poor Mr. Mansar is dead. He died at a comparatively early age of sixty-three, a very amiable man, who played the piano remarkably well."

"The violin," murmured his partner.

Jim was not interested in the musical accomplishments of the deceased Mr. Mansar.

"Is there no way of finding out what happened on that voyage?"

It was the second of the partners who spoke.

"We can produce the log book of the Battledore."

"I hope we can," corrected the other. "The Battledore was sunk during the Great War, torpedoed off the Needles, but Captain Pinnings, who was in command of her at the time, is alive and hearty."

"And his log book?" asked Jim.

"That we must investigate. We keep all log books at the Liverpool office, and I will write to-night to ask our managing clerk to send the book down, if it is in his possession."

"This is very urgent," said Jim earnestly. "You have been so kind that I would not press you if it were not a matter of the greatest importance. Would it be possible for me to go to Liverpool and see the log?"

"I think I can save you that trouble," said the elder of the two, whose names Jim never knew. "Mr. Harry is coming down to London to-morrow, isn't he?"

His friend nodded.

"Well, he can bring the book, if it exists. I will tell the clerk to telephone to Liverpool to that effect," and with this Jim had to content himself, though it meant another twenty-four hours' delay.

He reported progress to the lawyer, when he determined upon making a bold move. His first business was the protection of Eunice, and although he did not imagine that any immediate danger threatened her, she must be got out of 409, Grosvenor Square, at the earliest opportunity.

If Lady Mary were only in London, how simple it would be! As it was, he had neither the authority to command nor the influence to request.

He drove up to 409, Grosvenor Square, and was immediately shown into Digby Groat's study.

"How do you do, Mr. Steele," said that bland gentleman. "Take a seat, will you? It is much more comfortable than hiding under the table," he added, and Jim smiled.

"Now, what can I do for you?"

"I want to see Miss Weldon," said Jim.

"I believe the lady is out; but I will inquire."

He rang the bell and immediately a servant answered the summons.

"Will you ask Miss Weldon to step down here?"

"It is not necessary that I should see her here," said Jim.

"Don't worry," smiled Digby. "I will make my exit at the proper moment."

The maid returned, however, with the news that the lady had gone out.

"Very well," said Jim, taking up his hat, and with a smile as bland as his unwilling host's, "I will wait outside until she comes in."

"Admirable persistence!" murmured Digby. "Perhaps I can find her."

He went out and returned again in a few minutes with Eunice.

"The maid was quite misinformed," he said urbanely. "Miss Weldon had not gone out."

He favoured her with a little bow and left the room, closing the door behind him.

Eunice stood with her hands behind her, looking at the man on whom her hopes and thoughts had centred, and about whose conduct such a storm was still raging in her bosom.

"You want to see me, Mr. Steele?"

Her attitude shook his self-possession and drove from his mind all the carefully reasoned arguments he had prepared.

"I want you to leave this house, Eunice," he said.

"Have you a new reason?" she asked, though she hated herself for the sarcasm.

"I have the best of reasons," he said doggedly. "I am satisfied that you are the daughter of Lady Mary Danton."

Again she smiled.

"I think you've used that argument before, haven't you?"

"Listen, Eunice, I beg of you," he pleaded. "I can prove that you are Lady Mary's daughter. That scar on your wrist was made by Digby Groat when you were a baby. And there is no Eunice Weldon. We have proved that she died in Cape Town a year after you were born."

She regarded him steadily, and his heart sank.

"That is very romantic," she said, "and have you anything further to say?"

"Nothing, except the lady you saw in my room was your mother."

Her eyes opened wider and then he saw a little smile come and go like a ray of winter sunshine on her lips.

"Really, Jim," she said, "you should write stories. And if it interests you, I might tell you that I am leaving this house in a few days. I am going back to my old employment. I don't want you to explain who the woman was who has the misfortune to be without a telephone and the good fortune to have the key of your flat," she said, her anger swamping the pity she had for him. "I only want to tell you that you have shaken my faith in men more than Digby Groat or any other man could have done. You have hurt me beyond forgiveness."

For a moment her voice quivered, and then with an effort of will she pulled herself together and walked to the door. "Good-bye, Jim," she said, and was gone.

He stood as she had left him, stunned, unable to believe his ears. Her scorn struck him like a whip, the injustice of her view of him deprived him of speech.

For a second a blinding wave of anger drowned all other emotions, but this passed. He could have gone now, for there was no hope of seeing her again and explaining even if he had been willing to offer any explanation.

But he stayed on. He was anxious to meet Digby Groat and find from his attitude what part he had played in forming the girl's mind. The humour of the situation struck him and he laughed, though his laughter was filtered through a pain that was so nearly physical that he could not distinguish the one from the other.

Chapter 28

THE end was coming. Digby Groat took too sane a view of things to mistake the signs.

For two years he had been in negotiation with a land agent in San Paulo and had practically completed the purchase of an estate. By subterranean methods he had skilfully disguised the identity of the purchaser, and on that magnificent ranch he intended to spend a not unpleasant life. It might not come to a question of flight, in which case the ranch would be a diversion from the humdrum life of England. And more than ever was he determined that Eunice Weldon should accompany him, and share, at any rate, a year of his life. Afterwards—he shrugged his shoulders. Women had come into his life before, had at first fascinated, and then bored him, and had disappeared from his ken. Probably Eunice would go the same way, though he could not contemplate the possibility at the moment.

The hours of the morning passed all too slowly for Jim Steele. The partner brothers had said that their "Mr. Harry" would arrive at one o'clock, and punctually at that hour Jim was waiting in the outer office.

Mr. Harry's train, however, must have been late. It was nearer two when he came in, followed by a porter carrying a thick parcel under his arm. Presently the porter came out. "Will you go in, sir," he said respectfully, and Jim stepped quickly into the room.

Mr. Harry, whom he had thought of as a boy, was a grave man of fifty, and apparently the younger brother of the eldest partner.

"We have found the log of the Battledore," said that gentleman, "but I have forgotten the date."

"June 21st," said Jim.

The log lay open upon the big table, and its presence brought an atmosphere of romance into this quiet orderly office.

"Here we are," said the partner. "Battledore left Tilbury 9 a.m. on the tide. Wind east by south-east, sea smooth, hazy." He ran his fingers down. "This is what I think you want."

For Jim it was a moment of intense drama. The partner was reading some preliminary and suddenly he came to the entry which was to make all the difference in the world to the woman whom Jim loved dearer than life.

"'Heavy fog, speed reduced at 11.50 to half. Reduced to quarter speed at 12.1. Bosun reported that we had run down small rowing boat and that he had seen two persons in the water. Able seaman Grant went overboard and rescued child. The second person was not found. Speed increased, endeavoured to speak Dungeness, but weather too hazy for flag signals'—this was before the days of wireless, you must understand, Mr. Steele." Jim nodded.

"'Sex of child discovered, girl, apparent age a few months. Child handed to stewardess.'"

Entry followed entry, but there was no further reference to the child until he came to Funchal.

"In the island of Madeira," he explained. "'Arrived Funchal 6 a.m. Reported recovery of child to British Consul, who said he would cable to London.'"

The next entry was: "Dakka—a port on the West Coast of Africa and French protectorate," said the partner. "'Received cable from British Consul at Funchal saying no loss of child reported to London police.'"

There was no other entry which affected Jim until one on the third day before the ship arrived at Cape Town.

"'Mr. Weldon, a Cape Town resident who is travelling with his wife for her health, has offered to adopt the child picked up by us on June 2ist, having recently lost one of his own. Mr. Weldon being known to the Captain and vouched for by Canon Jesson'—this was apparently a fellow-passenger of his," explained the partner—"'the child was handed to his care, on condition that the matter was reported to the authorities in Cape Town.'"

A full description of the size, weight, and colouring of the little waif followed, and against the query "Marks on Body" were the words "Scar on right wrist, doctor thinks the result of a recent burn."

Jim drew a long sigh.

"I cannot tell you gentlemen how grateful I am to you. You have righted a great wrong and have earned the gratitude of the child who is now a woman."

"Do you think that this is the young lady?"

Jim nodded.

"I am sure," he said quietly. "The log of Captain Pinnings supplies the missing link of evidence. We may have to ask you to produce this log in court, but I hope that the claim of our client will not be disputed."

He walked down Threadneedle Street, treading on air, and the fact that while he had gained for Eunice—her name was Dorothy now, but she would be always Eunice to him—a fortune, he had lost the greatest fortune that could be bestowed upon a man, did not disturb his joy.

He had made a rough copy of the log, and with this in his hand he drove to Septimus Salter's office and without a word laid the extracts before him.

Mr. Salter read, and as he read his eyes lit up.

"The whole thing is remarkably clear," he said; "the log proves the identity of Lady Mary's daughter. Your investigations are practically complete?"

"Not yet, sir," smiled Jim. "We have first to displace Jane Groat and her son," he hesitated, "and we must persuade Miss Danton to leave that house."

"In that case," said the lawyer, rising, "I think an older man's advice will be more acceptable than yours, my boy, and I'll go with you."

A new servant opened the door, and almost at the sound of the knock, Digby came out of his study, urbane and as perfectly groomed as usual.

"I want to see Miss Weldon," said the lawyer, and Digby stiffened at the sight of him. He would have felt more uncomfortable if he had known what was in Salter's mind.

Digby was looking at him straightly; his whole attitude, thought Jim, was one of tense anxiety.

"I am sorry you cannot see Miss Weldon," he said, speaking slowly. "She left with my mother by an early Continental train and at this moment, I should imagine, is somewhere in the region of Paris."

"That is a damned lie!" said Jim Steele calmly.

Chapter 29

THEY stood confronting one another, two men with murder in their hearts.

"It is a lie!" repeated Jim. "Miss Weldon is either here or she has been taken to that hell house of yours in Somerset!"

For the time being Digby Groat was less concerned by Jim's vehement insult than he was by the presence of the lawyer.

"So you lend yourself to this blackguardly outrage," he sneered. "I should have thought a man of your experience would have refused to have been made a dupe of by this fellow. Anyway," he turned to Jim, "Miss Weldon wants no more to do with you. She has told me about that quarrel, and really, Steele, you have behaved very badly."

The man was lying. Jim did not think twice about that. Eunice would never have made a confidant of him.

"What is your interest in Miss Weldon?" asked Digby, addressing the lawyer.

"Outside of a human interest, none," said old Salter, and Jim was staggered.

"But——" he began.

"I think we had better go, Steele," Salter interrupted him with a warning glance.

They were some distance from the house before Jim spoke.

"But why didn't you tell him, Mr. Salter, that Eunice was the heiress of the Danton fortune?"

Salter looked at him with an odd queer expression in his bright blue eyes.

"Suppose all you fear has happened," he said gently. "Suppose this man is the villain that we both believe he is, and the girl is in his power. What would be, the consequence of my telling him that Eunice Weldon was in a position to strip him of every penny he possesses, to turn him out of his house and reduce him to penury?"

Jim bit his lip.

"I'm sorry, sir." he said humbly. "I'm an impetuous fool."

"So long as Digby Groat does not know that Eunice threatens his position she is comparatively safe. At any rate, her life is safe. Once we let him learn all that we know, she is doomed."

Jim nodded.' "Do you think, then, that she is in real danger?" he asked.

"I am certain that Mr. Digby Groat would not hesitate 'at murder to serve his ends," said the lawyer gruffly.

They did not speak again until they were in the office in Marlborough Street, and then Jim threw himself down in a chair with a groan and covered his face with his hands.

"It seems as if we are powerless," he said bitterly, and then, looking up, "Surely, Mr. Salter, the law is greater than Digby Groat. Are there no processes we can set in motion to pull him down?" It was very seldom old Septimus Salter smoked in his office, but this was an occasion for an extraordinary happening. He took from a cabinet an old meerschaum pipe and polishing it on the sleeve of his broad-cloth coat, slowly filled it, packing down the straggling strands of tobacco which overflowed the pipe, with exasperating calmness.

"The law, my boy, is greater than Digby Groat, and greater than you or I. Sometimes ignorant people laugh at it, sometimes they sneer at it, generally they curse it. But there it is, the old dilatory machinery, grinding slow and grinding exceedingly small. It is not confined to the issue of search warrants, of arrest and judgments. It has a thousand weapons to strike at the cheat and the villain, and, by God, every one of those weapons shall be employed against Digby Groat!"

Jim sprang to his feet and gripped the old man's hand. "And if the law cannot touch him," he said, "I will make a law of these two hands and strangle the life out of him."

Mr. Salter looked at him admiringly, but a little amused. "In which case, my dear Steele," he said dryly, "the law will take you in her two hands and strangle the life out of you, and it doesn't seem worth while, when a few little pieces of paper will probably bring about as effective a result as your wilful murder of this damnable scoundrel."

Immediately Jim began his inquiries. To his surprise he learnt that the party had actually been driven to Victoria Station. It consisted of Eunice and old Mrs. Groat. Moreover, two tickets for Paris had been taken by Digby and two seats reserved in the Pullman. It was through these Pullman reservations that the names of Eunice and the old woman were easy to trace, as Digby Groat intended they should be.

Whether they had left by the train, he could not discover.

He returned to the lawyer and reported progress.

"The fact that Jane Groat has gone does not prove that our client has also gone," said the lawyer sensibly.

"Our client?" said Jim, puzzled.

"Our client," repeated Septimus Salter with a smile. "Do not forget that Miss Danton is our client, and until she authorizes me to hand her interests elsewhere—"

"Mr. Salter," interrupted Jim, "when was the Danton estate handed over to Bennetts?"

"This morning," was the staggering reply, though Mr. Salter did not seem particularly depressed.

"Good heavens," gasped Jim, "then the estate is in Digby Groat's hands?"

The lawyer nodded.

"For a while," he said, "but don't let that worry you at all. You get along with your search. Have you heard from Lady Mary?"

"Who, sir?" said Jim, again staggered.

"Lady Mary Danton," said the lawyer, enjoying his surprise. "Your mysterious woman in black. Obviously it was Lady Mary. I never bad any doubt of it, but when I learnt about the Blue Hand, I was certain. You see, my boy," he said with a twinkle in his eyes, "I have been making a few inquiries in a direction which you have neglected."

"What does the Blue Hand mean?" asked Jim.

"Lady Mary will tell you one of these days, and until she does, I do not feel at liberty to take you into my confidence. Have you ever been to a dyer's, Steele?"

"A dyer's, sir; yes, I've been to a dye-works, if that is what you mean."

"Have you ever seen the hands of the women who use indigo?"

"Do you suggest that when she disappeared she went to a dye-works?" said Jim incredulously.

"She will tell you," replied the lawyer, and with that he had to be content.

The work was now too serious and the strings were too widely distributed to carry on alone. Salter enlisted the services of two ex-officers of the Metropolitan Police who had established a detective agency, and at a conference that afternoon the whole of the story, as far as it was known, was revealed to Jim's new helpers, ex-Inspector Holder and ex-Sergeant Field.

That afternoon Digby Groat, looking impatiently out of the window, saw a bearded man strolling casually along the garden side of the square, a pipe in his mouth, apparently absorbed in the contemplation of nature and the architectural beauty of Grosvenor Square. He did not pay as much attention to the lounger as he might have done, had not his scrutiny been interrupted by the arrival of Mr. Bennett, an angular, sandy-haired Scotsman, who was not particularly enamoured of his new employer.

"Well, Mr. Bennett, has old Salter handed over all the documents?"

"Yes, sir," said Bennett, "every one."

"You are sure he has not been up to any trickery?"

Mr. Bennett regarded him coldly.

"Mr. Septimus Salter, sir," he said quietly, "is an eminent lawyer, whose name is respected wherever it is mentioned. Great lawyers do not indulge in trickery."

"Well, you needn't get offended. Good Lord, you don't suppose he feels friendly towards you, do you?"

"What he feels to me, sir," said Mr. Bennett, his strong northern accent betraying his annoyance, "is a matter of complete indifference. It is what I think of him that we are discussing. The leases of the Lakeside Property have been prepared for transfer. You are not losing much time, Mr. Groat."

"No," said Digby, after a moment's thought. "The fact is, the people in the syndicate which is purchasing this property are very anxious to take possession. What is the earliest you can transfer?"

"To-morrow," was the reply. "I suppose "—he hesitated—"I suppose there is no question of the original heiress of the will—Dorothy Danton, I think her name is—turning up unexpectedly at the last moment?"

Digby smiled.

"Dorothy Danton, as you call her, has been food for the fishes these twenty years," he said. "Don't you worry your head about her."

"Very good," said Bennett, producing a number of papers from a black leather portfolio. "Your signature will be required on four of these, and the signature of your mother on the fifth."

Digby frowned.

"My mother? I thought it was unnecessary that she should sign anything. I have her Power of Attorney."

"Unfortunately the Power of Attorney is not sufficiently comprehensive to allow you to sign away certain royalty rights which descended to her through her father. They are not very valuable," said the lawyer, "but they give her lien upon Kennett Hall, and in these circumstances, I think you had better not depend upon the Power of Attorney in case there is any dispute. Mr. Salter is a very shrewd man, and when the particulars of this transaction are brought to his notice, I think it is very likely that, feeling his responsibility as Mr. Danton's late lawyer, he will enter a caveat."

"What is a caveat?"

"Literally," said Mr. Bennett, "a caveat emptor means 'let the purchaser beware,' and if a caveat is entered, your syndicate would not dare take the risk of paying you for the property, even though the caveat had no effect upon the estate which were transferred by virtue of your Power of Attorney."

Digby tugged at his little moustache and stared out of the window for a long time.

"All right, I'll get her signature."

"She is in Paris, I understand."

Digby shot a quick glance at him.

"How do you know?" he asked.

"I had to call at Mr. Salter's office to-day," he said, "to verify and agree to the list of securities which he handed me, and he mentioned the matter in passing."

Digby growled something under his breath.

"Is it necessary that you should see Salter at all?" he asked with asperity.

"It is necessary that I should conduct my own business in my own way," said Mr. Bennett with that acid smile of his.

Digby shot an angry glance at him and resolved that as soon as the business was completed, he would have little use for this uncompromising Scotsman. He hated the law and he hated lawyers, and he had been under the impression that Messrs. Bennett would be so overwhelmed with joy at the prospect of administering his estate that they would agree to any suggestion he made. He had yet to learn that the complacent lawyer is a figure of fiction, and if he is found at all, it is in the character of the seedy broken-down old solicitor who hangs about Police Courts and who interviews his clients in the bar parlour of the nearest public-house.

"Very good," he said, "give me the paper. I will get her to sign it."

"Will you go to Paris?"

"Yes," said Digby. "I'll send it across by—er—aeroplane."

The lawyer gathered up the papers and thrust them back into the wallet.

"Then I will see you at twelve o'clock to-morrow at the office of the Northern Land Syndicate."

Digby nodded.

"Oh, by the way, Bennett"—he called the lawyer back—"I wish you to put this house in the market. I shall be spending a great deal of my time abroad and I have no use for this costly property. I want a quick sale, by the way."

"A quick sale is a bad sale for the seller," quoth the lawyer, "but I'll do what I can for you, Mr. Groat. Do you want to dispose of the furniture?"

Digby nodded.

"And you have another house in the country?"

"That is not for sale," said Digby shortly.

When the lawyer had gone he went up to his room and changed, taking his time over his toilet.

"Now," he said as he drew on his gloves with a quiet smile, "I have to induce Eunice to be a good girl!"

Chapter 30

DIGBY GROAT made an unexpected journey to west. A good general, even in the hour of his victory, prepares the way for retreat, and the possibility of Kennett Hall had long appealed to Digby as a likely refuge in a case of emergency.

Kennett Hall was one of the properties which his mother had inherited and which, owing to his failure to secure her signature, had not been prepared for transfer to the land syndicate. It had been the home of the Danton family for 140 years. A rambling, neglected house, standing in a big and gloomy park, it had been untenanted almost as long as Digby could remember.

He had sent his car down in the early morning, but he himself had gone by train. He disliked long motor journeys, and though he intended coming back by road, he preferred the quietude and smooth progress of the morning railway journey.

The car, covered with dust, was waiting for him at the railway station, and the few officials who constituted the station staff watched him go out of the gate without evidence of enthusiasm.

"That's Groat who owns Kennett Hall, isn't it?" said the porter to the aged station-master.

"That's him," was the reply. "It was a bad day for this country when that property came into old Jane Groat's hands. A bad woman, that, if ever there was one."

Unconscious of the criticisms of his mother, Digby was bowling up the hill road leading to the gates of Kennett Hall. The gates themselves were magnificent specimens of seventeenth-century ironwork, but the lodges on either side were those ugly stuccoed huts with which the mid-Victorian architect "embellished" the estates of the great. They had not been occupied for twenty years, and bore the appearance of their neglect. The little gardens which once had flowered so cheerfully before the speckless windows, were overrun by weeds, and the gravel drive, seen through the gates, was almost indistinguishable from the grassland on either side.

The caretaker came running down the drive to unlock the gates. He was an ill-favoured man of fifty with a perpetual scowl, which even the presence of his master could not wholly eradicate.

"Has anybody been here, masters?" asked Digby.

"No, sir," said the man, "except the flying gentleman. He came this morning. What a wonderful thing flying is, sir! The way he came down in the Home Park was wonderful to see."

"Get on the step with the driver," said Digby curtly, who was not interested in his servitor's views of flying.

The car drove through a long avenue of elms and turned to breast a treeless slope that led up to the lower terrace. All the beauty and loveliness of Somerset in which it stood could not save Kennett Hall from the reproach of dreariness. Its parapets were crumbled by the wind and rain of long-forgotten seasons, and its face was scarred and stained with thirty winters' rains Its black and dusty windows seemed to leer upon the fresh clean beauty of the world, as though in pride of its sheer ugliness.

For twenty years no painter's brush had touched the drab and ugly woodwork: and the weeds grew high where roses used to bloom. Three great white seats of marble, that were placed against the crumbling terrace balustrade, were green with drippings from the neglected trees; the terrace floor was broken and the rags and tatters of dead seasons spread their mouldering litter of leaves and twigs and moss upon the marble walk where stately dames had trodden in those brave days when Kennett Hall was a name to inspire awe.

Digby was not depressed by his view of the property. He had seen it before, and at one time had thought of pulling it down and, erecting a modern building for his own comfort.

The man he had called Masters unlocked the big door and ushered him into the house.

The neglect was here apparent. As he stepped into the big bleak entrance he heard the scurry and scamper of tiny feet and smiled.

"You've got some rats here?"

"Rats?" said Masters in a tone of resignation, "there's a colony of them, sir. It is as much as I can do to keep them out of my quarters, but there's nothing in the east wing," he hastened to add. "I had a couple of terriers and ferrets here for a month keeping them down, and they're all on this side of the house." He jerked his head to the right.

"Is the flying gentleman here?"

"He's having breakfast, sir, at this minute."

Digby followed the caretaker down a long gloomy passage on the ground floor, and passed through the door that the man opened.

The bearded Villa nodded with a humorous glint in his eye as Digby entered. From his appearance and dress, he had evidently arrived by aeroplane.

"Well, you got here," said Digby, glancing at the huge meal which had been put before the man.

"I got here," said Villa with an extravagant flourish of his knife. "But only by the favour of the gods. I do not like these scout machines: you must get Bronson to pilot it back."

Digby nodded, and pulling out a rickety chair, sat down.

"I have given instructions for Bronson to come here-he will arrive to-night," he said.

"Good," muttered the man, continuing his meal.

Masters had gone, and Villa was listening to the receding sound of his footsteps upon the uncovered boards, before he asked:

"What is the idea of this, governor? You are not changing headquarters?"

"I don't know," replied Digby shortly, "but the Seaford aerodrome is under observation. At least, Steele knows, or guesses, all about it. I have decided to hire some commercial pilots to give an appearance of genuine business to the company."

Villa whistled.

"This place is no use to you, governor," he said, shaking his head. "They'd tumble to Kennett Hall—that's what you call it, isn't it?" He had an odd way of introducing slang words into his tongue, for he spoke in Spanish, and Digby smiled at "tumble."

"You're becoming quite an expert in the English language, Villa."

"But why are you coming here?" persisted the other. "This could only be a temporary headquarters. Is the game slipping?" he asked suddenly.

Digby nodded.

"It may come to a case of sauve qui peut," he said, "though I hope it will not. Everything depends upon—" He did not finish his sentence, but asked abruptly: "How far is the sea from here?"

"Not a great distance," was the reply. "I travelled at six thousand feet and I could see the Bristol Channel quite distinctly."

Digby was stroking his chin, looking thoughtfully at the table.

"I can trust you, Villa," he said, "so I tell you now, much as you dislike these fast machines, you've got to hold yourself in readiness to pilot me to safety. Again, I say that I do not think it will come to flight, but we must be prepared. In the meantime, I have a commission for you," he said. "It was not only to bring the machine that I arranged for you to come to this place."

Villa had guessed that.

"There is a man in Deauville to whom you have probably seen references in the newspapers, a man named Maxilla. He is a rich coffee planter of Brazil."

"The gambler?" said the other in surprise, and Digby nodded.

"I happen to know that Maxilla has had a very bad time-he lost nearly twenty million francs in one week, and that doesn't represent all his losses. He has been gambling at Aix and at San Sebastian, and I should think he is in a pretty desperate position."

"But he wouldn't be broke," said Villa, shaking his head. "I know the man you mean. Why, he's as rich as Croesus! I saw his yacht when you sent me to Havre. A wonderful ship, worth a quarter of a million. He has hundreds of square miles of coffee plantations in Brazil—"

"I know all about that," said Digby impatiently. "The point is, that for the moment he is very short of money. Now, do not ask me any questions, Villa: accept my word."

"What do you want me to do?" asked the man. "Go to Deauville, take your slow machine and fly there; see Maxilla—you speak Portuguese?"

Villa nodded.

"Like a native," he said. "I lived in Lisbon—"

"Never mind where you lived," interrupted Digby, unpleasantly. "You will see Maxilla, and if, as I believe, he is short of money, offer him a hundred thousand pounds for his yacht. He may want double that, and you must be prepared to pay it. Maxilla hasn't the best of reputations, and probably his crew—who are all Brazilians by the way—will be glad to sail under another flag. If you can effect the purchase, send me a wire, and order the boat to be brought round to the Bristol Channel to be coaled."

"It is an oil-running ship," said Villa.

"Well, it must take on supplies of oil and provisions for a month's voyage. The captain will come straight to me in London to receive his instructions. I dare say one of his officers can bring the boat across. Now, is that clear to you?"

"Everything is clear to me, my dear friend," said Villa blandly, "except two things. To buy a yacht I must have money."

"That I will give you before you go."

"Secondly," said Villa, putting the stump of his forefinger in his palm, "where does poor August Villa come into this?"

"You get away as well," said Digby.

"I see," said Villa.

"Maxilla must not know that I am the purchaser under any circumstances," Digby went on. "You may either be buying the boat for yourself in your capacity as a rich Cuban planter, or you may be buying it for an unknown friend. I will arrange to keep the captain and the crew quiet as soon as I am on board. You leave for Deauville tonight."

He had other preparations to make. Masters received an order to prepare two small rooms and to arrange for beds and bedding to be erected, and the instructions filled him with consternation.

"Don't argue with me," said Digby angrily. "Go into Bristol, into any town, buy the beds and bring them out in a car. I don't care what it costs. And get a square of carpet for the floor."

He tossed a bundle of notes into the man's band, and Masters, who had never seen so much money in his life, nearly dropped them in sheer amazement.

Chapter 31

DIGBY GROAT returned to town by car and reached Grosvenor Square in time for dinner. He had a hasty meal and then went up to his room and changed.

He passed the room that Eunice occupied and found Jackson sitting on a chair before the door.

"She's all right," said the man, grinning. "I've shuttered and padlocked the windows and I've told her that if she doesn't want me to make friendly calls she has to behave."

Digby nodded.

"And my mother—you gave her the little box?"

Again Jackson grinned.

"And she's happy," he said. "I never dreamt she was a dope, Mr. Groat—"

"There is no need for you to dream anything," said Digby sharply.

He had a call to make. Lady Waltham was giving a dance that night, and there would be present two members of the syndicate whom he was to meet on the following morning. One of these drew him aside during the progress of the dance.

"I suppose those transfers are quite in order for to-morrow," he said.

Digby nodded.

"Some of my people are curious to know why you want cash," he said, looking at Digby with a smile.

The other shrugged his shoulders.

"You seem to forget, my dear man," he said suavely, "that I am merely an agent in these matters, and that I am acting for my rather eccentric mother. God bless her!"

"That is the explanation which had occurred to me," said the financier. "The papers will be in order, of course? I seem to remember you saying that there was another paper which had to be signed by your mother."

Digby remembered with an unspoken oath that he had neglected to secure this signature. As soon as he could, he made his excuses and returned to Grosvenor Square.

His mother's room was locked, but she heard his gentle tap.

"Who is that?" she demanded in audible agitation.

"It is Digby."

"I will see you in the morning."

"I want to see you tonight," interrupted Digby sharply. "Open the door."

It was some time before she obeyed. She was in her dressing-gown, and her yellow face was grey with fear.

"I am sorry to disturb you, mother," said Digby, dosing the door behind him, "but I have a document which must be signed tonight."

"I gave you everything you wanted," she said tremulously, "didn't I, dear? Everything you wanted, my boy?"

She had not the remotest idea that he was disposing of her property.

"Couldn't I sign it in the morning?" she pleaded. "My hand is so shaky."

"Sign it now," he almost shouted, and she obeyed.

The Northern Land Syndicate was but one branch of a great finance corporation, and had been called into existence to acquire the Danton properties. In a large, handsomely furnished board-room, members of the syndicate were waiting. Lord Waltham was one; Hugo Vindt, the bluff, good-natured Jewish financier, whose fingers were in most of the business pies, was the second; and Felix Strathellan, that debonair man-about-town, was the important third—for he was one of the shrewdest land speculators in the kingdom.

A fourth member of the party was presently shown in in the person of the Scotch lawyer, Bennett, who carried under his arm a black portfolio, which he laid on the table.

"Good morning, gentlemen," he said shortly. Millionaires' syndicates had long failed to impress him.

"Good morning, Bennett," said his lordship. "Have you seen your client this morning?"

Mr. Bennett made a wry face as he unstrapped the portfolio.

"No, my lord, I have not," he said, and suggested by his tone that he was not at all displeased that he had missed a morning interview with Digby Groat.

"A queer fellow is Groat," said Vindt with a laugh. "He is not a business man, and yet he has curiously keen methods. I should never have guessed he was an Englishman: he looks more like a Latin, don't you think. Lord Waltham?"

His lordship nodded.

"A queer family, the Groats," he said. "I wonder how many of you fellows know that his mother is a kleptomaniac?"

"Good heavens," said Strathellan in amazement, "you don't mean that?"

His lordship nodded.

"She's quite a rum old lady now," he said, "though there was a time when she was as handsome a woman as there was in town. She used to visit us a lot, and invariably we discovered, when she had gone, that some little trinket, very often a perfectly worthless trifle, but on one occasion a rather valuable bracelet belonging to my daughter, had disappeared with her. Until I realized the true condition of affairs it used to worry me, but the moment I spoke to Groat, the property was restored, and we came to expect this evidence of her eccentricity. She's a lucky woman," he added.

"I wouldn't say that with a son like Digby," smiled Strathellan, who was drawing figures idly on his blotting-pad.

"Nevertheless, she's lucky," persisted his lordship. "If that child of the Dantons hadn't been killed, the Groats would have been as poor as Church mice."

"Did you ever meet Lady Mary, my lord?" asked Vindt.

Lord Waltham nodded.

"I met Lady Mary and the baby," he said quietly; "I used to be on dining terms with the Dantons. And a beautiful little baby she was."

"What baby is this?" asked a voice.

Digby Groat had come in in his noiseless fashion, and closed the door of the board-room softly behind him. The question was the first intimation they had of his presence, all except Lord Waltham, who, out of the corner of his eye, had seen his entrance.

"We were talking about Lady Mary's baby, your cousin."

Digby Groat smiled contemptuously.

"It will not profit us very much to discuss her." he said.

"Do you remember her at all, Groat?" asked Waltham.

"Dimly," said Digby with a careless shrug. "I'm not frightfully keen, on babies. I have a faint recollection that she was once staying in our house, and I associate her with prodigious howling! Is everything all right, Bennett?"

Bennett nodded.

"Here is the paper you asked for." Digby took it from his pocket and laid it before the lawyer, who unfolded it leisurely and read it with exasperating slowness.

"That is in order," he said. "Now, gentlemen, we will get to business."

Such of them who were not already seated about the table, drew up their chairs.

"Your insistence upon having the money in cash has been rather a nuisance, groat," said Lord Waltham, picking up a tin box from the floor and opening it. "I hate to have a lot of money in the office; it has meant the employment of two special watchmen."

"I will pay," said Digby good-humouredly, watching with greedy eyes as bundle after bundle of notes was laid upon the table.

The lawyer twisted round the paper and offered him a pen.

"You will sign here, Mr. Groat," he said.

At that moment Vindt turned his head to the clerk who had just entered.

"For me?" he said, indicating the letter in the man's hand.

"No, sir, for Mr. Bennett."

Bennett took the note, looked at the name embossed upon the flap, and frowned.

"From Salter," he said, "and it is marked 'urgent and important.'"

"Let it wait until after we have finished the business," said Digby impatiently.

"You had better see what it is," replied the lawyer, and took out a typewritten sheet of paper. He read it through carefully.

"What is it?" asked Digby.

"I'm afraid this sale cannot go through," answered the lawyer slowly. "Salter has entered a caveat against the transfer of the property."

Livid with rage Digby sprang to his feet.

"What right has he?" he demanded savagely. "He is no longer my lawyer: he has no right to act. Who authorized him?"

The lawyer had a queer expression on his face.

"This caveat," he said, speaking deliberately, "has been entered by Salter on behalf of Dorothy Danton, who, according to the letter, is still alive."

There was a painful silence, which the voice of Vindt broke.

"So that settles the transfer," he said. "We cannot go on with this business, you understand, Groat?"

"But I insist on the transfer going through," cried Digby violently. "The whole thing is a plot got up by that dithering old fool, Salter. Everybody knows that Dorothy Danton is dead! She has been dead for twenty years."

"Nevertheless," said Lord Waltham quietly, "we cannot move in face of the caveat. Without being a legal instrument, it places upon the purchasers of the property the fullest responsibility for their purchase."

"But I will sign the transfer," said Digby vehemently.

Lord Waltham shook his head.

"It would not matter if you signed twenty transfers," he said. "If we paid you the money for this property and it proved to be the property of Miss Danton, as undoubtedly it would prove, if she were alive, we, and only we, would be responsible. We should have to surrender the property and look to you to refund us the money we had invested in the estate. No, no, Groat, if it is, as you say, a bluff on the part of Salter—and upon my word, I cannot imagine a man of Salter's position, age and experience putting up empty bluff—then we can have a meeting on another day and the deal can go through. We are very eager to acquire these properties."

There was a murmur of agreement from both Strathellan and Vindt.

"But at present, as matters stand, we can do nothing, and you as a business man must recognize our helplessness in the matter."

Digby was beside himself with fury as he saw the money being put back in the tin box.

"Very well," he said. His face was pallid and his suppressed rage shook him as with an ague. But he never lost sight of all the possible developments of the lawyer's action. If he had taken, so grave a step in respect to the property, he would take action in other directions, and no time must be lost if he was to anticipate Salter's next move.

Without another word he turned on his heel and stalked down the stairs into the street. His car was waiting.

"To the Third National Bank," he said, as he flung himself into its luxurious interior.

He knew that at the Third National Bank was a sum nearly approaching a hundred thousand pounds which his parsimonious mother had accumulated during the period she had been in receipt of the revenues of the Danton estate. Viewing the matter as calmly as he could, he was forced to agree that Salter was not the man who would play tricks or employ the machinery of the law, unless he had behind him a very substantial backing of facts. Dorothy Danton! Where had she sprung from? Who was she? Digby cursed her long and heartily. At any rate, he thought, as his car stopped before the bank premises, he would be on the safe side and get his hands on all the money which was lying loose.

He wished now that when he had sent Villa to Deauville he had taken his mother's money for the purchase of the gambler's yacht. Instead of that he had drawn upon the enormous funds of the Thirteen.

He was shown into the manager's office, and he thought that that gentleman greeted him a little coldly.

"Good morning, Mr. Stevens, I have come to draw out the greater part of my mother's balance, and I thought I would see you first."

"I'm glad you did, Mr. Groat," was the reply. "Will you sit down?" The manager was obviously ill at ease. "The fact is," he confessed, "I am not in a position to honour any cheques you draw upon this bank."

"What the devil do you mean?" demanded Digby.

"I am sorry," said the manager, shrugging his shoulders, "but this morning I have been served with a notice that a caveat has been entered at the Probate Office, preventing the operation of the Danton will in your mother's favour. I have already informed our head office and they are taking legal opinion, but as Mr. Salter threatens to obtain immediately an injunction unless we agree to comply, it would be madness on my part to let you touch a penny of your mother's account. Your own account, of course, you can draw upon."

Digby's own account contained a respectable sum, he remembered.

"Very well," he said after consideration. "Will you discover my balance and I will close the account."

He was cool now. This was not the moment to hammer his head against a brick wall. He needed to meet this cold-blooded old lawyer with cunning and foresight. Salter was diabolically wise in the law and had its processes at his fingertips, and he must go wanly against the framed fighter or he would come to everlasting smash.

Fortunately, the account of the Thirteen was at another bank, and if the worst came to the worst—well, he could leave eleven of the Thirteen to make the best of things they could.

The manager returned presently and passed a slip across the table, and a few minutes afterwards Digby came back to his car, his pockets bulging with bank-notes.

A tall bearded man stood on the sidewalk as he came out and Digby gave him a cursory glance. Detective, he thought, and went cold. Were the police already stirring against him, or was this some private watcher of Salter's? He decided rightly that it was the latter.

When he got back to the house he found a telegram waiting. It was from Villa. It was short and satisfactory.

"Bought Pealigo hundred and twelve thousand pounds. Ship on its way to Avonmouth. Am bringing captain back by air. Calling Grosvenor nine o'clock."

The frown cleared away from his face as he read the telegram for the second tune, and as he thought, a smile lit up his yellow face. He was thinking of Eunice. The position was not without its compensations.

Chapter 32

EUNICE was sitting in the shuttered room trying to read when Digby Groat came in. All the colour left her face as she rose to meet him.

"Good evening. Miss Weldon," he said in his usual manner. "I hope you haven't been very bored."

"Will you please explain why I am kept here a prisoner?" she asked a little breathlessly. "You realize that you are committing a very serious crime——"

He laughed in her face.

"Well," he said almost jovially, "at any rate. Eunice, we can drop the mask. That is one blessed satisfaction! These polite little speeches are irksome to me as they are to you."

He took her hand in his.

"How cold you are, my dear," he said, "yet the room is warm!"

"When may I leave this house?" she asked in a low voice.

"Leave this house—leave me?" He threw the gloves be had stripped on to a chair and caught her by the shoulders. "When are we going? That is a better way of putting it. How lovely you are, Eunice!"

There was no disguise now. The mask was off, as he had said, and the ugliness of his black nature was written in his eyes.

Still she did not resist, standing stiffly erect like a figure of marble. Not even when he took her face in both his hands and pressed his lips to hers, did she move. She seemed incapable. Something inside her had frozen and she could only stare at him.

"I want you, Eunice! I have wanted you all the time. I chose you out of all the women in the world to be mine. I have waited for you, longed for you, and now I have you! There is nobody here, Eunice, but you and I. Do you hear, darling?"

Then suddenly a chord snapped within her. With an effort of strength which surprised him she thrust him off, her eyes staring in horror as though she contemplated some loathsome crawling thing. That look inflamed him. He sprang forward, and as he did, the girl in the desperation of frenzy, struck at him; twice her open hand came across his face. He stepped back with a yell. Before he could reach her she had flown into the bathroom and locked the door. For fully five minutes he stood, then he turned and walked slowly across to the dressing-table, and surveyed his face in the big mirror.

"She struck me!" this he said. He was as white as a sheet. Against his pale face the imprint of her hand showed lividly. "She struck me!" he said again wonderingly, and began to laugh.

For every blow, for every joint on every finger of the hand that struck the blow, she should have pain. Pain and terror. She should pray for death, she should crawl to him and clasp his feet in her agony. His breath came quicker and he wiped the sweat from his forehead with the back of his hand.

He passed out, locking the door behind him. His hand was on the key when he heard a sound and looking along the corridor, saw the door of his mother's room open and the old woman standing in the doorway.

"Digby," she said, and there was a vigour and command in her voice which made him frown. "I want you!" she said imperatively, and in amazement he obeyed her.

She had gone back to her chair when he came into the room.

"What do you want?" he demanded.

"Shut the door and sit down."

He stared at her dumbfounded. Not for a year had she dared address him in that tone.

"What the devil do you mean by ordering me—" he began.

"Sit down," she said quietly, and then he understood.

"So, you old devil, the dope is in you!"

"Sit down, my love child," she sneered. "Sit down, Digby Estremeda! I want to speak to you."

His face went livid.

"You—you—" he gasped.

"Sit down. Tell me what you have done with my property."

He obeyed her slowly, looking at her as though he could not believe the evidence of his ears.

"What have you done with my property?" she asked again. "Like a fool I gave you a Power of Attorney. How have you employed it? Have you sold—" she was looking at him keenly.

He was surprised into telling the truth.

"They have put an embargo—or some such rubbish—on the sale."

She nodded.

"I hoped they would," she said. "I hoped they would!"

"You hoped they would?" he roared, getting up.

Her imperious hand waved him down again. He passed his hand over his eyes like a man in a dream. She was issuing orders; this old woman whom he had dominated for years, and he was obeying meekly! He had given her the morphine to quieten her, and it had made her his master.

"Why did they stop the sale?"

"Because that old lunatic Salter swears that the girl is still alive—Dorothy Danton, the baby who was drowned at Margate!"

He saw a slow smile on her lined face and wondered what was amusing her.

"She is alive!" she said.

He could only glare at her in speechless amazement.

"Dorothy Danton alive?" he said. "You're mad, you old fool! She's gone beyond recall—dead—dead these twenty years!"

"And what brought her back to life, I wonder?" mused the old woman? "How did they know she was Dorothy? Why, of course you brought her back!" She pointed her skinny finger at her son. "You brought her, you are the instrument of your own undoing, my boy!" she said derisively. "Oh, you poor little fool—you clever fool!"

Now he had mastered himself.

"You will tell me all there is to be told, or, by God, you'll be sorry you ever spoke at all," he breathed.

"You marked her. That is why she has been recognized—you marked her!"

"I marked her?"

"Don't you remember, Digby," she spoke rapidly and seemed to find a joy in the hurt she was causing, "a tiny baby and a cruel little beast of a boy who heated a sixpence and put it on the baby's wrist?"

It came back to him instantly. He could almost hear the shriek of his victim. A summer day and a big room full of old furniture. The vision of a garden-through an open window and the sound of the bees… a small spirit-lamp where he had heated the coin… .

"My God!" said Digby, reeling back. "I remember!"

He stared at the mocking face of his mother for a second, then turned and left the room. As he did so, there came a sharp rat-tat at the door. Swiftly he turned into his own room and ran to the window.

One glance at the street told him all that he wanted to know. He saw Jim and old Salter... there must have been a dozen detectives with them.

The door would hold for five minutes, and there was time to carry out his last plan.

Chapter 33

A MINUTE later he appeared in Eunice Weldon's room. "I want you," he said, and there was a sinister look in his eye that made the girl cower back from him in fear that she could not master. "My dear," he said with that smile of his, "you need not be afraid, your friends are breaking into the house and in half an hour you will be free. What I intend doing to you is to put you in such a condition that you will not be able to give information against me until I am clear of this house. No, I am not going to kill you," he almost laughed, "and if you are not sensible enough to realize why I am taking this step, then you are a fool—and you are not a fool, Eunice."

She saw something bright and glittering in his hand and terror took possession of her.

"Don't touch me," she gasped. "I swear I will not tell," but he had gripped her arm.

"If you make a sound," his face was thrust into hers, "you'll regret it to the last day of your life."

She felt a sudden pricking sensation in her arm and tried to pull it away, but her arm was held as by a vice.

"There. It wasn't very painful, was it?"

She heard him utter a curse, and when he turned his face was red with rage.

"They've smashed in the gates," he said sharply.

She was walking toward him, her hand on the little puncture the needle had made, and her face was curiously calm.

"Are you going now?" she asked simply.

"We are going in a few minutes," said Digby, emphasizing the "we".

But even this she did not resent. She had fallen into a curious placid condition of mind which was characterized by the difficulty, amounting to an impossibility, of remembering what happened the previous minute. All she could do was to sit down on the edge of a chair, nursing her arm. She knew it hurt her, and yet she was conscious of no hurt. It was a curious impersonal sensation she had. To her, Digby Groat had no significance. He was a somebody whom she neither liked nor disliked. It was all very strange and pleasant.

"Put your hat on," he said, and she obeyed. She never dreamt of disobeying.

He led her to the basement and through a door which communicated with a garage. It was not the garage where he kept his own car—Jim had often been puzzled to explain why Digby kept his car so far from the house. The only car visible was a covered van, such as the average tradesman uses to deliver his goods.

"Get in," said Digby, and Eunice obeyed with a strange smile.

She was under the influence of that admixture of morphine and hyacin, which destroyed all memory and will.

"Sit on the floor," he ordered, and laced the canvas flap at the back. He reached under the driver's seat and pulled out a cotton coat which had once been white, but was now disfigured with paint and grease, buttoning it up to the throat. A cap he took from the same source and pulled it over his head, so that the peak well covered his eyes.

Then he opened the gates of a garage. He was in a mews, and with the exception of a woman who was talking to a milkman, the only two persons in sight, none saw the van emerge.

There was not the slightest suspicion of hurry on his part. He descended from his seat to close the gates and lock them, lit a pipe and, clambering up, set the little van going in the direction of the Bayswater Road.

He stopped only at the petrol station to take aboard a fair supply of spirit, and then he went on, still at a leisurely pace, passing through the outlying suburbs, until he came to the long road leading from Staines to Ascot. Here he stopped and got down.

Taking the little flat case from his pocket, and recharging the glass cylinder, he opened the canvas flap-at the back and looked in.

Eunice was sitting with her back braced against the side of the van, her head nodding sleepily. She looked up with a puzzled expression.

"It won't hurt you," said Digby. Again the needle went into her arm, and the piston was thrust home.

She screwed up her face a little at the pain and again fondled her arm.

"That hurt," she said simply.

Just outside Ascot a touring car was held up by two policemen and Digby slowed from necessity, for the car had left him no room to pass.

"We are looking for a man and a girl," said one of the policemen to the occupants of the car. "All right, sir, go on."

Digby nodded in a friendly way to the policeman.

"Is it all right, sergeant?"

"Off you go," said the sergeant, not troubling to look inside a van on which was painted the name of a reputable firm of London furnishers.

Digby breathed quickly. He must not risk another encounter. There would be a second barrier at the cross roads, where he intended turning. He must go back to London, he thought, the police would not stop a London-bound car. He turned into a secondary road and reached the main Bath road passing another barrier, where, as he had expected, the police did not challenge him, though they were holding up a string of vehicles going in the other direction. There were half a dozen places to which he could take her, but the safest was a garage he had hired at the back of a block of buildings in Paddington. The garage had been useful to the Thirteen, but had not been utilized for the greater part of a year, though he had sent Jackson frequently to superintend the cleaning.

He gained the west of London as the rain began to fall. Everything was in his favour. The mews in which the garage was situated was deserted and he had opened the gates and backed in the car before the occupants of the next garage were curious enough to come out to see who it was.

Digby had one fad and it had served him well before. It was to be invaluable now. Years before, he had insisted that every house and every room, if it were only a store-room, should have a lock of such a character that it should open to his master key.

He half led, half lifted the girl from the car, and she sighed wearily, for she was stiff and tired.

"This way," he said, and pushed her before him up the dark stairs, keeping her on the landing whilst he lit the gas.

Though it had not been dusted for the best part of a month, the room overlooking the mews was neat and comfortably furnished. He pulled down the heavy blind before he lit the gas here, felt her pulse and looked into her eyes.

"You'll do, I think," he said with a smile. "You must wait here until I come back. I am going to get some food."

"Yes," she answered.

He was gone twenty minutes, and on his return he saw that she had taken off her coat and had washed her hands and face. She was listlessly drying her hands when he came up the stairs. There was something pathetically childlike in her attitude, and a man who was less of a brute than Digby Groat would have succumbed to the appeal of her helplessness.

But there was no hint of pity in the thoughtful eyes that surveyed her. He was wondering whether it would be safe to give her another dose. In order to secure a quick effect he had administered more than was safe already. There might be a collapse, or a failure of heart, which would be as fatal to him as to her. He decided to wait until the effects had almost worn off.

"Eat," he said, and she sat at the table obediently.

He had brought in cold meat, a loaf of bread, butter and cheese. He supplemented this feast with two glasses of water which he drew in the little scullery.

Suddenly she put down her knife and fork.

"I feel very tired," she said.

So much the better, thought Digby. She would sleep now.

The back room was a bedroom. He watched her whilst she unfastened her shoes and loosened the belt of her skirt before she lay down. With a sigh, she turned over and was fast asleep before he could walk to the other side of the bed to see her face.

Digby Groat smoked for a long time over his simple meal. The girl was wholly in his power, but she could wait. A much more vital matter absorbed his attention. He himself had reached the possibility which he had long foreseen and provided against. It was not a pleasant situation, he thought, and found relief for his mind by concentrating his thoughts upon the lovely ranch in Brazil, on which, with average luck, he would spend the remainder of his days.

Presently he got up, produced from a drawer a set of shaving materials wrapped in a towel, and heating some water at the little gas-stove in the kitchen, he proceeded to divest himself of his moustache.

With the master key he unlocked the cupboard that ran the height of the room, and surveyed thoughtfully the stacks of dresses and costumes which filled the half a dozen shelves. The two top shelves were filled with boxes, and he brought out three of these and examined their contents. From one of these he took a beautiful evening gown of silver tissue, and laid it over the back of a chair. A satin wrap followed, and from another box he took white satin shoes and stockings and seemed satisfied by his choice, for he looked at them for a long time before he folded them and put them back where he had found them. His own disguise he had decided upon.

And now, having mapped out his plan, he dressed himself in a chauffeur's uniform, and went out to the telephone.

Chapter 34

"DEAD! Jane Groat dead?"

To Lady Mary the news came as a shock.

Jim, gaunt and hollow-eyed, sitting listlessly by the window of Mr. Salter's office, nodded.

"The doctors think it was an overdose of morphia that killed her," he said shortly.

Lady Mary was silent for a long while, then;

"I think perhaps now is a moment when I can tell you something about the Blue Hand," she said.

"Will it assist us?" asked Jim, turning quickly.

She shook her head.

"I am afraid it will not, but this I must tell you. The person against whom the Blue Hand was directed was not Digby Groat, but his mother. I have made one grave mistake recently," she said, "and it was to believe that Digby Groat was dominated by his mother. I was amazed to discover that so far from her dominating him, she was his slave, and the only explanation I can give for this extraordinary transition is Digby Groat's discovery that his mother was a drug-taker. Once he was strong enough to keep the drug from her the positions were reversed. The story of the Blue Hand," she said with her sad little smile, "is neither as fantastic nor as melodramatic as you might expect."

There was a long silence which neither of the men broke.

"I was married at a very early age, as you know." She nodded to Salter. "My father was a very poor nobleman with one daughter and no sons, and he found it not only difficult to keep up the mortgaged estates which he had inherited, but to make both ends meet even though he was living in the most modest way. Then he met Jonathan Danton's father, and between the two they fixed up a marriage between myself and Jonathan. I never met him until a week before my wedding-day. He was a cold, hard man, very much like his father, just to a fault, proud and stiff-necked, and to his natural hardness of demeanour was added the fretfulness due to an affected heart, which eventually killed him.

"My married life was an unhappy one. The sympathy that I sought was denied me. With all his wealth he could have made me happy, but from the first he seemed to be suspicious of me, and I have often thought that he hated me because I was a member of a class which he professed to despise. When our daughter was born I imagined that there would be a change in his attitude, but, if anything, the change was for the worse.

"I had met his sister, Jane Groat, and knew, in a vague kind of way, that some scandal had attached to her name-Jonathan never discussed it, but his father, in his lifetime, loathed Jane and would not allow her to put her foot inside his house. Jonathan hadn't the same prejudices. He knew nothing of her escapade with the Spaniard, Estremeda, and I only learnt of the circumstances by accident.

"Jane was a peculiar mixture. Some days she would be bright and vivacious, and some days she would be in the depths of gloom, and this used to puzzle me, until one day we were at tea together at our house in Park Lane. She had come in a state of nerves and irritability which distressed me. I thought that her little boy was giving her trouble, for I knew how difficult he was, and how his cruel ways, even at that tender age, annoyed her. I nearly said distressed her," she smiled, "but Jane was never distressed at things like that. We were having a cup of tea when she put her hand in her bag and took out a small bottle filled with brown pellets.

"'I really can't wait any longer, Mary,' she said, and swallowed one of the pills. I thought it was something for digestion, until I saw her eyes begin to brighten and her whole demeanour change, then I guessed the truth.

"'You're not taking drugs, are you, Jane? 'I asked.

"'I'm taking a little morphine,' she replied. 'Don t be shocked, Mary. If you had my troubles, and a little devil of a boy to look after, as I have, you'd take drugs too!'

"But that was not her worst weakness, from my point of view. What that was I learnt after my husband sailed to America on business.

"Dorothy was then about seven or eight months old, a bonny, healthy, beautiful child, whom my husband adored in his cold, dour fashion. One morning Jane came into my room while I was dressing, and apologizing for her early arrival, asked me if I would go shopping with her. She was so cheerful and gay that I knew she had been swallowing some of those little pellets, and as I was at a loose end that morning I agreed. We went to several stores and finished up at Clayneys, the big emporium in Brompton Road. I noticed that Jane made very few purchases, but this didn't strike me as being peculiar, because Jane was notoriously mean, and I don't think she had a great deal of money either. I did not know Clayneys. I had never been to the shop before. This explanation is necessary in view of what followed. Suddenly, when we were passing through the silk department, Jane turned to me with a startled expression and said to me under her breath, 'Put this somewhere.'

"Before I could expostulate, she had thrust something into the interior of my muff. It was a cold day and I was carrying one of those big pillow muffs which were so fashionable in that year. I had hardly done so before somebody tapped me on the shoulder. I turned to see a respectable-looking man who said sharply, 'I'll trouble you to accompany me to the manager's office.'

"I was dazed and bewildered, and the only thing I recollect was Jane whispering in my ear, 'Don't give your name.' She apparently was suspect as well, for we were both taken to a large office, where an elderly man interviewed us. 'What is your name?' he asked. The first name I could think of was my maid, Madge Benson. Of course, I was half mad. I should have told them that I was Lady Mary Danton and should have betrayed Jane upon the spot. My muff was searched and inside was found a large square of silk, which was the article Jane had put into it.

"The elderly man retired with his companion to a corner of the room and I turned to Jane. 'You must get me out of this; it is disgraceful of you, Jane. Whatever made you do it?'

"'For God's sake, don't say a word,' she whispered. 'Whatever happens, I will take the responsibility. The magistrate—'

"'The magistrate?' I said in horror. 'I shall not go before a magistrate?'

"'You must, you must; it would break Jonathan's heart, and he would blame you if I came into court. Quick.' She lowered her voice and began speaking rapidly. 'I know the magistrate at Paddington and I will go to him and make a confession of the whole thing. When you come up to-morrow you will be discharged. Mary, you must do this for me, you must!'

"To cut a long story short, the manager came back and, summoning a policeman, gave me into custody. I neither denied my crime nor in any way implicated Jane. I found afterwards that she explained to the proprietor that she was a distant relation of mine and she had met me in the shop by accident. How can I depict the horror of that night spent in a police-court cell? In my folly I

106

even thanked God that my name had not been given. The next morning I came before the magistrate, and did not doubt that Jane had kept her word. There was nobody in the court who knew me. I was brought up under the name of Madge Benson and the elderly man from Clayneys went into the witness-box and made his statement. He said that his firm had been losing considerable quantities through shop-lifting, and that he had every reason to believe I was an old hand.

"Humiliating as this experience was, I did not for one moment doubt that the magistrate would find some excuse for me and discharge me. The shame of that moment as I stood there in the dock, with the curious crowd sneering at me! I cannot even speak of it to-day without my cheeks burning. The magistrate listened in silence, and presently he looked at me over his glasses and I waited.

"'There has been too much of this sort of thing going on,' said he, 'and I am going to make an example of you. You will go to prison with hard labour for one month.'

"The court, the magistrate, the people, everything and everybody seemed to fade out, and when I came to myself I was sitting in a cell with the jailer's wife forcing water between my teeth. Jane had betrayed me. She had lied when she said she would go to the magistrate, but her greatest crime had yet to be committed.

"I had been a fortnight in Holloway Gaol when she came to visit me. I was not a strong woman and they put me to work with several other prisoners in a shed where the prison authorities were making experiments with dyes. You probably don't know much about prisons," she said, "but in every county gaol through England they make an attempt to keep the prisoners occupied with some one trade. In Maidstone the printing is done for all the prisons in England—I learnt a lot about things when I was inside Holloway! In Shepton Mallet the prisoners weave. In Exeter they make harness. In Manchester they weave cotton, and so on.

"The Government were thinking of making one of the prisons a dye-works. When I came to the little interview-room to see Jane Groat, I had forgotten the work that had stained both my hands, and it was not until I saw her starting at the hands gripping the bars that I realized that the prison had placed upon me a mark which only time would eradicate.

"'May, look!' she stammered. 'Your hands are blue!'

"My hands were blue," said Lady Mary bitterly. "The Blue Hand became the symbol of the injustice this woman had worked.

"I did not reproach her. I was too depressed, too broken to taunt her with her meanness and treachery. But she promised eagerly that she would tell my husband the truth, and told me that the baby was being taken care of, and that she had sent it with her own maid to Margate. She would have kept the baby at her own house, she said, and probably with truth, but she feared the people, seeing the baby, would wonder where I was. If the baby was out of town, I too might be out of town.

"And then occurred that terrible accident that sent, as I believed, my darling baby to a horrible death. Jane Groat saw the advantage which the death gave to her. She had discovered in some underhand fashion the terms of my husband's will, terms which were unknown to me at the time. The moment Dorothy was gone she went to him with the story that I had been arrested and convicted for shop-lifting, and that the baby, whom it was my business to guard, had been left to the neglectful care of a servant and was dead.

"The shock killed Jonathan. He was found dead in his study after his sister had left him. The day before I came out of prison I received a note from Jane telling me boldly what had happened.

She made no attempt to break to me gently the news of my darling baby's death. The whole letter was designed to produce on me the fatal effect that her news had produced on poor Jonathan. Happily I had some money and the property in the City, which my husband, in a moment of generosity, which I am sure he never ceased to regret, had given to me. At my father's suggestion I turned this into a limited liability company, the shares of which were held, and are still held, by my father's lawyer.

"Soon after my release my father inherited a considerable fortune, which on his death came to me. With that money I have searched the world for news of Dorothy, news which has always evaded me. The doubt in my mind as to whether Dorothy was dead or not concentrated on my mistrust of Jane. I believed, wrongly, as I discovered, that Jane knew my girlie was alive. The Blue Hand was designed to terrorize her into a confession. As it happened, it only terrorized the one person in the world I desired to meet—my daughter!"

Salter had listened in silence to the recital of this strange story which Lady Mary had to tell.

"That clears up the last mystery," he said.

Chapter 35

EUNICE woke and, opening her eyes, tried hard to remember what had happened. Her last clear recollection was of her room in Grosvenor Square. The last person—she shivered as she recalled the moment—was Digby Groat, and he was coming towards her—she sat up in bed and reeled with the pain in her head. Where was she? She looked round. The room was meanly furnished, a heavy green blind had been drawn over the small window, but there was enough light in the room to reveal the shabby wardrobe, the common iron bed on which she lay, the cheap washstand and the threadbare carpet that covered the floor.

She was fully dressed and feeling horribly grimy. She almost wished at that moment she was back in Grosvenor Square, with its luxurious bathroom and its stinging shower-baths.

But where was she? She got off the bed, and, staggering across the room, she pulled aside the blind. She looked out upon the backs of drab buildings. She was in London, then. Only London could provide that view. She tried to open the door—it was locked, and as she turned the handle she heard footsteps outside.

"Good morning," said Digby Groat, unlocking the door.

At first she did not recognize him in his chauffeur uniform and without his moustache.

"You?" she said in horror. "Where am I? Why have you brought me here?"

"If I told you where you were you would be no wiser," said Digby coolly. "And the reason you are with me must be fairly obvious. Be sensible and have some breakfast."

He was looking at her with a keen professional eye. The effect of the drug had not worn off, he noticed, and she was not likely to give him a great deal of trouble.

Her throat was parched and she was ravenously hungry. She sipped at the coffee he had made, and all the time her eyes did not leave his.

"I'll make a clean breast of it," he said suddenly. "The fact is, I have got into very serious trouble and it is necessary that I should get away."

"From Grosvenor Square?" She opened her eyes wide in astonishment. "Aren't you going back to Grosvenor Square?"

He smiled.

"It is hardly likely." he said sarcastically; "your friend Steele—"

"Is he there?" she cried eagerly, clasping her hands. "Oh, tell me, please."

"If you expect me to sing your lover's praises you're going to get a jar!" said Digby, without heat. "Now eat some food and shut up." His tone was quiet but menacing, and she thought it best not to irritate him.

She was only beginning to understand her own position. Digby had run away and taken her with him. Why did she go? she wondered. He must have drugged her! And yet—she remembered the hypodermic syringe and instinctively rubbed her arm.

Digby saw the gesture and could almost read her thoughts. How lovely she was, he mused. No other woman in the world, after her experience of yesterday, could face the cold morning clear-eyed and flawless as she did. The early light was always kind to her, he remembered. The brightness of her soft eyes was undiminished, untarnished was the clarity of her complexion. She was a thing of delight, a joy to the eye, even of this connoisseur of beauty, who was not easily moved by mere loveliness.

"Eunice," he said, "I am going to marry you."

"Marry me," she said, startled. "Of course, you will do nothing of the kind, Mr. Groat. I don't want to marry you."

"That is quite unimportant," said Digby, and leaning forward over the table, he lowered his voice. "Eunice, do you realize what I am offering you and the alternative?"

"I will not marry you," she answered steadily, "and no threat you make will change my mind." His eyes did not leave hers.

"Do you realize that I can make you glad to marry me," he said, choosing his words deliberately, "and that I will stop at nothing—nothing?"

She made no reply, but he saw her colour change.

"Now understand me, my dear, once and for all. It is absolutely necessary that I should marry you, and you can either agree to a ceremony or you can take the consequence, and you know what that consequence will be."

She had risen to her feet and was looking down at him, and in her eyes was a contempt which would have wilted any other man than he.

"I am in your power," she said quietly, "and you must do what you will, but consciously I will never marry you. You were able to drug me yesterday, so that I cannot remember what happened between my leaving your house and my arrival in this wretched place, and possibly you can produce a similar condition, but sooner or later, Digby Groat, you will pay for all the wrong that you have done to the world. If I am amongst the injured people who will be avenged, that is God's will."

She turned to leave the room, but he was at the door before her and pulled her arm violently towards him.

"If you scream," he said, "I will choke the life out of you."

She looked at him with contempt.

"I shall not scream."

Nor did she even wince when the bright needle passed under the skin of her forearm.

"If anything happens to me," she said in a voice scarcely above a whisper, "I will kill myself in your presence, and with some weapon of yours." Her voice faded away and he watched her.

For the first time, he was afraid. She had touched him on a sensitive point—his own personal safety. She knew. What had put that idea into her head, he wondered, as he watched the colour come and go under the influence of the drug? And she would do it! He sweated at the thought. She might have done it here, and he could never have explained his innocence of her murder.

"Phew!" said Digby Groat, and wiped his forehead.

Presently, he let her hand drop and guided her to a chair.

Again, her hand touched her arm, tenderly, and then:

"Get up," said Digby, and she obeyed. "Now go to your room and stay there until I tell you I want you."

Chapter 36

THAT afternoon he had a visitor. He was, apparently, a gentleman who was anxious to rent a garage, and he made one or two inquiries in the mews before he called at Digby Groat's temporary home. Those people who troubled to observe him, noticed that he stayed a considerable time within this garage, and when he came out he seemed satisfied with his negotiations. He was in truth Villa, who had come in answer to an urgent wire.

"Well," said Digby, "is everything ready?"

"Everything is ready, dear friend," said Villa amiably. "I have the three men you want. Bronson is one, Fuentes and Silva are the others; they are known to you?"

Digby nodded. Bronson was an army aviator who had left the service under a cloud. Digby had employed him once before, to carry him to Paris—Bronson ran a passenger carrying service which Digby had financed. The other two he knew as associates of Villa—Villa had queer friends.

"Bronson will be in a field just outside Rugby. I told him to pretend he had made a false landing."

"Good," said Digby. "Now you understand that I shall be travelling north in the disguise of an old woman. A car must be waiting a mile short of the station and Fuentes must reach the line with a red hand-lamp and signal the train to stop. When it stops he can clear and by that time I shall be well away. I know Rugby well and this sketch-map will tell you everything." He handed a sheet of paper to Villa. "The car must be waiting at the end of the lane marked B. on the plan—the house—is it in good condition?"

"There's a house on the property," said Villa, "but it is rather a tumbledown affair."

"It can't be worse than Kennett Hall," said Digby. "That will do splendidly. You can keep the girl there all night and bring her to Kennett Hall in the morning. I will be there to receive you. To-morrow afternoon, just before sundown, we will take our final flight to the sea."

"What about Bronson?"

"Bronson will have to be settled with," said Digby. "but you can leave that to me."

He had his own views about Bronson which it was not expedient at the moment to discuss.

"How are you going to get to the Hall?" asked the interested Villa.

"You can leave that to me also," said Digby with a frown. "Why are you so curious? I will tell you this much, that I intend taking on the car and travelling through the night."

"Why not take the girl by the car?" demanded the persistent Villa.

"Because I want her to arrive at Kennett Hall by the only way that is safe. If the Hall is being watched, there is a chance of getting away again before they close in on us. No, I will be there before daybreak, and make a reconnaissance. In a case like this, I can trust nobody but myself, and what is more. Villa, I know the people who are watching me. Now, do you understand?"

"Perfectly, my friend," said Villa jovially; "as to that little matter of sharing out—"

"The money is here," said Digby, tapping his waist, "and you will have no cause to complain. There is much to be done yet—we have not seen the worst of our adventures."

For Eunice Weldon the worst was, for the moment, a splitting headache which made it an agony to lift her head from the pillow. She seemed to have passed through the day in a condition which was neither wakefulness nor sleep. She tried to remember what had happened and where she was, but the effort was so painful that she was content to lie with her throbbing head, glad that she was left alone. Several times the thought of Digby Groat came through her mind, but he was so inexplicably confused with Jim Steele that she could not separate the two personalities.

Where she was she neither knew nor cared. She was lying down and she was quiet—that satisfied her. Once she was conscious of a sharp stinging sensation in her right arm, and soon after she must have gone to sleep again, only to wake with her head racked with shooting pains as though somebody was driving red-hot nails into her brain.

At last it became so unendurable that she groaned, and a voice near her—an anxious voice, she thought—said;

"Have you any pain?"

"My head," she murmured. "It is dreadful!"

She was conscious of a "tut" of impatience, and almost immediately afterwards somebody's arm was round her neck and a glass was held to her lips.

"Drink this," said the voice.

She swallowed a bitter draught and made a grimace of distaste.

"That was nasty," she said.

"Don't talk," said the voice. Digby was seriously alarmed at the condition in which he found her when he had returned from a visit of reconnaissance. Her colour was bad, her breathing difficult and her pulse almost imperceptible. He had feared this, and yet he must continue his "treatment."

He looked down at her frowningly and felt some satisfaction when he saw the colour creep back to the wax-like face, and felt the throb of the pulse under his fingers.

As to Eunice, the sudden release from pain which came almost immediately after she had taken the draught, was so heavenly that she would have been on her knees in gratitude to the man who had accomplished the miracle, and with relief from pain came sleep.

Digby heaved a sigh of relief and went back to his work. It was very pleasant work for him, for the table was covered with little packages of five thousand dollar gold bills, for he had been successful in drawing the funds of the Thirteen and exchanging them for American money. He did not want to find himself in Brazil with a wad of English notes which he could not change because the numbers had been notified.

His work finished, he strapped the belt about his waist and proceeded leisurely to prepare for the journey. A grey wig changed the appearance of his face, but he was not relying upon that disguise. Locking the door, he stripped himself of his clothes and began to dress deliberately and carefully.

It was nearly eight o'clock that night when Eunice returned to consciousness. Beyond an unquenchable thirst, she felt no distress. The room was dimly illuminated by a small oil-lamp that stood on the washstand, and the first thing that attracted her eye, after she had drunk long and eagerly from the glass of water that stood on the table by the side of the bed, was a beautiful evening dress of silver tissue which hung over the back of the chair. Then she saw pinned to the side of the pillow a card. It was not exactly the same shade of grey that Digby and she had received in the early stages of their acquaintance. Digby had failed to find the right colour in his search at the local stationers, but he had very carefully imitated the pen-print with which the mysterious woman in black had communicated her warnings, and the girl reading at first without understanding and then with a wildly beating heart, the message of the card saw her safely assured.

"Dress in the clothes you will find here, and if you obey me without question I will save you from an ignominious fate. I will call for you but you must not speak to me. We are going to the north in order to escape Digby Groat."

The message was signed with a rough drawing of the Blue Hand.

She was trembling in every limb, for now the events of the past few days were slowly looming through the fog with which the drugs had clouded her brain. She was in the power of Digby Groat, and the mysterious woman in black was coming to her rescue. It did not seem possible. She stood up and almost collapsed, for her head was humming and her knees seemed incapable of sustaining her weight. She held on to the head of the bedstead for several minutes before she dared begin to dress.

She forgot her raging thirst, almost forgot her weakness, as with trembling hands she fastened the beautiful dress about her and slipped on the silk stockings and satin shoes. Why did the mysterious woman in black choose this conspicuous dress, she wondered, if she feared that Digby Groat would be watching for her? She could not think consecutively. She must trust her rescuer blindly, she thought. She did her hair before the tiny mirror and was shocked to see her face. About her eyes were great dark circles; she had the appearance of one who was in a wasting sickness.

"I'm glad Jim can't see you, Eunice Weldon," she said, and the thought of Jim acted as a tonic and a spur.

Her man! How she had hurt him. She stopped suddenly in the act of brushing her hair. She remembered their last interview. Jim said she was the daughter of Lady Mary Danton! It couldn't be true, and yet Jim had said it, and that gave it authority beyond question. She stared at her reflection, and then the effort of thought made her head whirl again and she sat down.

"I mustn't think, I mustn't think," she muttered, and yet thoughts and doubts, questions and speculations, crowded in upon her. Lady Mary Danton was her mother! She was the woman who had come into Jim's flat. There was a tap at the door and she started. Was it Digby Groat? Digby who had brought her here?

"Come in," she said faintly.

The door opened but the visitor did not enter, and she saw, standing on the little landing, a woman in black, heavily veiled, who beckoned to her to follow. She rose unsteadily and moved towards her.

"Where are we going?" she asked, and then, "Thank you, thank you a thousand times, for all you are doing for me!"

The woman made no reply, but walked down the stairs, and Eunice went after her.

It was a dark night; rain was falling heavily and the mews was deserted except for the taxi-cab which was drawn up at the door. The woman opened the door of the cab and followed Eunice into its dark interior.

"You must not ask questions," she whispered. "There is a hood to your coat. Pull it over your head."

What did it mean? Eunice wondered.

She was safe, but why were they going out of London? Perhaps Jim awaited her at the end of the journey and the danger was greater than she had imagined. Whither had Digby Groat gone, and how had this mysterious woman in black got him out of the way? She put her hand to her head. She must wait. She must have patience. All would be revealed to her in good time—and she would see Jim!

The two people who were interested in the departure of the eleven-forty-five train for the north, did not think it was unusual to see a girl in evening dress, accompanied by a woman in mourning, take their places in a reserved compartment. It was a train very popular with those visitors to London who wanted to see a theatre before they left, and the detective who was watching on the departure platform, scrutinizing every man who was accompanied by a woman, gave no attention to the girl in evening dress and, as they thought, her mother. Perhaps if she had not been so attired, they might have looked more closely—Digby Groat was a great student of human nature.

Lady Mary, in her restlessness, had come to Euston to supplement the watch of the detectives, and had passed every carriage and its occupants under review just before Eunice had taken her seat.

"Sit in the corner," whispered the "woman," "and do not look at the platform. I am afraid Groat will be on the look-out for me."

The girl obeyed and Lady Mary, walking back, seeing the young girl in evening dress, whose face was hidden from her, never dreamt of making any closer inspection. The detective strolled along the platform with her towards the entrance.

"I am afraid there will be no more trains to-night, my lady," said the bearded officer, and she nodded. "I should think they've left by motor-car."

"Every road is watched now," said Lady Mary quietly, "and it is impossible for them to get out of London by road."

At the moment the train, with a shrill whistle, began to move slowly out of the station.

"May I look now?" said Eunice, and the "woman" in black nodded.

Eunice turned her head to the platform and then with a cry, started up.

"Why, why," she cried wildly, "there is Mrs. Fane—Lady Mary, my mother!"

Another instant, and she was dragged back to her seat, and a hateful voice hissed in her ear; "Sit down!" The "woman" in black snapped down the blind and raised "her" veil. But Eunice knew that it was Digby Groat before she saw the yellow face of the man.

Chapter 37

THE recognition had been mutual. Lady Mary had seen that white face, those staring eyes, for a second, and then the train had rolled quickly past her, leaving her momentarily paralysed.

"There, there!" she gasped, pointing. "Stop the train!"

The detective looked round. There was no official in sight, and he tore back to the barriers, followed by Lady Mary. He could discover nobody with authority to act.

"I'll find the station-master," he cried. "Can you telephone anywhere?"

There was a telephone booth within a few yards and her first thought was of Jim.

Jim was sitting in his room, his head in his hands, when the telephone bell rang, and he went listlessly to answer the call. It was Lady Mary speaking.

"Eunice is on the northern train that has just left the station," she said, speaking rapidly. "We are trying to stop it at Willesden, but I am afraid it will be impossible. Oh, for God's sake do something, Jim!"

"On the northern train?" he gasped. "How long has it left?"

"A few seconds ago… ."

He dropped the receiver, threw open the door and ran downstairs. In that moment his decision had been taken. Like a flash there had come back to his mind a sunny afternoon when, with Eunice at his side, he had watched a daring little boy pulling himself across the lines by the telegraph wire which crossed the railway from one side to the other. He darted into the courtyard and as he mounted the wall he beard the rumble and roar of the train in the tunnel.

It would be moving slowly because the gradient was a stiff one. From which tunnel would it emerge? There were two black openings and it might be from either. He must risk that, he thought, and reaching up for a telegraph wire, swung himself over the coping. The wires would be strong enough to hold a boy. Would they support him? He felt them sagging and heard an ominous creak from the post which was in the courtyard, but he must risk that too. Hand over hand he went, and presently he saw with consternation the gleam of a light from the farther tunnel. In frantic haste he pulled himself across. There was no time for caution. The engine, labouring heavily, had passed before he came above the line. Now he was over the white-topped carriages, and his legs were curled up to avoid contact with them. He let go and dropped on his foot. The movement of the carriage threw him down and he all but fell over the side, but gripping to a ventilator, he managed to scramble to his knees.

As he did so he saw the danger ahead. The train was running into a second tunnel. He had only time to throw himself flat on the carriage, before he was all but suffocated by the sulphur fumes which filled the tunnel. He was on the right train, he was certain of that, as he lay gasping and coughing, but it would need all his strength to hold himself in position when the driver began to work up speed.

He realized, when they came out again into the open, that it was raining, and raining, heavily. In a few minutes he was wet through, but he clung grimly to his perilous hold. Would Lady Mary succeed in stopping the train at Willesden? The answer came when they flashed through that junction, gathering speed at every minute.

The carriages rocked left and right and the rain-splashed roofs were as smooth as glass. It was only by twining his legs about one ventilator, and holding on to the other, that he succeeded in retaining his hold at all. But it was for her sake. For the sake of the woman he loved, he told himself, when utter weariness almost forced him to release his grip. Faster and faster grew the speed of the train, and now in addition to the misery the stinging rain caused him, he was bombarded by flying cinders and sparks from the engine.

His coat was smouldering in a dozen places, in spite of its sodden condition, his eyes were grimed and smarting with the dust which the rain washed into them, and the agony of the attacks of cramp, which were becoming more and more frequent, was almost unendurable. But he held on as the train roared through the night, flashing through little wayside stations, diving into smoky tunnels, and all the time rocking left and right, so that it seemed miraculous that it was able to keep the rails.

It seemed a century before there came from the darkness ahead a bewildering tangle of red and green lights. They were reaching Rugby and the train was already slowing. Suddenly it stopped with unusual suddenness and Jim was jerked from his hold. He made a wild claw at the nearest ventilator, but he missed his hold and fell with a thud down a steep bank, rolling over and over... another second, and he fell with a splash into water.

The journey had been one of terror for Eunice Danton. She understood now the trick that had been played upon her. Digby Groat had known she would never leave willingly and had feared to use his dope lest her appearance betrayed him. He had guessed that in his disguise of the woman in black she would obey him instantly, and now she began to understand why he had chosen evening dress for her.

"Where are you taking me?" she asked.

He had drawn the blinds of the carriage and was smoking a cigarette.

"If I had known you would ask that question," he said sarcastically, "I would have had a guide book prepared. As it is, you must possess your soul in patience, and wait until you discover your destination."

There was only one carriage on the train which was not a corridor car, and Digby had carefully chosen that for his reservation. It was a local car that would be detached at Rugby, as he knew, and the possibility of an interruption was remote. Once or twice he had looked up to the ceiling and frowned. The girl, who had caught a scratching sound, as though somebody was crawling along the roof of the carriage, watched him as he pulled down the window and thrust out head and shoulders. He drew in immediately, his face wet with rain.

"It is a filthy night," he said as he pulled down the blinds again. "Now, Eunice, be a sensible girl. There are worse things that could happen to you than to marry me."

"I should like to know what they were," said Eunice calmly. The effect of the drug had almost worn off and she was near to her normal self.

"I have told you before," said Digby, puffing a ring of smoke to the ceiling, "that if your imagination will not supply you with a worse alternative, you are a singularly stupid young person, and you are not stupid." He stopped. Suddenly he changed his tone and, throwing the cigarette on to the ground, he came over to her and sat by her side. "I want you, Eunice," he said, his voice trembling and his eyes like fiery stars. "Don't you understand I want you? That you are necessary to me. I couldn't live without you now. I would sooner see you dead, and myself dead too, than hand you to Jim Steele, or any other man." His arm was about her, his face so close to hers that she could feel his quick breath upon her cheek. "You understand?" he said in a low voice. "I would sooner see you dead. That is an alternative for you to ponder on."

"There are worse things than death."

"I'm glad you recognize that," said Digby, recovering his self-possession with a laugh. He must not frighten her at this stage of the flight. The real difficulties of the journey were not yet passed.

As to Eunice, she was thinking quickly. The train must stop soon, she thought, and though he kill her she would appeal for help. She hated him now, with a loathing beyond description—seeing in him the ugly reality, and her soul shrank in horror from the prospect he had opened up to her. His real alternative she knew and understood only too well. It was not death—that would be merciful and final. His plan was to degrade her so that she would never again hold up her head, nor meet Jim's tender eyes. So that she would, in desperation, agree to marriage to save her name from disgrace, and her children from shame.

She feared him more now in his grotesque woman garb, with that smile of his playing upon his thin lips, than when he had held her in his arms, and his hot kisses rained on her face. It was the brain behind those dark eyes, the cool, calculating brain that had planned her abduction with such minute care, that she had never dreamt she was being duped—this was what terrified her. What was his plan now? she wondered. What scheme had he evolved to escape from Rugby, where he must know the station officials would be looking for him?

Lady Mary had seen her and recognized her and would have telegraphed to the officials to search the train. The thought of Lady Mary started a new line of speculation. Her mother! That beautiful woman of whom she had been jealous. A smile dawned on her face, a smile of sheer joy and happiness, and Digby Groat, watching her, wondered what was the cause.

She puzzled him more than he puzzled her.

"What are you smiling at?" he asked curiously, and as she looked at him the smile faded from her face. "You are thinking that you will be rescued at Rugby," he bantered.

"Rugby," she said quickly. "Is that where the train stops?" And he grinned.

"You're the most surprising person. You are constantly trapping me into giving you information," he mocked her. "Yes, the train will stop at Rugby." He looked at his watch and she heard him utter an exclamation. "We are nearly there," he said, and then he took from the little silk bag he carried in his role of an elderly woman a small black case, and at the sight of it Eunice shrank back.

"Not that, not that," she begged. "Please don't do that."

He looked at her.

"Will you swear that you will not make any attempt to scream or cry out so that you will attract attention?"

"Yes, yes," she said eagerly. "I will promise you."

She could promise that with safety, for if the people on the platform did not recognize her, her case was hopeless.

"I will take the risk," he said. "I am probably a fool, but I trust you. If you betray me, you will not live to witness the success of your plans, my friend."

Chapter 38

SHE breathed more freely when she saw the little black case dropped into the bag, and then the speed of the train suddenly slackened and stopped with such a violent jerk that she was almost thrown from the seat.

"Is there an accident?"

"I don't think so," said Digby, showing his teeth mirthlessly. He had adjusted his wig and his bonnet and now he was letting down the window and looking out into the night. There came to his ears a sound of voices up the line and a vista of signal lamps. He turned to the girl as he opened the door.

"Come along," he commanded sharply, and she stood aghast.

"We are not in the platform."

"Come out quickly," he snarled. "Remember you promised."

With difficulty she lowered herself in the darkness and his arm supported her as she dropped to the permanent way. Still clutching her arm, they stumbled and slid down the steep embankment and came presently to a field of high grass. Her shoes and stockings were sodden by the rain which was falling more heavily than ever, and she could scarcely keep her feet, but the hand that gripped her arm did not relax, nor did its owner hesitate. He seemed to know the way they were going, though to the girl it was impossible to see a yard before her.

The pitiless rain soaked her through and through before she had half crossed the field. She heard Digby curse as he caught his foot in his skirt, and at any other tune she might have laughed at the picture she conjured up of this debonair man, in his woman's dress. But now she was too terrified to be even amused.

But she had that courage which goes with great fear. The soul courage which rises superior to the weakness of the flesh.

Once Digby stopped and listened. He heard nothing but the patter of the rain and the silvery splash of the water as it ran from the bushes. He sank on his knees and looked along the ground, striving to get a skyline, but the railway embankment made it impossible. The train was moving on when the girl looked back, and she wondered why it had stopped so providentially at that spot.

"I could have sworn I heard somebody squelching through the mud," said Digby. "Come along, there is the car."

She caught the faint glimmer of a light and immediately afterwards they left the rough and soggy fields and reached the hard road, where walking was something more of a pleasure.

The girl had lost one shoe in her progress and now she kicked off the other. It was no protection from the rain, for the thin sole was soaked through, so that it was more comfortable walking in her stockinged feet.

The distance they had traversed was not far. They came from the side-lane on to the main road, where a closed car was standing, and Digby hustled her in, saying a few low words to the driver, and followed her.

"Phew, this cursed rain," he said, and added with a laugh! "I ought not to complain. It has been a very good friend to me."

Suddenly there was a gleam of light in the car. He had switched on a small electric lamp.

"Where are your shoes?" he demanded.

"I left them in the field," she said.

"Damn you, why did you do that?" he demanded angrily. "You think you were leaving a clue for your lover, I suppose?"

"Don't be unreasonable, Mr. Groat. They weren't my shoes, so they couldn't be very much of a clue for him. They were wet through, and as I had lost one I kicked off the other."

He did not reply to this, but sat huddled in a comer of the car, as it ran along the dark country road.

They must have been travelling for a quarter of an hour when the car stopped before a small house and Digby jumped out. She would have followed him, but he stopped her.

"I will carry you," he said.

"It is not necessary," Eunice replied coldly.

"It is very necessary to me," he interrupted her. "I don't want the marks of your stockinged feet showing on the roadside."

He lifted her in his arms; it would have been foolish of her to have made resistance, and she suffered contact with him until he set her down in a stone passage in a house that smelt damp and musty.

"Is there a fire here?" He spoke over his shoulders to the chauffeur.

"Yes, in the back room. I thought maybe you'd want one, boss."

"Light another," said Digby. He pushed open the door, and the blaze from the fire was the only light in the room.

Presently the driver brought in an oil motor-lamp. In its rays Digby was a ludicrous spectacle. His grey wig was soaked and clinging to his face; his dress was thick with mud, and his light shoes were in as deplorable a condition as the girl's had been.

She was in a very little better case, but she did not trouble to think about herself and her appearance. She was cold and shivering and crept nearer to the fire, extending her chilled hands to the blaze.

Digby went out. She heard him still speaking in his low mumbling voice, but the man who replied was obviously not the chauffeur, though his voice seemed to have a faintly familiar ring. She wondered where she had heard it before, and after awhile she identified its possessor. It was the voice of the man whom she and Jim had met coming down the steps of the house in Grosvenor Square.

Presently Digby came back carrying a suitcase.

"It is lucky for you, my friend, that I intended you should change your clothes here," he said as he threw the case down. "You will find everything in there you require."

He pointed to a bed which was in the corner of the room.

"We have no towels, but if you care to forgo your night's sleep, or sleep in blankets, you can use the sheets to dry yourself," he said.

"Your care for me is almost touching," she said scornfully, and he smiled.

"I like you when you are like that," he said in admiration. "It is the spirit in you and the devil in you that appeal to me. If you were one of those puling, whining misses, all shocks and shivers, I would have been done with you a long time ago. It is because I want to break that infernal pride of yours, and because you offer me a contest, that you stand apart from, and above, all other women."

She made no reply to this, and waited until he had gone j out of the room before she looked for some means of securing the door. The only method, apparently, was to place a chair under the door-knob, and this she did, undressing quickly and utilizing the sheet as Digby had suggested.

The windows were shuttered and barred. The room itself, except for the bed and the chair, was unfurnished and dilapidated. The paper was hanging in folds from the damp walls, and the under part of the grate was filled with the ashes of fires that had burnt years before, and the smell of decay almost nauseated her.

Was there any chance of escape? she wondered. She tried the shuttered window, but found the bars were so thick that it was impossible to wrench them from their sockets without the aid of a hammer. She did not dream that they would leave the door unguarded, but it was worth trying, and she waited until the house seemed quiet before she made her attempt.

Stepping out into the dark passage, she almost trod on the hand of Villa, who was lying asleep in the passage. He was awake instantly.

"Do you want anything, miss?" he asked.

"Nothing," she replied, and went back to the room. It was useless, useless, she thought bitterly, and she must wait to see what the morrow brought forth.

Her principal hope lay in her—her mother. How difficult that word was to say! How much more difficult to associate a name, the mention of which brought up the picture of the pleasant-faced woman who had been all that a mother could be to her in South Africa, with that gracious lady she had seen in Jim Steele's flat!

She lay down, not intending to sleep, but the warmth of the room and her own tiredness made her doze. It seemed she had not slept more than a few minutes when she woke to find Villa standing by her side with a huge cup of cocoa in his hand.

"I'm sorry I can't give you tea, miss," he said.

"What time is it?" she asked in surprise.

"Five o'clock. The rain has stopped and it is a good morning for flying."

"For flying?" she repeated in amazement.

"For flying," said Villa, enjoying the sensation he had created. "You are going a little journey by aeroplane."

Chapter **39**

JIM STEELE had had as narrow an escape from death as he had experienced in the whole course of his adventurous life. It was not a river into which he tumbled, but a deep pool, the bottom of which was a yard thick with viscid mud, in which his feet and legs were held as by hidden hands.

Struggle as he did, he could not release their grip, and he was on the point of suffocation when his groping hands found a branch of a tree which, growing on the edge of the pond, had drooped one branch until its end was under water. With the strength of despair, he gripped, and drew himself up by sheer force of muscle. He had enough strength left to drag himself to the edge of the pond, and there he lay, oblivious to the rain, panting and fighting for his breath.

In the old days of the war, his comrades of the Scout Squadron used to tick off his lives on a special chart which was kept in the mess-room. He had exhausted the nine lives, with which they had credited him, when the war ended, and all further risk seemed to an end.

"There go two more!" he gasped to himself. His words must have been inspired, for as he drew himself painfully to his bruised knees he heard a voice not a dozen yards away, and thanked God again. It was Digby Groat speaking.

"Keep close to my side," said Digby.

"I will," muttered Jim, and walked cautiously in the direction where he had heard the voice, but there was nobody in sight. The train, which had been stationary on the embankment above— he had forgotten the train—began to move, and in the rumble of its wheels, any sound might well be drowned.

He increased his pace, but still he did not catch sight of the two people he was tracking. Presently he heard footsteps on a roadway, but only of a man.

They had reached better going than the field, thought Jim, and moved over in the same direction. He found the lane, and as he heard the footsteps receding at the far end he ran lightly forward, hoping to overtake them before they reached the car, the red rear-light of which he could see. The wheels were moving as he reached the open road, and he felt for his revolver. If he could burst the rear tyres he could hold them. Jim was a deadly shot. Once, twice, he pressed the trigger, but there was no more than a "click," as the hammer struck the sodden cartridge, and before he could extract the dud and replace it the car was out of range.

He was aching in every limb. His arms and legs were cramped painfully, but he was not deterred. Putting the useless pistol in his pocket, he stepped off at a jog-trot, following in the wake of the car.

He was a magnificent athlete and he had, too, the intangible gift of class, that imponderable quality which distinguishes the great race-horse from the merely good. It served a double purpose, this exercise. It freed the cramped muscles, it warmed his chilled body and it cleared the mind. He had not been running for ten minutes before he had forgotten that within the space of an hour he had nearly been hurled to death from the roof of a train and had all but choked to death in the muddy depths of a pond.

On, on, without either slackening or increasing his pace, the same steady lop-lopping stride that had broken the heart of the Oxford crack when he had brought victory to the light-blue side at Queen's Park.

It was half an hour before he came in sight of the car, and he felt well rewarded, although he had scarcely glimpsed it before it had moved on again.

Why had it stopped? he wondered, checking his pace to a walk. It may have been tyre trouble. On the other hand, they might have stopped at a house, one of Digby Groat's numerous depots through the country.

He saw the house at last and went forward with greater caution, as he heard a man's voice asking the time.

He did not recognize either Villa or Bronson, for though he had heard Villa speak, he had no very keen recollection of the fact. "What to do?" murmured Jim.

The house was easily approachable, but to rush in with a defective revolver would help neither him nor the girl. If that infernal pond had not been there! He groaned in the spirit. That he was wise in his caution he was soon to discover. Suddenly a man loomed up before him and Jim stopped dead on the road. The man's back was towards him, and he was smoking as he walked up and down, taking his constitutional, for the rain had suddenly ceased. He passed so close as he turned back that, had he stretched out his band towards the bushes under which Jim was crouching, he would not have failed to touch him.

In a little while a low voice called:

"Bronson!"

"Bronson!" thought Jim. "I must remember that name!"

The man turned and walked quickly back to the house, and the two talked in a tone so low that not a syllable reached Jim.

At the risk of discovery he must hear more, and crept up to the house. There was a tiny porch before the door and under this the two men were standing.

"I will sleep in the passage," said the deep-throated Villa. "You can take the other room if you like."

"Not me," said the man called Bronson. "I'd rather stand by the machine all night. I don't want to sleep anyway."

"What machine?" wondered Jim. "Was there another motor-car here?"

"Will the boss get there to-night?" asked Villa.

"I can't tell you, Mr. Villa," replied Bronson. "He might not, of course, but if there are no obstacles he'll be at the Hall before daybreak. It is not a very good road."

At the Hall! In a flash it dawned upon Jim. Kennett Hall! The pile of buildings which Mrs. Weatherwale had pointed out to him as the one-time ancestral home of the Dantons. What a fool he had been not to remember that place when they were discussing the possible shelters that Digby Groat might use!

Both Villa and Bronson were smoking now and the fragrance of the former man's cigar came to the envious Jim.

"She won't give any trouble, will she, Mr. Villa?" asked Bronson.

"Trouble?" Villa laughed. "Not she. She'll be frightened to death. I don't suppose she's ever been in an aeroplane before."

So that was the machine. Jim's eyes danced. An aeroplane… where? He strained his eyes to beyond the house, but it was too dark to distinguish anything.

"Nothing funny will happen to that machine of yours in the rain?"

"Oh no," said Bronson. "I have put the sheet over the engines. I have frequently kept her out all night."

Then you're a bad man, thought Jim, to whom an aeroplane was a living, palpitating thing. So Eunice was there and they were going to take her by aeroplane somewhere. What should he do? There was time for him to go back to Rugby and inform the police, but—

"Where is Fuentes?" asked Bronson. "Mr. G. said he would be here."

"He's along the Rugby Road," replied Villa. "I gave him a signal pistol to let us know in case they send a police-car after us. If you aren't going to bed, Bronson, I will, and you can wait out here and keep your eye open for any danger."

Fuentes was in it, too, and his plan to get back to Rugby would not work. Nevertheless, the watchful Fuentes had allowed Jim to pass, though it was likely that he was nearer to Rugby than the place where he had come out on to the road. They might not get the girl away on the machine in the darkness, but who knows what orders Digby Groat had left for her disposal in case a rescue was attempted? He decided to wait near, hoping against hope that a policeman cyclist would pass.

Villa struck a match to start a new cigar and in its light Jim had a momentary glimpse of the two men. Bronson was in regulation air-kit. A leather coat reached to his hips, his legs were encased in leather breeches and top-boots. He was about his height, Jim thought, as an idea took shape in his mind. What an end to that adventure! Jim came as near to being excited as ever he had been in his life.

Presently Villa yawned.

"I'm going to lie down in the passage, and if that dame comes out, she's going to have a shock," he said. "Good night. Wake me at half-past four."

Bronson grunted something and continued his perambulations up and down the road. Ten minutes passed, a quarter of an hour, half an hour, and the only sound was the dripping of the ram from the trees, and the distant clatter and rumble of the trains as they passed through Rugby.

To the north were the white lights of the railway sidings and workshops; to the west, the faint glow in the sky marked the position of a town. Jim pulled his useless pistol from his pocket and stepped on to the roadway, crouching down, so that when he did rise, he seemed to the astonished Bronson to have sprung out of the ground. Something cold and hard was pushed under the spy's nose.

"If you make a sound, you son of a thief!" said Jim, "I'll blow your face off! Do you understand that?"

"Yes," muttered the man, shivering with fright.

Jim's left hand gripped his collar. The automatic pistol under his nose was all too obvious, and Felix Bronson, a fearful man for whom the air alone had no terror, was cowed and beaten.

"Where is the bus?" asked Jim in a whisper.

"In the field behind the house," the man answered in the same tone. "What are you going to do? Who are you? How did you get past—"

"Don't ask so many questions," said Jim; "lead the way—not that way," as the man turned to pass the house.

"I shall have to climb the fence if I don't go that way," said Bronson sullenly.

"Then climb it." said Jim, "it will do you good, you lazy devil!"

They walked across the field, and presently Jim saw a graceful outline against the dark sky.

"Now take off your clothes," he said peremptorily.

"What do you mean?" demanded the startled Bronson. "I can't undress here!"

"I'm sorry to shock your modesty, but that is just what you are going to do," said Jim; "and it will be easier to undress you alive than to undress you dead, as I know from my sorrowful experience in France."

Reluctantly Bronson stripped his leather coat.

"Don't drop it on the grass," said Jim, "I want something dry to wear."

In the darkness Bronson utilized an opportunity that he had already considered. His hand stole stealthily to the hip-pocket of his leather breeches, but before it closed on its objective Jim had gripped it and spun him round, for Jim possessed other qualities of the cat besides its lives.

"Let me see that lethal weapon. Good," said Jim, and flung his own to the grass. "I am afraid mine is slightly damaged, but I'll swear that yours is in good trim. Now, off with those leggings and boots."

"I shall catch my death of cold." Bronson's teeth were chattering.

"In which case," said the sardonic Jim, "I shall send a wreath; but I fear you are not born to die of cold in the head, but of a short sharp jerk to your cervical vertebra."

"What is that?" asked Bronson.

"It is German for neck," said Jim, "and if you think I am going to stand here giving you lectures on anatomy whilst you deliver the goods, you have made a mistake—strip!"

Chapter **40**

UNDER menace of Jim Steele's pistol, Mr. Bronson stripped and shivered. The morning was raw, and the clothes that Jim in his mercy handed to the man to change were not very dry. Bronson said as much, but evoked no sympathy from Jim. He stood shivering and shaking in the wet clothes, whilst his captor strapped his wrists behind.

"Just like they do when they hang you," said Jim to cheer him up. "Now, my lad, I think this handkerchief round your mouth and a nearly dry spot under a hedge is all that is required to make the end of a perfect night."

"You're damned funny," growled Bronson in a fury, "but one of these days——"

"Don't make me sing," said Jim, "or you'll be sorry."

He found him a spot under a hedge, which was fairly dry and sheltered from observation, and there he entertained his guest until the grey in the sky warned him that it was time to wake Villa.

Mr. Villa woke with a curse.

"Come in and have some cocoa."

"Bring it out here," said Jim. He heard the man fumbling with the lock of the door and raised his pistol.

Something inside Jim Steele whispered: "Put that pistol away," and he obeyed the impulse, as with profit he had obeyed a hundred others.

Men who fight in the air and who win their battles in the great spaces of the heavens are favoured with instincts which are denied to the other mortals who walk the earth.

He had time to slip the pistol in his pocket and pull the goggles down over his eyes before the door opened and Villa sleepily surveyed him in the half-light.

"Hullo, you're ready to fly, are you?" he said with a guffaw. "Well, I shan't keep you long."

Jim strolled away from the house, pacing the road as Bronson had done the night before.

What had made him put the pistol away? he wondered. He took it out furtively and slipped the cover. It was unloaded!

He heard the man calling.

"Put it down," he said, when he saw the cup in his hand.

He drank the cocoa at a gulp, and making his way across the field to the aeroplane he pulled on the waterproof cover, tested the engine and pulled over the prop.

Eunice had swallowed the hot cocoa and was waiting when Villa came in. What the day would bring forth she could only guess. Evidently there was some reason why Digby Groat should not wait for her, and amongst the many theories she had formed was one that he had gone on in order to lead his pursuers from her track. She felt better now than she had done since she left the house in Grosvenor Square, for the effect of the drug had completely gone, save for a tiredness which made walking a wearisome business. Her mind was clear, and the demoralizing tearfulness which the presence of Digby evoked had altogether dissipated.

"Now, young miss, are you ready?" asked Villa. He was, at any rate. He wore a heavy coat and upon his head was a skin cap. This, with his hairy face and his broad stumpy figure, gave him the appearance of a Russian in winter attire. Why did he wrap himself up so on a warm morning? she wondered. He carried another heavy coat in his hand and held it up for her to put on.

"Hurry up, I can't wait for you all day. Get that coat on."

She obeyed.

"I am ready," she said coldly.

"Now, my dear, step lively!"

Jim, who had taken his place in the pilot's seat, heard Villa's deep voice and looking round saw the woman he loved.

She looked divinely beautiful by the side of that squat, bearded man who was holding her forearm and urging her forward.

"Now, up with you."

He pushed her roughly into one of the two seats behind the pilot, and Jim dared not trust himself to look back.

"I'll swing the prop. for you, Bronson," said Villa, making his way to the propeller, and Jim, whose face was almost covered by the huge fur-lined goggles, nodded. The engine started with a splutter and a roar and Jim slowed it.

"Strap the lady," he shouted above the sound of the engine, and Villa nodded and climbed into the fuselage with extraordinary agility for a man of his build.

Jim waited until the broad strap was buckled about the girl's waist, and then he let out the engine to its top speed. It was ideal ground for taking off, and the plane ran smoothly across the grass, faster and faster with every second. And then, with a touch of the lever, Jim set the elevator down and the girl suddenly realized that the bumping had stopped and all conscious motion had ceased. The Scout had taken the air.

Eunice had never flown in an aeroplane before, and for a moment she forgot her perilous position in the fascination of her new and wonderful experience. The machine did not seem to leave the earth. Rather it appeared as though the earth suddenly receded from the aeroplane and was sinking slowly away from them. She had a wonderful feeling of exhilaration as the powerful Scout shot through the air at a hundred miles an hour, rising higher and higher as it circled above the field it had left, a manoeuvre which set Villa wondering, for Bronson should have known the way back to Kennett Hall without bothering to find his landmark.

But Bronson, so far from being at the wheel, at that moment was lying bound hand and feet beneath a bush in the field below, and had Villa looked carefully through his field glasses he would not have failed to see the figure of the man wearing Jim's muddy clothes. Villa could not suspect that the pilot was Jim Steele, the airman whose exploits in the abstract he had admired, but whose life he would not at this moment have hesitated to take.

"It is lovely!" gasped Eunice, but her voice was drowned in the deafening thunder of the engines.

They were soaring in great circles, and above were floating the scarves of mist that trailed their ravelled edges to the sun, which tinted them so that it seemed to her the sky's clear blue was laced with golden tissue. And beneath she saw a world of wonder: here was spread a marvellous mosaic, green and brown and grey, each little pattern rigidly defined by darked lines, fence and hedge and wall. She saw the blood-red roof of house and the spread of silver lakes irregular in shape, and to her eye like gouts of mercury that some enormous hand had shaken haphazard on the earth.

"Glorious!" her lips said, but the man who sat beside her had no eye for the beauty of the scene.

126

Communication between the pilot and his passengers was only possible through the little telephone, the receiver of which Jim had mechanically strapped to his ear, and after awhile he heard Villa's voice asking:

"What are you waiting for? You know the way?"

Jim nodded.

He knew the way back to London just as soon as he saw the railway.

The girl looked down in wonder on the huge chequer-board intercepted by tiny white and blue ribbons.

They must be roads, and canals, she decided, and those little green and brown patches were the fields and the pastures of Warwickshire. How glorious it was on this early summer morning to be soaring through the cloud-wisps that flecked the sky, wrack from the storm that had passed overnight. And how amazingly soothing was the loneliness of wings! She felt aloof from the world and all its meanness. Digby Groat was no more than that black speck she could see, seemingly stationary, on the white tape of a road. She knew that speck was a man and he was walking. And within that circle alone was love and hate, desire and sacrifice.

Then her attention was directed to Villa. He was red in the face and shouting something into the telephone receiver, something she could not hear, for the noise of the engines was deafening.

She saw the pilot nod and turn to the right and the movement seemed to satisfy Villa, for he sank back in his seat.

Little by little, the nose of the aeroplane came back to the south, and for a long time Villa did not realize the fact. It was the sight of the town which he recognized that brought the receiver of the telephone to his lips.

"Keep to the right, damn you, Bronson. Have you lost your sense of direction?"

Jim nodded, and again the machine banked over, only to return gradually to the southerly course; but now Villa, who had directed the manoeuvre, was alert.

"What is wrong with you, Bronson?" and Jim heard the menace in his voice.

"Nothing, only I am avoiding a bad air current," he answered, and exaggerated as the voice was by the telephone, Villa did not dream that it was anybody but Bronson to whom he was speaking.

Jim kept a steady course westward, and all the time he was wondering where his destination was supposed to have been. He was a raving lunatic, he thought, not to have questioned Bronson before he left him, but it had never occurred to him that his ignorance on the subject would present any difficulties.

He was making for London, and to London he intended going. That had been his plan from the first, and now, without disguise, he banked left, accelerated his engines and the Scout literally leapt forward.

"Are you mad?" It was Villa's voice in his ear, and he made no reply, and then the voice sank to a hiss: "Obey my instructions or we crash together!"

The barrel of an automatic was resting on his shoulder. He looked round, and at that moment Eunice recognized him and gave a cry.

Villa shot a swift glance at her, and then leapt forward and jerked at Jim's shoulders, bringing his head round.

"Steele!" he roared, and this time the pistol was under Jim's ear. "You obey my instructions, do you hear?"

Jim nodded.

"Go right, pick up Oxford and keep it to your left until I tell you to land."

There was nothing for it now but to obey. But Jim did not fear. Had the man allowed him to reach London it might have been well for all parties. As Villa was taking an aggressive line, and had apparently recognized him, there could be only one end to this adventure, pistol or no pistol. He half twisted in his narrow seat, and looked back at Eunice with an encouraging smile, and the look he saw in her eyes amply repaid him for all the discomfort he had suffered.

But it was not to look at her eyes that he had turned. His glance lingered for a while on her waist, and then on the waist of Villa, and he saw all that he wanted to know. He must wait until the man put his pistol away; at present Villa held the ugly-looking automatic in his hand. They passed over Oxford, a blur of grey and green, for a mist lay upon the city, making it difficult to pick out the buildings.

Soon Jim's attention was directed elsewhere. One of his engines had begun to miss and he suspected water was in the cylinder. Still, he might keep the machine going for awhile. A direction was roared in his ear, and he bore a little more west. It seemed that the engine difficulty had been overcome, for she was running sweetly. Again he glanced back. The pistol was tucked in the breast of Villa's leather jacket, and probably would remain there till the end of the journey. To wait any longer would be madness.

Eunice, watching the scene below in a whirl of wonder, suddenly felt the nose of the aeroplane dive down, as though it were aiming directly for earth. She experienced no sense of fear, only a startled wonder, for as suddenly the nose of the aeroplane came up again with a rush and the sky seemed to turn topsy-turvy. There was a tremendous strain at the leather belt about her waist, and looking "down" she found she was staring at the sky! Then she was dimly conscious of some commotion on her right and shut her eyes in instinctive apprehension. When she opened them again Villa was gone! Jim had looped the loop, and, unprepared for this form of attack, Villa, who was not secured to the machine, had lost his balance and fallen. Down, down, the tiny fly shape twirled and rolled with outstretched arms and legs, tragically comic in its grotesqueness…
.

Jim turned his head away and this time swung completely round to the girl, and she saw his lips move and his eyes glance at the telephone which the man had left.

She picked up the mouthpiece with trembling hands. Something dreadful had happened. She dare not look down: she would have fainted if she had made the attempt.

"What has happened?" she asked in a quavering voice.

"Villa has parachuted to the ground," lied Jim soothingly. "Don't worry about him. He's not in any danger—in this world," he added under his breath.

"But, Jim, how did you come here?"

"I'll have to explain that later," he shouted back, "my engine is misbehaving."

This time the trouble was much more serious, and he knew that the journey to London he had contemplated would be too dangerous to attempt. He was not at sufficient height to command any ground he might choose, and he began to search the countryside for a likely landing. Ahead of him, fifteen miles away, was a broad expanse of green, and a pin-point flicker of white caught his eye. It must be an aerodrome, he thought, and the white was the ground signal showing the direction of the winds. He must reach that haven, though, had he been alone, he would not have hesitated to land on one of the small fields beneath him.

Here the country is cut up into smaller pastures than in any other part of England, and to land on one of those fields with its high hedges, stiff and stout stone walls, would mean the risk of a crash, and that was a risk he did not care to take.

As he grew nearer to the green expanse he saw that he had not been mistaken. The sheet was obviously planted for the purpose of signalling, and a rough attempt had been made to form an arrow. He shut off his engines and began to glide down, and the wheels touched the earth so lightly that Eunice did not realize that the flight was ended.

"Oh, it was wonderful, Jim," she cried as soon as she could make herself heard, "but what happened to that poor man? Did you—"

There was a flippant reply on Jim's lips, but when he saw the white face and the sorrowful eyes he decided it was not a moment for flippancy. He, who had seen so many better men than Villa die in the high execution of their duty, was not distressed by the passing of a blackguard who would have killed him and the girl without mercy.

He lifted Eunice and felt her shaking under the coat she wore. And so they met again in these strange circumstances, after the parting which she had thought was final. They spoke no word to one another. He did not kiss her, nor did she want that evidence of his love. His very presence, the grip of his hands, each was a dear caress which the meeting of lips could not enhance.

"There's a house here," said Jim, recovering his breath. "I must take you there and then go and telegraph dear old Salter."

He put his arm about her shoulder, and slowly they walked across the grasses gemmed with wild flowers. Knee-deep they paced through the wondrous meadowland, and the scent of the red earth was incense to the benediction which had fallen on them.

"This house doesn't seem to be occupied," said Jim, "and it is a big one, too."

He led the way along a broad terrace, and they came to the front of the building. The door stood open, and there the invitation ended. Jim looked into a big dreary barn of a hall, uncarpeted and neglected.

"I wonder what place this is," said Jim, puzzled.

He opened a door that led from the hall to the left. The room into which he walked was unfurnished and bore the same evidence of decay as the hall had shown. He crossed the floor and entered a second room, with no other result. Then he found a passageway.

"Is anybody here?" he called, and turned immediately. He thought he heard a cry from Eunice, whom he had left outside on the terrace admiring the beauty of the Somerset landscape. "Was that you, Eunice?" he shouted, and his voice reverberated through the silent house.

There was no reply. He returned quickly by the way he had come, but when he reached the terrace Eunice was gone! He ran to the end, thinking she had strolled back to the machine, but there was no sign of her. He called her again, at the top of his voice, but only the echoes answered. Perhaps she had gone into the other room. He opened the front door and again stepped in.

As he did so Xavier Silva crept from the room on the left and poised his loaded cane. Jim heard the swish of the stick and, half turning, took the blow short on his shoulder. For a second he was staggered, and then driving left and right to the face of the man he sent him spinning.

Before he could turn, the noose of a rope dropped over his head and he was jerked to the ground, fighting for breath.

Chapter 41

WHILST Jim had been making his search of the deserted house, Eunice had strolled to the edge of the terrace, and, leaning on the broken balustrade, was drinking in the beauty of the scene. Thin wraiths of mist still lingered in the purple shadows of the woods and lay like finest muslin in the hollows. In the still air the blue-grey smoke of the cottagers' fires showed above the tree-tops, and the sun had touched the surface of a stream that wound through a distant valley, so that it showed as a thread of bubbling gold amidst the verdant green.

Somebody touched her gently on the shoulder. She thought it was Jim.

"Isn't it lovely, Jim?"

"Very lovely, but not half as lovely as you, my dear."

She could have collapsed at the voice. Swinging round she came face to face with Digby Groat, and uttered a little cry.

"If you want to save Steele's life," said Digby in a low urgent tone, "you will not cry out, you understand?"

She nodded.

He put his arm round her shoulder and she shivered, but it was no caress he offered. He was guiding her swiftly into the house. He swung open a door and, pushing her through, followed. There was a man in the room, a tall, dour man, who held a rope in his hand.

"Wait, Masters," whispered Digby. "We'll get him as he comes back." He had heard the footsteps of Jim in the hall and then suddenly there was a scuffle.

Eunice opened her lips to cry a warning, but Digby's hand covered her mouth and his face was against her ear.

"Remember what I told you," he whispered.

There was a shout outside, it was from Xavier, and Masters dashed out ahead of his employer. Jim's back was turned to the open door, and Digby signalled. Immediately the rope slipped round Jim's neck and he was pulled breathlessly to the ground; his face grew purple and his hands were tearing at the cruel noose. They might have choked him then and there, but that Eunice, who had stood for a moment paralysed, flew out of the room and, thrusting Masters aside, knelt down and with her own trembling hands released the noose about her lover's neck.

"You beasts, you beasts!" she cried, her eyes flashing her hate.

In an instant Digby was on her and had lifted her clear.

"Rope him," he said laconically, and gave his attention to the struggling girl. For now Eunice was no longer quiescent. She fought with all her might, striking at his face with her hands, striving madly to free herself of his grip.

"You little devil!" he cried breathlessly, when he had secured her wrists and had thrust her against the wall. There was an ugly red mark where her nails had caught his face, but in his eyes there was nothing but admiration.

"That is how I like you best," he breathed. "My dear, I have never regretted my choice of you! I regret it least at this moment!"

"Release my hands!" she stormed. She was panting painfully, and, judging that she was incapable of further mischief, he obeyed.

"Where have you taken Jim? What have you done with him?" she asked, her wide eyes fixed on his. There was no fear in them now. He had told her that he had seen the devil in her. Now it was fully aroused.

"We have taken your young friend to a place of safety," said Digby. "What happened this morning, Eunice?"

She made no reply.

"Where is Villa?"

Still she did not answer.

"Very good," he said. "If you won't speak I'll find a way of making your young man very valuable."

"You'd make him speak!" she said scornfully. "You don't know the man you're dealing with. I don't think you've ever met that type in the drawing-rooms you visited during the war. The real men were away in France, Digby Groat. They were running the risks you shirked, facing the dangers you feared. If you think you can make Jim Steele talk, go along and try!"

"You don't know what you're saying," he said, white to the lips, for her calculated insult had touched him on the raw. "I can make him scream for mercy."

She shook her head.

"You judge all men by yourself," she said, "and all women by the poor little shop-girls you have broken for your amusement."

"Do you know what you're saying?" he said, quivering with rage. "You seem to forget that I am——"

"I forget what you are!" she scoffed. The colour had come back to her face and her eyes were bright with anger. "You're a half-breed, a man of no country and no class, and you have all the attributes of a half-breed. Digby Groat, a threatener of women and an assassin of men, a thief who employs other thieves to take the risks whilst he takes the lion's share of the loot. A quack experimenter, who knows enough of medicines to drug women and enough of surgery to torture animals—I have no doubt about you!"

For a long time he could not speak. She had insulted him beyond forgiveness, and with an uncanny instinct had discovered just the things to say that would hurt him most.

"Put out your hands," he almost yelled, and she obeyed, watching him contemptuously as he bound them together with the cravat which he had torn from his neck.

He took her by the shoulders and, pushing her feet from her ungently, sat her in a corner.

"I'll come back and deal with you, my lady," he growled.

Outside in the hall Masters was waiting for him, and the big, uncouth man was evidently troubled.

"Where have you put him?"

"In the east wing, in the old butler's rooms," he said, ill at ease. "Mr. Groat, isn't this a bad business?"

"What do you mean, bad business?" snarled Digby.

"I've never been mixed up in this kind of thing before," said Masters. "Isn't there a chance that they will have the law on us?"

"Don't you worry, you'll be well paid," snapped his employer, and was going away when the man detained him.

"Being well paid won't keep me out of prison, if this is a prison job," he said. "I come of respectable people, and I've never been in trouble all my life. I'm well known in the country, and although I'm not very popular in the village, yet nobody can point to me and say that I've done a prison job."

"You're a fool," said Digby, glad to have some one to vent his rage upon. "Haven't I told you that this man has been trying to run off with my wife?"

"You didn't say anything about her being your wife," said Masters, shaking his head and looking suspiciously at the other, "and, besides, she's got no wedding-ring. That's the first thing I noticed. And that foreign man hadn't any right to strike with his cane—it might have killed him."

"Now look here, Masters," said Digby, controlling himself, for it was necessary that the man should be humoured, "don't trouble your head about affairs that you can't understand. I tell you this man Steele is a scoundrel who has run away with my wife and has stolen a lot of money. My wife is not quite normal, and I am taking her away for a voyage… " He checked himself. "Anyway, Steele is a scoundrel," he said.

"Then why not hand him over to the police," said the uneasy Masters, "and bring him before the justices? That seems to me the best thing to do, Mr. Groat. You're going to get a bad name if it comes out that you treated this gentleman as roughly as you did."

"I didn't treat him roughly," said Digby coolly, "and it was you who slipped the rope round his neck."

"I tried to get it over his shoulders," explained Masters hastily; "besides, you told me to do it."

"You'd have to prove that," said Digby, knowing that he was on the right track. "Now listen to me, Masters. The only person who has committed any crime so far has been you!"

"Me?" gasped the man. "I only carried out your orders."

"You'd have to prove that before your precious justices," said Digby, with a laugh, and dropped his hand on the man's shoulder, a piece of familiarity which came strangely to Masters, who had never known his employer in such an amiable mood. "Go along and get some food ready for the young lady," he said, "and if there is any trouble, I'll see that you get clear of it. And here." He put his hand in his pocket and took out a wad of notes, picked two of them out and pressed them into the man's hand. "They are twenty-pound banknotes, my boy, and don't forget it and try to change them as fivers. Now hurry along and get your wife to find some refreshment for the young lady."

"I don't know what my wife's going to say about it," grumbled the man, "when I tell her—"

"Tell her nothing," said Digby sharply. "Damn you, don't you understand plain English?"

At three o'clock that afternoon a hired car brought two passengers before the ornamental gate of Kennett Hall, and the occupants, failing to secure admission, climbed the high wall and came trudging up towards the house.

Digby saw them from a distance and went down to meet the bedraggled Bronson and the dark-skinned Spaniard who was his companion. They met at the end of the drive, and Bronson and his master, speaking together, made the same inquiry in identical terms;

"Where is Villa?"

Chapter 42

THE room into which Jim was thrust differed little from those chambers he had already seen, save that it was smaller. The floorboards were broken, and there were holes in the wainscot which he understood long before he heard the scamper of the rats' feet.

He was trussed like a fowl, his hands were so tightly corded together that he could not move them, and his ankles roped so that it was next to impossible to lever himself to his feet.

"What a life!" said Jim philosophically, and prepared himself for a long, long wait.

He did not doubt that Digby would leave immediately, and Jim faced the prospect of being left alone in the house, to make his escape or die. He was fully determined not to die, and already his busy mind had evolved a plan which he would put into execution as soon as he knew he was not under observation.

But Digby remained in the house, as he was to learn.

An hour passed, and then the door was snapped open and Digby came in, followed by a man at the sight of whom Jim grinned. It was Bronson, looking ludicrous in Jim's clothes, which were two sizes too large for him.

"They discovered you, did they, Bronson!" he chuckled. "Well, here am I as you were, and presently somebody will discover me, and then I shall be calling on you in Dartmoor, some time this year, to see how you are going along. Nice place Dartmoor, and the best part of the prison is Block B.—central heating, gas, hot water laid on, and every modern convenience except tennis—"

"Where is Villa?" asked Digby.

"I don't know for a fact," said Jim pleasantly, "but I can guess."

"Where is he?" roared Bronson, his face purple with rage.

Jim smiled, and in another minute the man's open hand had struck him across the face, but still Jim smiled, though there was something in his eyes that made Bronson quail.

"Now, Steele, there's no sense in your refusing to answer," said Digby. "We want to know what you have done with Villa. Where is he?"

"In hell," said Jim calmly. "I'm not a whale on theology, Groat, but if men are punished according to their deserts, then undoubtedly your jovial pal is in the place where the bad men go and there is little or no flying."

"Do you mean that he is dead?" asked Digby, livid.

"I should think he is," said Jim carefully. "We were over five thousand feet when I looped the loop from sheer happiness at finding myself once again with a joy-stick in my hand, and I don't think your friend Villa had taken certain elementary precautions. At any rate, when I looked round, where was Villa? He was flying through the air on his own, Groat, and my experience is that when a man starts flying without his machine, the possibility of making a good landing is fairly remote."

"You killed him," said Bronson between his teeth, "damn you!"

"Shut up," snapped Digby. "We know what we want to know. Where did you throw him out?"

"Somewhere around," said Jim carelessly. "I chose a deserted spot. I should have hated it if he had hurt anybody when he fell."

Digby went out of the room without a word, and locked the door behind him, and did not speak until he was back in the room where he had left Villa less than a week before. He shuddered as he thought of the man's dreadful end.

The two Spaniards were there, and they had business which could not be postponed. Digby had hoped they would rely on his promise and wait until he had readied a place of safety before they insisted on a share-out, but they were not inclined to place too high a value upon their chief's word. Their share was a large one, and Digby hated the thought of paying them off, but it had to be done. He had still a considerable fortune. No share had gone to the other members of the gang.

"What are your plans?" asked Xavier Silva.

"I'm going to Canada," replied Digby. "You may watch the agony columns of the newspapers for my address."

The Spaniard grinned.

"I shall be watching for something more interesting," he said, "for my friend and I are returning to Spain. And Bronson, does he go with you?"

Digby nodded.

It was necessary, now that Villa had gone, to take the airman into his confidence. He had intended leaving his shadow in the lurch, a fact which Bronson did not suspect. He sent the two men into the grounds to give the machine an examination, and Jim, sitting in his room, heard the noise of the engine and struggled desperately to free his hands. If he could only get up to his feet! All his efforts must be concentrated upon that attempt.

Presently the noise ceased; Xavier Silva was a clever mechanic, and he had detected that something was wrong with one of the cylinders.

"Tuning up!" murmured Jim.

So he had more time than he had hoped for.

He heard a step on the stone terrace, and through the window caught a glimpse of Bronson passing. Digby had sent the man into the village to make judicious inquiries as to Villa's fate.

Curiously enough, the three men who had watched the approaching aeroplane from the terrace of Kennett Hall had been unconscious of Villa's doom, although they were witnesses of the act. They had seen the loop in the sky and Digby had thought no more than that Bronson was showing off to the girl, and had cursed him roundly for his folly. Villa's body must be near at hand. How near, Bronson was to discover at the village inn.

After the man had left, Digby went to look at his second prisoner, and found her walking up and down the room into which she had been put for safety.

"Did you like your aeroplane journey, Eunice?" he asked blandly.

She did not reply.

"Rather thrilling and exciting, wasn't it? And were you a witness to the murder of my friend Villa?"

She looked up at him.

"I don't remember that your friend Villa was murdered," she said, ready to defend Jim of any charge that this man might trump up against him.

He read her thoughts.

"Don't worry about Mr. Steele," he said dryly. "I am not charging him with murder. In fact, I have no time. I am leaving tomorrow night as soon as it is dark, and you are coming with me by aeroplane."

She did not answer this.

"I am hoping that you won't mind a brief immersion in the sea," he said. "I cannot guarantee that we can land on my yacht."

She turned round. On his yacht! That, then, was the plan. She was to be carried off to a yacht, and the yacht was to take her—where?

There was a clatter of feet in the outer room and he opened the door. One glance at Bronson's face told him that he had important news.

"Well?" he asked sharply.

"They've found Villa's body. I saw a reporter at the inn," said the man breathlessly.

"Do they know who it is?" asked Digby, and Bronson nodded.

"What?" asked Digby, startled. "They know his name is Villa?"

Again the man nodded.

"They found a paper in his pocket, a receipt for the sale of a yacht," he said, and through the open doorway Eunice saw the man shrink back.

"Then they know about the yacht?"

The news confounded him and shook him from his calm. If the police knew about the yacht his difficulties became all but insuperable, and the danger which threatened him loomed up like a monstrous overwhelming shape. Digby Groat was not built to meet such stunning emergencies and he went all to pieces under the shock.

Eunice, watching him through the open door, saw his pitiable collapse. In a second he had changed from the cool, self-possessed man who had sneered at danger into a babbling fretful child who cursed and wrung his hands, issuing incoherent orders only to countermand them before his messenger had left the room.

"Kill Steele!" he screamed. "Kill him, Bronson. Damn him—no, no, stay! Get the machine ready... we leave to-night."

He turned to the girl, glaring at her.

"We leave to-night, Eunice! To-night you and I will settle accounts!"

Chapter 43

HER heart sank, and it came to her, with terrifying force, that her great trial was near at hand. She had taunted Digby with his cowardice, but she knew that he would show no mercy to her, and unwillingly she had played into his hands by admitting that she knew she was the heiress to the Danton fortune and that she had known his character, and yet had elected to stay in his house.

The door was slammed and locked, and she was left alone. Later she heard for the second time the splutter and crash of the aeroplane's engines as the Spaniard tuned them up.

She must get away—she must, she must! She looked round wildly for some means of escape. The windows were fastened. There was no other door from the room. Her only hope was Jim, and Jim, she guessed, was a close prisoner.

Digby lost no time. He dispatched Silva in the car, telling him to make the coast as quickly as possible, and to warn the captain of the Pealigo to be ready to receive him that night. He wrote rapidly a code of signals. When in sight of the sea Bronson was to fire a green signal light, to which the yacht must respond. A boat must be lowered on the shoreward side of the yacht ready to pick them up. After the messenger had left he remembered that he had already given the same orders to the captain, and that it was humanly impossible for the Spaniard to reach the yacht that night.

Digby had in his calmer moments made other preparations. Two inflated life-belts were taken to the aeroplane and tested, signal pistols, landing lights, and other paraphernalia connected with night flying were stowed in the fuselage. Bronson was now fully occupied with the motor of the aeroplane, for the trouble had not been wholly eradicated, and Digby Groat paced up and down the terrace of the house, fuming with impatience and sick with fear.

He had not told the girl to prepare, that must be left to the very last. He did not want another scene. For the last time he would use his little hypodermic syringe and the rest would be easy.

Fuentes joined him on the terrace, for Fuentes was curious for information.

"Do you think that the finding of Villa's body will bring them after us here?"

"How do I know?" snapped Digby, "and what does it matter, anyway? We shall be gone in an hour?"

"You will," said the Spaniard pointedly, "but I shan't. I have no machine to carry me out of the country, and neither has Xavier, though he is better off than I am—he has the car. Couldn't you take me?"

"It is utterly impossible," said Digby irritably. "They won't be here to-night, and you needn't worry yourself. Before the morning, you will have put a long way between you and Kennett Hall."

He spoke in Spanish, the language which the man was employing, but Fuentes was not impressed.

"What about that man?" He jerked his thumb to the west wing, and a thought occurred to Digby. Could he persuade his hitherto willing slave to carry out a final instruction?

"He is your danger," he said. "Do you realize, my dear Fuentes, that this man can bring us all to destruction? And nobody knows he is here, except you and me."

"And that ugly Englishman," corrected Fuentes.

"Masters doesn't know what has happened to him. We could tell him that he went with us!"

He looked at the other keenly, but Fuentes was purposely stupid.

"Now what do you say, my dear Fuentes," said Digby, "shall we allow this man to live and give evidence against us, when a little knock on the head would remove him for ever?"

Fuentes turned his dark eyes to Digby's, and he winked.

"Well, kill him, my dear Groat," he mocked. "Do not ask me to stay behind and be found with the body, for I have a wholesome horror of English gaols, and an unspeakable fear of death."

"Are you afraid?" asked Digby.

"As afraid as you," said the Spaniard. "If you wish to kill him, by all means do so. And yet, I do not know that I would allow you to do that," he mused, "for you would be gone and I should be left. No, no, we will not interfere with our courageous Englishman. He is rather a fine fellow." Digby turned away in disgust.

The "fine fellow" at that moment had, by almost super-human effort, raised himself to his feet. It had required something of the skill of an acrobat and the suppleness and ingenuity of a contortionist, and it involved supporting himself with his head against the wall for a quarter of an hour whilst he brought his feet to the floor; but he had succeeded.

The day was wearing through and the afternoon was nearly gone before he had accomplished this result. His trained ear told him that the aeroplane was now nearly ready for departure, and once he had caught a glimpse of Digby wearing a lined leather jacket. But there was no sign of the girl. As to Eunice, he steadfastly kept her out of his thoughts. He needed all his courage and coolness, and even the thought of her, which, in spite of his resolution, flashed across his mind, brought him agonizing distress.

He hopped cautiously to the window and listened. There was no sound and he waited until Bronson—he guessed it was Bronson—started the engines again. Then with his elbow he smashed out a pane of glass, leaving a jagged triangular piece firmly fixed in the ancient putty. Carefully he lifted up his bound hands, straining at the rope which connected them with the bonds about his feet, and which was intended to prevent his raising his hands higher than the level of his waist.

By straining at the rope and standing on tiptoe, he brought the end of the connecting link across the sharp jagged edge of the glass. Two strokes, and the rope was severed. His hands were still bound and to cut through them without injury to himself was a delicate operation. Carefully he sawed away, and first one and then the other cord was cut through. His hands were red and swollen, his wrists had no power until he had massaged them.

He snapped off the triangular piece of glass and applied it to the cords about his feet, and in a minute he was free. Free, but in a locked room. Still, the window-sash should not prove an insuperable obstacle. There was nothing which he could use as a weapon, but his handy feet smashed at the frames, only to discover that they were of iron. Jonathan Danton's father had had a horror of burglars, and all the window-frames on the lower floor had been made in a foundry. The door was the only egress left and it was too stout to smash.

He listened at the keyhole. There was no sound. The light was passing from the sky and night was coming on. They would be leaving soon, he guessed, and grew frantic. Discarding all caution, he kicked at the panels, but they resisted his heavy boots, and then he heard a sound that almost stopped his heart beating.

A shrill scream from Eunice. Again and again he flung his weight at the door, but it remained immovable, and then came a shout from the ground outside. He ran to the window and listened.

"They are coming, the police!"

It was the Spaniard's throbbing voice. He had run until he was exhausted. Jim saw in stagger past the window and heard Digby say something to him sharply. There was a patter of feet and silence.

Jim wiped the sweat from his forehead with the sleeve of his coat and looked round desperately for some means of getting out of the room. The fireplace! It was a big, old-fashioned fire-basket, that stood on four legs in a yawning gap of chimney. He looked at it; it was red with rust and it had the appearance of being fixed, but he lifted it readily. Twice he smashed at the door and the second time it gave way, and dropping the grate with a crash he flew down the passage out of the house.

As he turned the comer he heard the roar of the aeroplane and above its drone the sound of a shot. He leapt the balustrade, sped through the garden and came in sight of the aeroplane as it was speeding from him.

"My God!" said Jim with a groan, for the machine had left the ground and was zooming steeply up into the darkening sky.

And then he saw something. From the long grass near where the machine had been a hand rose feebly and fell again. He ran across to where he had seen this strange sight. In a few minutes he was kneeling by the side of Fuentes. The man was dying. He knew that long before he had seen the wound in his breast.

"He shot me, senor," gasped Fuentes, "and I was his friend... I asked him to take me to safety... and he shot me!"

The man was still alive when the police came on the spot; still alive when Septimus Salter, in his capacity of Justice of the Peace, took down his dying statement.

"Digby Groat shall hang for this, Steele," said the lawyer; but Jim made no reply. He had his own idea as to how Digby Groat would die.

Chapter 44

THE lawyer explained his presence without preliminary, and Jim listened moodily.

"I came with them myself because I know the place," said Mr. Salter, looking at Jim anxiously. "You look ghastly, Steele. Can't you lie down and get some sleep?"

"I feel that I shall never sleep until I have got my hand on Digby Groat. What was it you saw in the paper? Tell me again. How did they know it was Villa?"

"By a receipt in his pocket," replied Salter. "It appears that Villa, probably acting on behalf of Digby Groat, had purchased from Maxilla, the Brazilian gambler, his yacht, the Pealigo—"

Jim uttered a cry.

"That is where he has gone," he said. "Where is the Pealigo?"

"That I have been trying to find out," replied the lawyer, shaking his head, "but nobody seems to know. She left Havre a few days ago, but what her destination was, nobody knows. She has certainly not put in to any British port so far as we can ascertain. Lloyd's were certain of this, and every ship, whether it is a yacht, a liner, or a cargo tramp, is reported to Lloyd's."

"That is where he has gone," said Jim.

"Then she must be in port," said old Salter eagerly. "We can telegraph to every likely place—"

Jim interrupted him with a shake of his head.

"Bronson would land on the water and sink the machine. It is a very simple matter," he said. "I have been in the sea many times and there is really no danger, if you are provided with life-belts, and are not strapped to the seat. It is foul luck your not coming before."

He walked weakly from the comfortable parlour of the inn where the conversation had taken place.

"Do yon mind if I am alone for a little while? I want to think," he said.

He turned as he was leaving the room.

"In order not to waste time, Mr. Salter," he said quietly, "have you any influence with the Admiralty? I want the loan of a seaplane."

Mr. Salter looked thoughtful.

"That can be fixed," he said. "I will get on to the 'phone straight away to the Admiralty and try to get the First Sea Lord. He will do all that he can to help us."

Whilst the lawyer telephoned, Jim made a hasty meal. The pace had told on him and despair was in his heart.

The knowledge that Digby Groat would eventually be brought to justice did not comfort him. If Eunice had only been spared he would have been content to see Digby make his escape, and would not have raised his hand to stop him going. He would have been happy even if, in getting away, the man had been successful in carrying off the girl's fortune. But Eunice was in his wicked hands and the thought of it was unendurable.

He was invited by the local police-sergeant to step across to the little lock-up to interview the man Masters, who was under arrest, and as Mr. Salter had not finished telephoning, he crossed the village street and found the dour man in a condition of abject misery.

"I knew he'd bring me into this," bewailed, "and me with a wife and three children and not so much as a poaching case against me! Can't you speak a word for me, sir?"

Jim's sense of humour was never wholly smothered and the cool request amused him.

"I can only say that you tried to strangle me," he said. "I doubt whether that good word will be of much service to you."

"I swear I didn't mean to," pleaded the man. "He told me to put the rope round your shoulders and it slipped. How was I to know that the lady wasn't his wife who'd run away with you?"

"So that is the story he told you?" said Jim.

"Yes, sir," the man said eagerly. "I pointed out to Mr. Groat that the lady hadn't a wedding-ring, but he said that he was married all right and he was taking her to sea—"

"To sea?"

Masters nodded.

"That's what he said, sir—he said she wasn't right in her head and the sea voyage would do her a lot of good."

Jim questioned him closely without getting any further information. Masters knew nothing of the steamer on which Digby and his "wife" were to sail, or the port at which he would embark.

Outside the police station Jim interviewed the sergeant.

"I don't think this man was any more than a dupe of Groat's," he said, "and I certainly have no charge to make against him."

The sergeant shook his head.

"We must hold him until we have had the inquest on the Spaniard," he said, and then, gloomily, "To think that I had a big case like this right under my nose and hadn't the sense to see it!"

Jim smiled a little sadly.

"We have all had the case under our noses, sergeant, and we have been blinder than you!"

The threat of a renewed dose of the drug had been sufficient to make Eunice acquiescent. Resistance, she knew, was useless. Digby could easily overpower her for long enough to jab his devilish needle into her arm.

She had struggled at first and had screamed at the first prick from the needle-point. It was that scream Jim had heard.

"I'll go with you; I promise you I will not give you any trouble," she said. "Please don't use that dreadful thing again."

Time was pressing and it would be easier to make his escape if the girl did not resist than if she gave him trouble.

The propeller was ticking slowly round when they climbed into the fuselage.

"There is room for me, senor. There must be room for me!"

Digby looked down into the distorted face of the Spaniard who had come running after him.

"There is no room for you, Fuentes," he said. "I have told you before. You must get away as well as you can."

"I am going with you!"

To Digby's horror, the man clung desperately to the side of the fuselage. Every moment was increasing their peril, and in a frenzy he whipped out his pistol.

"Let go," he hissed, "or I'll kill you," but still the man held on.

There were voices coming from the lower path, and, in his panic, Digby fired. He saw the man crumple and fall and yelled to Bronson: "Go, go!"

Eunice, a horrified spectator, could only stare at the thing which had been Digby Groat, for the change which had come over him was extraordinary. He seemed to have shrunk in stature. His face was twisted, like a man who had had a stroke of paralysis.

She thought this was the case, but slowly he began to recover.

He had killed a man! The horror of this act was upon him, the fear of the consequence which would follow overwhelmed him and drove him into a momentary frenzy. He had killed a man! He could have shrieked at the thought. He, who had so carefully guarded himself against punishment, who had manoeuvred his associates into danger, whilst he himself stood in a safe place, was now a fugitive from a justice which would not rest until it had lain him by the heel.

And she had seen him, she, the woman at his side, and would go into the box and testify against him! And they would hang him! In that brick-lined pit of which Jim Steele had spoken. All these thoughts flashed through his mind in a second, even before the machine left the ground, but with the rush of cold air and the inevitable exhilaration of flight, he began to think calmly again.

Chapter 45

BRONSON had killed him, that was the comforting defence. Bronson, who was now guiding him to safety, and who would, if necessary, give his life for him. Bronson should bear the onus of that act.

They were well up now, and the engines were a smooth "b-r-r" of sound. A night wind was blowing and the plane rocked from side to side. It made the girl feel a little sick, but she commanded her brain to grow accustomed to the motion, and after a while the feeling of nausea wore off.

They could see the sea now. The flashing signals of the lighthouses came from left and right. Bristol, a tangle of fiery spots, lay to their left, and there were tiny gleams of light on the river and estuary.

They skirted the northern shore of the Bristol Channel and headed west, following the coastline. Presently the machine turned due south, leaving behind them the land and its girdle of lights. Twenty minutes later Bronson fired his signal pistol. A ball of brilliant green fire curved up and down and almost immediately, from the sea, came an answering signal. Digby strapped the girl's life-belt tighter, and saw to the fastening of his own.

"Fix my belt." It was Bronson shouting through the telephone, and Digby, leaning forward, fastened the life-belt about the pilot's waist. He fastened it carefully and added a, stout strap, tying the loose end of the leather in a knot. Down went the machine in a long glide toward the light which still burnt, and now the girl could see the outlines of the graceful yacht and the green and red lights it showed. They made a circle, coming lower and lower every second, until they were spinning about the yacht not more than a dozen feet from the sea. Bronson shut off his engines and brought the machine upon the water, less than fifty feet from the waiting boat.

Instantly the aeroplane sank under them, leaving them in the sea. It was a strange sensation, thought the girl, for the water was unusually warm.

She heard a shriek and turned, and then Digby caught her hand.

"Keep close to me," he said in a whimpering voice, "you might be lost in the darkness."

She knew that he was thinking of himself. A light flared from the oncoming boat, and she looked round. In spite of herself, she asked:

"Where is the man?"

Bronson was nowhere in sight. Digby did not trouble to turn his head or answer. He reached up and gripped the gunwale of the boat and in a minute Eunice was lifted out of the water. She found herself in a small cutter which was manned by brown-faced men, whom she thought at first were Japanese.

"Where is Bronson?" she asked again in a panic, but Digby did not reply. He sat immovable, avoiding her eyes, and she could have shrieked her horror. Bronson had gone down with the aeroplane! The strap which Digby had fastened about his waist, he had cunningly attached to the seat itself, and had fastened it so that it was impossible for the pilot to escape.

He was the first up the gangway on to the white deck of the yacht, and turning, he offered his hand to her.

"Welcome to the Pealigo," he said in his mocking voice.

Then it was not fear that had kept him silent. She could only look at him.

142

"Welcome to the Pealigo, my little bride," he said, and she knew that the man who had not hesitated to murder his two comrades in cold blood would have no mercy on her.

A white-coated stewardess came forward, and said something in a language which Eunice did not understand. She gathered that the woman was deputed to show her the way to the cabin. Glad to be free from the association of Digby, she passed down the companion-way, through a lobby panelled in rosewood, into a cabin, the luxury of which struck her, even though her nerves were shattered, and she was incapable of taking an interest in anything outside the terrible fact that she was alone on a yacht with Digby Groat.

Extravagance had run riot here, and the Brazilian must have lavished a fortune in the decoration and appointments.

The saloon ran the width of the ship and was as deep as it was broad. Light was admitted from portholes cunningly designed, so that they had the appearance of old-fashioned casement windows. A great divan, covered in silk, ran the length of the cabin on one side, whilst the other was occupied by a silver bedstead, hung with rose silk curtains. Rose-shaded lights supplied the illumination, and the lamps were fashioned like torches and were held by beautiful classical figures placed in niches about the room.

She came to the conclusion that it was a woman's room and wondered if there were any other women on board but the stewardess. She asked that woman, but apparently she knew no English, and the few words in Spanish which she had learnt did not serve her to any extent.

The suite was complete, she discovered, for behind the heavy silken curtains at the far end of the cabin there was a door which gave to a small sitting-room and a bath-room. It must be a woman's. In truth, it was designed especially by Senor Maxilla for his own comfort.

Lying on the bed was a complete change of clothing. It was brand-new and complete to the last detail. Digby Groat could be very thorough.

She dismissed the woman, and bolting the door, made a complete change, for the third time since she had left Grosvenor Square.

The boat was under way now. She could feel the throb of its engines, and the slight motion that it made in the choppy sea. The Pealigo was one of the best sea boats afloat, and certainly one of the fastest yachts in commission.

She had finished her changing when a knock came at the door and she opened it to find Digby standing on the mat.

"You had better come and have some dinner," he said.

He was quite his old self, and whatever emotions had disturbed him were now completely under control.

She shrank back and tried to close the floor, but now he was not standing on ceremony. Grasping her arm roughly, he dragged her out into the passage.

"You're going to behave yourself while you're on this ship," he said. "I'm master here, and there is no especial reason why I should show you any politeness."

"You brute, you beast!" she flamed at him, and he smiled.

"Don't think that because you're a woman it is going to save you anything in the way of punishment," he warned her. "Now be sensible and come along to the dining-saloon."

"I don't want to eat," she said.

"You will come into the dining-saloon whether you want to or not."

The saloon was empty save for the two and a dark-skinned waiter, and, like her own cabin, it was gorgeously decorated, a veritable palace in miniature, with its dangling electrolier, its flowers, and its marble mantelpiece at the far end.

The table was laid with a delicious meal, but Eunice felt she would choke if she took a morsel.

"Eat," said Digby, attacking the soup which had been placed before him.

She shook her head.

"If you don't," and his eyes narrowed, "if you don't, my good soul, I will find a way of making you eat," he said. "Remember," he put his hand in his pocket, pulled out the hateful little black case (it was wet, she noticed) and laid it on the table, "at any rate, you will be obedient enough when I use this!"

She picked up her spoon meekly and began to drink the soup, and he watched her with an amused smile.

She was surprised to find how hungry she was, and made no attempt to deny the chicken en casserole, nor the sweet that followed, but resolutely she refused to touch the wine that the steward poured out for her, and Digby did not press her.

"You're a fool, you know, Eunice." Digby lit a cigar without asking permission, and leaning back in his chair, looked at her critically. "There is a wonderful life ahead for you if you are only intelligent. Why worry about a man like Steele? A poor beggar, without a penny in the world—"

"You forget that I have no need of money, Mr. Groat," she said with spirit. Any reference to Jim aroused all that was savage in her. "I have not only the money which you have not stolen from my estate, but when you are arrested and In prison, I shall recover all that you have now, including this yacht, if it is yours."

Her answer made him chuckle.

"I like spirit," he said. "You can't annoy me, Eunice, my darling. So you like our yacht-our honeymoon yacht?" he added.

To this, she made no reply.

"But suppose you realise how much I love you"-he leant over and caught her hand in both of his and his eyes devoured her. "Suppose you realise that, Eunice, and knew I would give my life-my very soul-to make you happy, wouldn't that make a difference?"

"Nothing would make a difference to my feelings, Mr Groat," she said. "The only chance you have of earning my gratitude is to put in at the nearest port and set me ashore."

"And where do I set myself?" he asked coolly. "Be as intelligent as you are beautiful, Eunice. No, no, I shall be very glad to make you happy, so long as I get a little of the happiness myself, but I do not risk imprisonment and death-". He shivered, and hated himself that he had been surprised into this symptom of fear and hated her worst, having noticed that.

"Where are we going?" she asked.

"We are bound to South America," said Digby, "and it may interest you to learn that we are following a track which is not usually taken by the South American traffic. We shall skirt Ireland and take what Americans call the Western Ocean route, until we are within 1000 miles of long island, when we shall turn due south. By this way we avoid being sighted by the American ships, and we also avoid—"

The man who came in at that moment, Eunice thought must be the captain.

He was three rings of gold about his wrist, but he was not her ideal of a seaman. Under-sized, lame in one foot, his parchment face of stiff black hair almost convinced her that this was a Japanese boat after all.

"You must meet the captain," said Digby, introducing him, "and you had better make friends with him."

Eunice thought that the chances of her making friends with that uncompromising little man were remote.

"What is it, captain?" asked Digby in Portuguese.

"We have just picked up a wireless; I thought you'd like to see it."

"I had forgotten we had wireless," said Digby as he took the message from the man's hand.

It was ill-spelt, having been written by a Brazilian who had no knowledge of English and had set down the message letter by letter as he received it. Slipping the errors of transmission, Digby read;

"To all ships westward, southward, and homeward bound. Keep a sharp look out for the yacht Pealigo and report by wireless, position and bearing, to Inspector Rite, Scotland Yard."

Eunice did not understand what they were talking about, but she saw a frown settle on Digby's forehead, and guessed that the news was bad. If it was bad for him, then it was very good for her, she thought, and her spirits began to rise.

"You had better go to bed, Eunice." said Digby. "I want to talk to the captain."

She rose, and only the captain rose with her.

"Sit down," said Digby testily. "You are not here to do the honours to Mrs. Digby Groat."

She did not hear the last words, for she was out of the saloon as quickly as she could go. She went back to her own cabin, shut the door, and put up her band to shoot home the bolt, but while she had been at dinner somebody had been busy. The bolt was removed and the key of the door was gone!

Chapter 46

EUNICE stared at the door. There was no mistake. The bolts had recently been removed and the raw wood showed where the screws had been taken out.

The Pealigo was rolling now, and she had a difficulty in keeping her balance, but she made her way round the cabin, gathering chairs, tables, everything that was movable, and piling them up against the door. She searched the drawers of the bureau for some weapon which might have been left by its former occupant, but there was nothing more formidable than a golden-backed hairbrush which the plutocratic Maxilla had overlooked.

The bathroom yielded nothing more than a long-handled brush, whilst her sitting-room made no return for her search.

She sat watching the door as the hours passed, but no attempt was made to enter the cabin. A bell rang at intervals on the deck: she counted eight. It was midnight. How long would it be before Digby Groat came?

At that moment a pale-faced Digby Groat, his teeth chattering, sat in the cabin of the wireless operator, reading a message which had been picked up. Part was in code, and evidently addressed to the Admiralty ships cruising in the vicinity, but the longer message was in plain English and was addressed:

"To the chief officers of all ships. To the Commanders of H.M. ships: to all Justices of the Peace, officers of the police Great Britain and Ireland. To all Inspectors, sub-inspectors of the Royal Irish Constabulary:

"Arrest and detain Digby Groat, height five foot nine, stoutly built, complexion sallow, had small moustache but believed to have shaven. Speaks Spanish, French, Portuguese, and is a qualified surgeon and physician, believed to be travelling on the S.Y. Pealigo, No, XVM. This man is wanted on a charge of wilful murder and conspiracy; a reward of five thousand pounds will be paid by Messrs. Salter & Salter, Solicitors, of London, for his arrest and detention. Believe he has travelling with him, under compulsion, Dorothy Danton, age 22. Groat is a dangerous man and carries fire-arms."

The little captain of the Pealigo took the thin cigar from his teeth and regarded the grey ash attentively, though he was also looking at the white-faced man by the operator's side.

"So you see, senhor," he said suavely, "I am in a most difficult position."

"I thought you did not speak English," said Digby, finding his voice at last.

The little captain smiled.

"I read enough English to understand a reward of five thousand pounds, senhor," he said significantly. "And if I did not, my wireless operator speaks many languages, English included, and he would have explained to me, even if I had not been able to understand the message myself."

Digby looked at him bleakly.

"What are you going to do?" he asked.

"That depends upon what you are going to do," said the Brazilian. "I am no traitor to my salt, and I should like to serve you, but you readily understand that this would mean a terrible thing for me, if, knowing that you were wanted by the English police, I assisted you to make an escape? I am not a stickler for small things," he shrugged his shoulders, "and Senhor Maxilla did much that I closed my eyes to. Women came into his calculations, but murder never."

"I am not a murderer, I tell you," stormed Digby vehemently, "and you are under my orders. Do you understand that?"

He jumped up and stood menacingly above the unperturbed Brazilian, and in his hand had appeared an ugly-looking weapon.

"You will carry out my instructions to the letter, or, by God, you'll know all about it!"

But the captain of the Pealigo had returned to the contemplation of his cigar. He reminded Digby somewhat of Bronson, and the yellow-faced man shivered as at an unpleasant thought.

"It is not the first time I have been threatened with a revolver," said the captain coolly. "Years ago when I was very young, such things might have frightened me, but to-day I am not young. I have a family in Brazil who are very expensive; my pay is small, otherwise I would not follow the sea and be every man's dog to kick and bully as he wishes. If I had a hundred thousand pounds, senhor, I should settle down on a plantation which I have bought and be a happy and a silent man for the rest of my life."

He emphasized "silent," and Digby understood.

"Couldn't you do that for a little less than a hundred thousand?" he asked.

"I have been thinking the matter out very carefully. We shipmen have plenty of time to think, and that is the conclusion that I have reached, that a hundred thousand pounds would make all the difference between a life of work and a life of ease." He was silent for a moment and then went on. "That is why I hesitated about the reward. If the radio had said a hundred thousand pounds, senhor, I should have been tempted."

Digby turned on him with a snarl.

"Talk straight, will you?" he said. "You want me to pay you a hundred thousand pounds, and that is the price for carrying me to safety; otherwise you will return to port and give me up."

The captain shrugged his shoulders.

"I said nothing of the sort, senhor," he said. "I merely mentioned a little private matter in which I am glad to see you take an interest. The senhor also wishes for a happy life in Brazil with the beautiful lady he brought on board, and the senhor is not a poor man, and if it is true that the beautiful lady is an heiress, he could be richer."

The operator looked in. He was anxious to come back to his own cabin, but the captain, with a jerk of his head, sent him out again.

He dropped his voice a tone.

"Would it not be possible for me to go to the young lady and say: 'Miss, you are in great danger, and I too am in danger of losing my liberty, what would you pay me to put a sentry outside your door; to place Senhor Digby Groat in irons, in the strong-room? Do you think she would say a hundred thousand pounds, or even a half of her fortune, senhor?"

Digby was silent.

The threat was real and definite. It was not camouflaged by any fine phrases; as plainly as the little Brazilian could state his demands, he had done so.

"Very good." Digby got up from the edge of the table where he had sat, with downcast eyes, turning this and that and the other plan over in his mind. "I'll pay you."

"Wait, wait," said the captain. "Because there is another alternative that I wish to put to you, senhor," he said. "Suppose that I am her friend, or pretend to be, and offer her protection until we reach a port where she can be landed? Should we not both receive a share of the great reward?"

"I will not give her up," said Digby between his teeth. "You can cut that idea out of your head, and also the notion about putting me in irons. By God, if I thought you meant it—" He glowered at the little man, and the captain smiled.

"Who means anything in this horrible climate?" he said lazily. "You will bring the money to-morrow to my cabin, perhaps—no, no, to-night," he said thoughtfully.

"You can have it to-morrow."

The captain shrugged his shoulders; he did not insist, and Digby was left alone with his thoughts.

There was still a hope; there were two. They could not prove that he shot Fuentes, and it would be a difficult matter to pick up the yacht if it followed the course that the captain had marked for it, and in the meantime there was Eunice. His lips twisted, and the colour came into his face. Eunice! He went along the deck and down the companion-way, but there was a man standing in the front of the door of the girl's cabin, a broad-shouldered brown-faced man, who touched his cap as the owner appeared, but did not budge.

"Stand out of the way," said Digby impatiently. "I want to go into that room."

"It is not permitted," said the sailor.

Digby stepped back a pace, crimson with anger.

"Who gave orders that I should not pass?"

"The capitano," said the man.

Digby flew up the companion-ladder and went in search of the captain. He found him on the bridge.

"What is this?" he began, and the captain snapped something at him in Portuguese, and Digby, looking ahead, saw a white-fan-shaped light stealing along the sea.

"It is a warship, and she may be engaged in manoeuvres," said the captain, "but she may also be looking for us."

He gave an order, and suddenly all the lights on the ship were extinguished. The Pealigo swung round in a semicircle and headed back the way she had come.

"We can make a detour and get past her," explained the captain, and Digby forgot the sentry at the door in the distress of this new danger.

Left and right wheeled the searchlight, but never once did it touch the Pealigo. It was searching for her, though they must have seen her lights, and now the big white ray was groping at the spot where the yacht had turned. It missed them by yards.

"Where are we going?" asked Digby fretfully.

"We are going back for ten miles, and then we'll strike between the ship and Ireland, which is there." He pointed to the horizon, where a splash of light trembled for a second and was gone.

"We are losing valuable time," said Digby fretfully.

"It is better to lose time than to lose your liberty," said the philosophical captain.

Digby clutched the rail and his heart turned to water, as the searchlight of the warship again swung round. But fortune was with them. It might, as the captain said, be only a ship carrying out searchlight practice, but on the other hand, in view of the wireless messages which had been received, it seemed certain that the cruiser had a special reason for its scrutiny.

It was not until they were out of the danger zone that Digby remembered the mission that had brought him to the bridge.

"What do you mean by putting a man on guard outside that girl's door?" he asked.

The captain had gone to the deckhouse, and was bending over the table examining an Admiralty chart. He did not answer until Digby had repeated the question, then he looked up and straightened his back.

"The future of the lady is dependent, entirely, on the fulfilment of your promise, illustrious," he said in the flamboyant terminology of his motherland.

"But I promised—"

"You have not performed."

"Do you doubt my words?" stormed Digby.

"I do not doubt, but I do not understand," said the captain. "If you will come to my cabin I will settle with you."

Digby thought a while; his interest in Eunice had evaporated with the coming of this new danger, and there was no reason why he should settle that night. Suppose he was captured, the money would be wasted. It would be useless to him also, but this, in his parsimonious way, did not influence him.

He went down to his cabin, a smaller and less beautifully furnished one than that occupied by Eunice, and pulling an arm-chair to the neat little desk, he sat down to think matters over. And as the hours passed, his perspective shifted. Somehow, the danger seemed very remote, and Eunice was very near, and if any real danger came, why, there would be an end of all things, Eunice included, and his money would be of no more value to him than the spray which flapped against the closed porthole.

Beneath the bureau was a small, strong safe, and this he unlocked, taking out the broad money-belt which he had fastened about his waist before he began the journey. He emptied one bulging pocket, and laid a wad of bills upon the desk. They were gold bonds of ten thousand dollar denomination, and he counted forty, put the remainder back in the pocket from whence he had taken it, and locked the belt in the safe.

It was half-past five and the grey of the new day showed through the portholes. He thrust the money in his pocket and went out to talk to the captain.

He shivered in the chill wind of morning as he stepped out on the deck and made his way for'ard. The little Brazilian, a grotesque figure, wrapped in his overcoat and muffled to the chin, was standing moodily staring across the grey waste. Without a word Digby stepped up to him and thrust the bundle of notes into his hand. The Brazilian looked at the money, counted it mechanically, and put it into his pocket. "Your Excellency is munificent," he said. "Now take your sentry from the door," said Digby sharply.

"Wait here," said the captain, and went below. He returned in a few minutes.

Chapter 47

SHE had heard the tap of her first visitor at one o'clock in the morning. It had come when Digby Groat was sitting in his cabin turning over the possibilities of misfortune which the future held, and she had thought it was he.

The handle of the door turned and it opened an inch; beyond that it could not go without a crash, for the chairs and tables that Eunice had piled against it. She watched with a stony face and despair in her heart, as the opening of the door increased.

"Please do not be afraid," said a voice.

Then it was not Digby! She sprang to her feet. It might be some one worse, but that was impossible.

"Who is it?" she asked.

"It is I, the captain," said a voice in laboured English.

"What is it you want?"

"I wish to speak to you, mademoiselle, but you must put away these things from behind the door, otherwise I will call two of my sailors, and it will be a simple matter to push them aside."

Already he had prized open the door to the extent of two or three inches, and with a groan Eunice realized the futility of her barricade. She dragged the furniture aside and the little captain came in smiling, hat in hand, closing the door after him.

"Permit me, mademoiselle," he said politely, and moved her aside while he replaced the furniture; then he opened the door and looked out, and Eunice saw that there was a tall sailor standing with his back to her, evidently on guard. What did this mean, she wondered? The captain did not leave her long in ignorance.

"Lady," he said in an accent which it was almost impossible to reproduce, "I am a poor sailor-man who works at his hazardous calling for two hundred miserable milreis a month. But because I am poor, and of humble—" he hesitated and used the Portuguese word for origin—which she guessed at—"it does not mean that I am without a heart." He struck his breast violently. "I have a repugnancio to hurting female women!"

She was wondering what was coming next: would he offer to sell his master at a price? If he did, she would gladly agree, but the new hope which surged up within her was dissipated by his next words.

"My friend Groat," he said, "is my master. I must obey his orders, and if he says 'Go to Callio,' or to Rio de Janeiro, I must go."

Her hopes sunk, but evidently he had something more to say.

"As the captain I must do as I am told," he said, "but I cannot and will not see a female hurted. You understand?"

She nodded, and the spark of hope kindled afresh.

"I myself cannot be here all the time, nor can my inconquerable sailors, to see that you are not hurted, and it would look bad for me if you were hurted—very bad!"

Evidently the worthy captain was taking a very far-sighted view of the situation, and had hit upon a compromise which relieved him at least of his responsibility toward his master.

"If the young lady will take this, remembering that Jose Montigano was the good friend of hers, I shall be repaid."

"This" was a silvery weapon. She took the weapon in her hand with a glad cry.

"Oh, thank you, thank you, captain," she said, seizing his hand.

"Remember," he raised a warning finger. "I cannot do more. I speak now as man to woman. Presently I speak as captain to owner. You understand the remarkable difference?"

He confused her a little, but she could guess what he meant.

He bowed and made his exit, but presently he returned.

"To put the chairs and tables against the floor is no use," he said, shaking his head. "It is better—" He pointed significantly to the revolver, and with a broad grin closed the door behind him.

Digby Groat knew nothing of this visit: it satisfied him that the sentry had been withdrawn, and that now nothing stood between him and the woman whom, in his distorted, evil way, he loved, but her own frail strength. He tapped again. It pleased him to observe these threadbare conventions for the time being, yet when no answer came to his knock, he opened the door slowly and walked in.

Eunice was standing at the far end of the cabin; the silken curtains had been drawn aside, and the door leading to her sitting saloon was open. Her hands were behind her and she was fully dressed.

"My dear," said Digby, in his most expansive manner, "why are you tiring your pretty eyes? You should have been in bed and asleep."

"What do you want?" she demanded.

"What else could a man want, who had such a beautiful wife, but the pleasure of her conversation and companionship," he said with an air of gaiety.

"Stand where you are," she called sharply as he advanced, and the authority in her tone made him halt.

"Now, Eunice," he said, shaking his head, "you are making a lot of trouble when trouble is foolish. You have only to be sensible, and there is nothing in the world that I will not give you."

"There is nothing in the world that you have to give, except the money which you have stolen from me," she said calmly. "Why do you talk of giving, when I am the giver, and there is nothing for you to take but my mercy?"

He stared at her, stricken dumb by the coolness at the moment of her most deadly danger, and then with a laugh he recovered his self-possession and strolled towards her, his dark eyes aflame.

"Stand where you are," said Eunice again, and this time she had the means to enforce her command.

Digby could only stare at the muzzle of the pistol pointed towards his heart, and then he shrank back.

"Put that thing away!" he said harshly. "Damn you, put it away! You are not used to fire-arms, and it may explode."

"It will explode," said Eunice. Her voice was deep and intense, and all the resentment she had smothered poured forth in her words. "I tell you, Digby Groat, that I will shoot you like a dog, and glory in the act. Shoot you more mercilessly than you killed that poor Spaniard, and look upon your body with less horror than you showed."

"Put it away, put it away! Where did you get it?" he cried. "For God's sake, Eunice, don't fool with that pistol; you don't want to kill me, do you?"

"There are times when I want to kill you very badly," she said, and lowered the point of the revolver at the sight of the man's abject cowardice.

He wiped his forehead with a silk handkerchief, and she could see his knees trembling.

"Who gave you that pistol?" he demanded violently. "You didn't have it when you left Kennett Hall, that I'll swear. Where did you find it? In one of those drawers?" He looked at the bureau, one of the drawers of which was half open.

"Does it matter?" she asked. "Now, Mr. Groat, you will please go out of my cabin and leave me in peace."

"I had no intention of hurting you," he growled. He was still very pale. "There was no need for you to flourish your revolver so melodramatically. I only came in to say good night."

"You might have come about six hours earlier," she said. "Now go."

"Listen to me, Eunice," said Digby Groat; he edged forward, but her pistol covered him, and he jumped. "If you're going to play the fool, I'll go," he said, and followed the action by the deed, slamming the door behind him.

She heard the outer door open and close, and leant against the brass column of the bed for support, for she was near to the end of her courage. She must sleep, she thought, but first she must secure the outer door. There was a lock on the lobby door; she had not noticed that before. She had hardly taken two steps through the cabin door before an arm was flung round her, she was pressed back, and a hand gripped the wrist which still carried the weapon. With a wrench he flung it to the floor, and in another moment she was in his arms.

"You thought I'd gone "—he lifted her, still struggling, and carried her back to the saloon. "I want to see you," he breathed; "to see your face, your glorious eyes, that wonderful mouth of yours, Eunice." He pressed his lips against hers; he smothered with kisses her cheeks, her neck, her eyes.

She felt herself slipping from consciousness; the very horror of his caresses froze and paralysed her will to struggle. She could only gaze at the eyes so close to hers, fascinated as by the glare of the deadly snake.

"You are mine now, mine, do you hear?" he murmured into her ear. "You will forget Jim Steele, forget everything except that I adore you," and then he saw her wild gaze pass him to the door, and turned.

The little captain stood there, his hands on his hips, watching, his brown face a mask.

Digby released his hold of the girl, and turned on the sailor.

"What the hell are you doing here? Get out." he almost screamed.

"There is an aeroplane looking for us," said the captain. "We have just picked up her wireless."

Digby's jaw dropped. That possibility had not occurred to him.

"Who is she? What does the wireless say?"

"It is a message we picked up saying, 'Nothing sighted. Am heading due south.' It gave her position," added the captain, "and if she is coming due south I think Mr. Steele will find us."

Digby fell back a pace, his face blanched.

"Steele," he gasped.

The captain nodded.

"That is the gentleman who signs the message. I think it would be advisable for you to come on deck."

"I'll come on deck when I want," growled Digby. There was a devil in him now. He was at the end of his course, and he was not to be thwarted.

"Will the good gentleman come on deck?"

"I will come later. I have some business to attend to here."

152

"You can attend to it on deck," said the little captain calmly.

"Get out," shouted Digby.

The captain's hand did not seem to move; there was a shot, the deafening explosion of which filled the cabin, and a panel behind Digby's head splintered into a thousand pieces.

He glared at the revolver in the Brazilian's hand, unable to realize what had happened.

"I could have shot you just as easily," said the Brazilian calmly, "but I preferred to send the little bullet near your ear. Will you come on deck, please?"

Digby Groat obeyed.

Chapter **48**

WHITE and breathless he leant against the bulwark glowering at the Brazilian, who had come between him and the woman whose rum he had planned.

"Now," he said, "you will tell me what you mean by this, you swine!"

"I will tell you many things that you will not like to hear," said the captain.

A light dawned upon Digby.

"Did you give the girl that revolver?"

The Brazilian nodded.

"I desired to save you from yourself, my friend," he said. "In an hour the gentleman Steele will be within sight of us; I can tell where he is within a few miles. Do you wish that he should come on board and discover that you have added something to murder that is worse than murder?"

"That is my business," said Digby Groat, breathing so quickly that he felt he would suffocate unless the pent-up rage in him found some vent.

"And mine," said the captain, tapping him on the chest. "I tell you, my fine fellow, that that is my business also, for I do not intend to live within an English gaol. It is too cold in England and I would not survive one winter. No, my fine fellow, there is only one thing to do. It is to run due west in the hope that we escape the observation of the airship man; if we do not, then we are——" He snapped his fingers.

"Do as you like," said Digby, and turning abruptly walked down to his cabin.

He was beaten, and the end was near. He took from a drawer a small bottle of colourless liquid, and emptied its contents into a glass. This he placed in a rack conveniently to his hand. The effect would not be violent. One gulp, and he would pass to sleep and there the matter would end for him. That was a comforting thought to Digby Groat.

If they escaped——! His mind turned to Eunice. She could wait; perhaps they would dodge through all these guards that the police had put, and they would reach that land for which he yearned. He could not expect the captain, after receiving the wireless messages of warning, to take the risks. He was playing for safety, thought Digby, and did not wholly disapprove of the man's attitude.

When they were on the high seas away from the ocean traffic, the little Brazilian would change his attitude, and then—Digby nodded. The captain was wise; it would have been madness on his part to force the issue so soon.

Eunice could not get away; they were moving in the same direction to a common destination, and there were weeks, hot and sunny weeks, when they could sit under the awning on this beautiful yacht and talk. He would be rational and drop that cave-man method of wooing. A week's proximity and freedom from restraint might make all the difference in the world, if— There was a big if, he recognized. Steele would not rest until he had found him, but by that time Eunice might be a complacent partner.

He felt a little more cheerful, locked away the glass and its contents in a cupboard, and strolled up to the deck. He saw the ship now for the first time in daylight, and it was a model of what a yacht should be. The deck was snowy white; every piece of brass-work glittered, the coiled sheets looked to have been dipped in chalk, and under that identical awning great basket chairs awaited him invitingly.

He glanced round the horizon; there was no ship in sight. The sea sparkled in the rays of the sun, and over the white wake of the steamer lay a deep black pall of smoke, for the Pealigo was racing forward at twenty-two knots an hour. The captain, at any rate, was not playing him false. He was heading west, judged Digby.

Far away on the right was an irregular purple strip, the line of the Irish coast; the only traffic they would meet now, he considered, was the western-bound steamers on the New York route. But the only sign of a steamer was a blob of smoke on the far-off eastern horizon.

The chairs invited him, and he sat down and stretched his legs luxuriously.

Yes, this was a better plan, he thought, and as his mind turned again to Eunice, she appeared at the head of the companion-way. At first she did not see him, and walking to the rail, seemed to be breathing in the beauties of the morning.

How exquisite she looked! He did not remember seeing a woman who held herself as she did. The virginal purity of her face, the glory of her colouring, the svelte woman figure of her—they were worth waiting for, he told himself again.

She turned her head and saw him and made a movement as though she were going back to her cabin, but he beckoned to her, and to his surprise, she walked slowly toward him.

"Don't get up," she said coldly. "I can find a chair myself. I want to speak to you, Mr. Groat."

"You want to speak to me," he said in amazement, and she nodded.

"I have been thinking that perhaps I can induce you to turn this yacht about and land me in England."

"Oh, you have, have you?" he said sharply. "What inducement can you offer other than your gracious self?"

"Money," she answered. "I do not know by what miracle it has happened, but I believe I am an heiress, and worth"—she hesitated—"a great deal of money. If that is the case, Mr. Groat, you are poor."

"I'm not exactly a pauper," he said, apparently amused. "What are you offering me?"

"I'm offering you half my fortune to take me back to England," she said.

"And what would you do with the other half of your fortune?" he mocked her. "Save me from the gallows? No, no, my young friend, I have committed myself too deeply to make your plan even feasible. I'm not going to bother you again, and I promise you I will wait until we have reached our destination before I ask you to share my lot. I appreciate your offer and I dare say it is an honest one," he went on, "but I have gone too far literally and figuratively to turn back. You hate me now, but that feeling will change."

"It will never change," she said as she rose. "But I see that I am wasting my time with you," and with a little nod, she would have gone had he not caught her hand and drawn her back.

"You love somebody else, I suppose?"

"That is an impertinence," she said. "You have no right to question me."

"I am not questioning you, I am merely making a statement which is beyond dispute. You love somebody else, and that somebody is Jim Steele." He leant forward. "You can make up your mind for this, that sooner than give you to Jim Steele, I will kill you. Is that plain?"

"It is the kindest thing you have said," she smiled contemptuously as she rose.

155

Chapter 49

A LITTLE smudge of smoke far away to the south, sent Jim Steele racing away on a fool's errand, for the ship proved to be nothing more interesting than a fruit-boat which had ignored his wireless inquiry because the only man who operated the instrument was asleep in his bunk. Jim saw the character of the ship when he was within two miles of it, and banked over, cutting a diagonal course north-west.

Once or twice he glanced back at his "passenger," but Inspector Maynard was thoroughly at home and apparently comfortable.

Jim was growing anxious. At the longest he could not keep in the air for more than four hours, and two of those precious hours were already gone. He must leave himself sufficient "juice" to make the land and this new zigzag must not occupy more than half an hour.

He had purposely taken the machine to a great height to enlarge his field of vision, and that meant a still further burden upon his limited supply of petrol.

He was almost despairing when he saw in the far distance a tiny white arrow of foam—the ship whose wake it was he could not see. His hand strayed to the key of his little wireless and he sent a message quivering through the ether. There was no response. He waited a minute and again the key clattered and clicked. Again a silence and he flashed an angry message. Then through his ear-pieces he heard a shrill wail of sound—the steamer was responding.

"What ship is that?"

He waited, never "doubting that he would learn it was some small merchant vessel. There was a whine, and then:

"P-E-A-L-I-G-O." was the reply.

Digby had gone forward to see what the men were doing who were swung over the side. He was delighted to discover that they were painting out the word Pealigo and were substituting Malaga. He went up to the captain in his most amiable mood.

"That is a good thought of yours," he said, "changing the name, I mean."

The captain nodded.

"By your orders, of course," he said.

"Of course," smiled Digby, "by my orders."

All the time he was standing there chatting to the Brazilian he noticed that the man constantly turned his eyes to the north, scanning the sky.

"You don't think that the aeroplane will come so far out, do you? How far are we from the coast?"

"We are a hundred and twelve miles from the English coast," said the skipper, "and that isn't any great distance for a seaplane."

Digby with unusual joviality slapped him on the back.

"You are getting nervous," he said. "He won't come now."

A man had come on to the bridge whom Digby recognized as the wireless operator. He handed a message to the captain, and he saw the captain's face change.

"What is it?" he asked quickly.

Without a word the man handed the written slip.

"Ship heading south, send me your name and number."

156

"Who is it from?" asked Digby, startled at this voice from nowhere.

The captain, supporting his telescope against a stanchion, scanned the northern skies.

"I see nothing," he said with a frown. "Possibly it came from one of the land stations; there is no ship in sight."

"Let us ask him who he is," said Digby.

The three went back to the wireless room and the operator adjusted his ear-pieces. Presently he began writing, after a glance up at the captain, and Digby watched fascinated the movements of the pencil.

"Heave to. I am coming aboard you."

The captain went out on the deck and again made a careful examination of the sky.

"I can't understand it," he said.

"The signal was close, senhor captain—it was less than three miles away," broke in the operator.

The captain rubbed his nose.

"I had better stop," he said.

"You'll do nothing of the kind," stormed Digby.

"You'll go on until I tell you to stop."

They returned to the bridge, and the captain stood with one hand on the telegraph, undecided.

And then right ahead of them, less than half a mile away, something fell into the water with a splash.

"What was that?" said Digby.

He was answered immediately. From the place where the splashing had occurred arose a great mass of billowing smoke which sped along the sea, presenting an impenetrable veil. Smoke was rising from the sea to their right, and the captain, shading his eyes, looked up. Directly over them it seemed was a silvery shape, so small as to be almost invisible if the sun had not caught the wing-tips and painted them silver.

"This, my friend," said the captain, "is where many things happen." He jerked over the telegraph to stop.

"What is it?" asked Digby.

"It was a smoke-bomb, and I prefer a smoke-bomb half a mile away to a real bomb on my beautiful ship," said the captain.

For a moment Digby stared at him, and then with a scream of rage he sprang at the telegraph and thrust it over to full-ahead. Immediately he was seized from behind by two sailors, and the captain brought the telegraph back to its original position.

"You will signal to the senhor aviator, to whom you have already told the name of the ship, if you have obeyed my orders," he said to the operator, "and say that I have put Mr. Digby Groat in irons!"

And five minutes later this statement was nearly true.

Down from the blue dropped that silvery dragon-fly, first sweeping round the stationary vessel in great circles until it settled like a bird upon the water close to the yacht's side.

The captain had already lowered a boat, and whilst they were fixing the shackles on a man who was behaving like a raving madman in his cabin below, Jim Steele came lightly up the side of the ship and followed the captain down the companion-way.

Above the rumble of the yacht's machinery Eunice had heard the faint buzz of the descending seaplane, but had been unable to distinguish it until the yacht stopped, then she heard it plainly enough and ran to the porthole, pulling aside the silk curtain.

Yes, there it was, a buzzing insect of a thing, that presently passed out of sight on the other side. What did it mean? What did it mean, she wondered. Was it—and then the door flew open and a man stood there. He was without collar or waistcoat, his hair was rumpled, his face bleeding, and one link of a steel handcuff was fastened about his wrist. It was Digby Groat, and his face was the face of a devil.

She shrank back against the bed as he came stealthily toward her, the light of madness in his eyes, and then somebody else came in, and he swung round to meet the cold level scrutiny of Jim Steele.

With a yell like a wild beast, Digby sprang at the man he hated, but the whirling steel of the manacle upon his hand never struck home. Twice Jim hit him, and he fell an inert heap on the ground. In another second Eunice was in her lover's arms, sobbing her joy upon the breast of his leather jacket.

Made in the USA
Monee, IL
14 December 2021

85505750R00087